DRUNK in Love

LOVE, DECEIT AND FRIENDSHIP

NATHAN WELCH

DRUNK IN LOVE

BY

NATHAN WELCH

ISBN-13: 978-0-9887621-8-3
Library of Congress Control Number: On File

Paperback Edition, April 2014

Publisher's Note
This is a work of fiction. Any names historical events, real people, living and dead, or the locales are intended only to give the fiction a setting in historic reality. Other names, characters, places, businesses and incidents are either the product of the author's imagination or are used fictiously, and their resemblance, if any, to real life counterparts is entirely coincidental.

DC Bookdiva Publications
#245 4401-A Connecticut Ave
NW, Washington, DC 20008
www.dcbookdiva.com
facebook.com/thedcbookdiva
twitter.com/dcbookdiva

Dedication

THIS NOVEL IS DEDICATED TO ALL THE MEN
AND WOMEN WHO GO THROUGH ALL THE
MOTIONS AND HEARTACHES WHILE
SEARCHING FOR LOVE AND HAPPINESS...
DON'T GIVE UP UNTIL LOVE GETS YA!!!

Drunk In Love

Prologue

The memories of her infidelity always haunted Vanessa whenever she sat down to eat breakfast or any other meal with her family, the one-night stand she had with the madman from her job and the horrific rape, which led to the in-house separation from her faithful husband.

Russell decided to work things out with Vanessa solely on the strength of their daughter. He didn't want to explain to his daughter why he left home and only came to visit them on the weekends. That's the road he wanted to take, but the love Russell had for his daughter and Vanessa made him stick around for now. By staying, Russell chose to sleep in a different bedroom and not talk to his wife. He only talked to Vanessa during family meals and that was it!

"Hey Daddy!" Russell heard Dejah calling him, which brought him hurtling away from his thoughts - back to the kitchen table in the house where he lived with his beautiful daughter and his wife the Betrayer!

He heard Dejah asking, "Daddy, can we go to the park today? Just me, you, and Mommy, you know, like old times?"

Dejah was quite the slickster and more focused than ever. Vanessa saw the crazed and angry look in her husband's chinky brown eyes - a look that screamed that he wanted to tell Dejah the truth once and for all.

"Dejah, baby, why don't you and Daddy just go to the park? Mommy has a lot of work to do. Maybe I'll go with you guys some other time."

Russell grunted in disgust as she finished talking. He glared at her evilly.

This cheating-ass bitch has some nerve! Now she's lying to our daughter! What's next?

"Okay Mommy," Dejah said joyously before turning to her father. "Daddy, you can take me -" she suddenly stopped in mid-sentence and just bad-eyed her father. "Daddy, what's that?" Dejah asked, pointing at the red pinpoint of the laser on his chest.

Russell looked down and saw the red dot moving slowly up onto the Polo horse emblem near his heart. It didn't take a rocket scientist to figure out what the red dot was.

What the fuck! he thought before going after his daughter. Fear consumed Russell as he instinctively grabbed hold of his daughter and dove quickly to the kitchen floor. Microseconds later, rapid gunfire penetrated his sham of a Happy Home.

Drunk In Love

Briana Evans
Dayton, Ohio

For patient #107, there was nowhere to go but forward in an effort to get to the bottom of her problems. Love is a Hellhole for the spirit. It kills some, while others it breaks down. Like a bag of glass bottles and leaves them bitter, vengeful, hateful, and scared to ever commit to another person in life.

Some stagger out of relationships cowed and repentant, while many exit walking tall, resolved to do it better the next time around. On all people, love leaves its mark. No one who gives their all and does time in a relationship is ever the same person they were before entering it. It's very sad, but it's an unavoidable truth. There had only been one or two exceptions to this rule.

Then you have people like Briana Evans who pretend never to notice they have issues. Opening the door, the twenty-nine-year-old medical physician with the rich chocolate skin and hourglass curves on her mouthwatering staggering body took in the spacious, furnished office and smiled.

This is what escape from reality looked like to a woman in the midst of hard times. When a peach-colored carpeted floor, oil painting-covered walls, a cherry oak-laden desk, and high arching windows overlooking downtown were the circumference of a woman's week, that room with its plush futon and sectional sofas looked like a vacation getaway with the fragrance of clear blue waters and jasmine oils thrown in.

It looked and reminded her of hope.

Several right answers. With a carefully modulated attitude - part quietly reassured self-possession, part repentance, and part deference, Briana felt she could make her shrink really believe she was on her way to recovery. *Whatever the hell that means,* she thought. She decided to be cool, play it straight, and walk. It had been a simple formula one that had worked on numerous occasions. She felt, *Hell, why not work it one more time?*

The tall, dark, and handsome psychologist greeted Briana as she stepped inside his office. While deciding on a seat, Briana was suddenly surprised to hear him starting the appointment.

"Good afternoon, Ms. Evans."

"Please, I've been coming here to see you for close to six months now. I think it's okay if you called me Briana, Doc."

The psychologist turned towards Briana and smiled. While studying his neutral but expectant expression, Briana also analyzed his grey cardigan sweater, expensive Prada specs, and matching grey slacks with a small cuff over his Gucci loafers. Even she had to admit that he was disconcertingly good-looking and in the prime of his life. None of the light appeared to have disappeared out of his large, bourbon-hued eyes - the kind of eyes she loved looking deep into while searching for the truth.

"Okay, Briana, sorry… Let's move forward, shall we?" He held his hands up in mock surrender.

"Stop with the guilt trip, Jackson," she blurted tonelessly while glancing back and forth as though the wealth of the plush seating was a hard choice. She eventually chose her favorite leather futon.

Briana took a seat and got comfortable quickly, looking up genially, thinking, *I wonder how much of my $250 per visit is paying for this large, airy, and beautiful room?* The money really didn't hurt her, though, since she made a little over $137,000 a year.

"So Briana, what brings you here on such a sudden notice? You're not scheduled until the day after tomorrow."

There was a purposeful pause.

Drunk In Love

Briana thought of a half dozen replies that burst like Pop Rocks on her tongue. She rejected them all. She waited out the moment, maintaining perfect eye contact with her shrink. "Well, Doc, I'm at a point in my life where I want a shot at love again." She gave him an affable smile before continuing. "I'm twenty-nine years old. In another year, the big Three-O will hit me like a ton of bricks. I mean, I'm successful and all that, but I want and need that warm dick to come home to every night and curl up beside. Excuse the vulgarity of my statement, but you get what I'm saying, right?"

"Yes, please continue," he urged, knowing the best sessions always came from him listening to his patients problems instead of talking to them.

"I mean all I need is a man to love me for me and not have all the extra bullshit attached to him, you know?"

No man had asked Briana out on a date in over two years. That was around the time her last serious relationship failed, and she had no plans to ask out any men. Briana tried to imagine how she would react to an invitation for a date. She felt that men had nothing to give and nothing to share with her but their dicks. She felt she could get by on her sex toys, which lasted longer on batteries and didn't give her all the headaches men presented.

Looking over his glasses from behind his desk, the psychologist's expression never changed. He couldn't understand why a successful and gorgeous woman like Briana couldn't find love in Ohio. *But for $250 per consult, I'll listen to her problems until my ears bleed,* he thought while choosing his words carefully.

"Ms. Eva- I mean, Briana - there's plenty of single men out there without all the excess baggage you speak of. What I'm trying to find out is what the real reason is why you're so scared of taking a chance at finding love and happiness?"

Briana hated hearing that question. Two years after her nasty break-up, the very words "love and happiness" twisted

3

like a dagger in her uterus, bringing back the horrible memories of her fiancé sprawled naked on their bedroom floor under the buxom brunette from next door. Who was bouncing up and down on his hard pole, riding him like a porn actress in a heated sex scene.

It was random and pointless, and for no reason. He couldn't explain why he cheated on her after she did everything to please him. She stared at her shrink, trying not to remember the day that made her stop trusting all men.

"I'm scared of commitment, okay? There, I said it! You happy now?" she said in an angry tone. She shifted a little like she was uncomfortable by the confession. She gave him a small shrug. "I guess I get it from my mother. When she left my Daddy after twenty-six years of marriage and started being a whore around town, I got into a self-destructive pattern of mimicking her ways."

Briana blamed her mother instead of coming clean about her nasty break-up. Most women feel inferior and insufficient as a woman and have serious self-esteem issues when their man cheats on them. Briana fell into this category, but she was still in the denial phase about the situation.

"If you find that special guy, it is likely that you will continue this pattern?"

"Honestly, Doc?" She sighed. "I honestly can't say. I mean, I don't think I'll do it again just for kicks. I'm tired of that juvenile stuff. I want more now and I think I'm old enough to handle more, you know?"

Briana caught his darting glance and wondered how it would feel to make love to her sexy shrink. Her pussy pulsated with the lustful thoughts. She had to cross her legs to keep the moist love juices from oozing out of her twat.

"Well, you listen to me Briana. You can't move forward unless you release those old demons. If you don't, you'll only be stunting your growth in life. There's a person out there for everyone. You know if Flava Flav can have a million sexy women chasing behind him on television then there's definitely love out there waiting on you."

"So what you saying, Doc, I'm ugly?" she threw at him just to mess with him.

"No, no, not at all! I was just - never mind that example. What I'm trying to say is that there's a man out there waiting on you to love you for you. Don't let him pass you by because you're stuck on some preconceived notion about men. About your mom and whatever else that's stopping you from finding true love. Remember the story about the little train that could?"

She nodded, licking her lips in an enticing manner as the shrink continued. She visualized him throwing her over his desk. Ripping her clothes off roughly, and fucking her into a sexually-gratifying coma. At that moment, she realized that all her sex toys couldn't give her what she really wanted and needed in life: a man who loved her.

"You just apply that story to your pursuit of the perfect companion and don't give up until you're barefoot, pregnant, and cooking soul food for your man." He smiled.

Briana smiled and sighed. "I don't know, Doc...I really don't know," she muttered, wondering if her shrink was single. She wouldn't mind being barefoot, pregnant, and cooking for him for the rest of her life.

"How much do you make a year, Doc?" she asked with a flirting smile.

He stared at her coldly.

"I was just asking, Mr. Meanie," Briana said in a baby-like voice while staring at him, and then she broke into a congenial grin.

So much for him being my soul mate, she thought as he gave her a few more pointers on finding the perfect male companion before ending the session.

Casey Cooper
Dayton's Central Booking

The minimum security holding cells below the courthouse did not have the usual body searches and lockdowns for inmate counts three times a day. There weren't any Holes or Solitary Confinement Dungeons. It was a twelve cell holding facility for all criminals coming off the streets.

The holding facility also became very useful for people that got sent to the jail for being held in contempt in an honorable courtroom - a place that Casey Cooper, the hotshot defense attorney, had never seen until today.

To her, the place felt like prison.

She couldn't believe Judge Nelson had the gall to use his authority abusively. He had cited her in contempt of court for something silly, but Casey knew the real reason behind the Judge's anger. He wanted to get back at her for dumping his old ass. What did he expect? He had sculpted gray hair with the rigid texture of a helmet and a face just as unmoving.

While waiting to post bail, Casey had some regrets about sleeping with the older control freak. She only had sex with him to see if she could gain a few victories in his courtroom, which had always been a very hard courtroom to win in. Now her unethical actions came back and bit her in her honey-bronzed curvaceous butt.

Looking at the wall outside of her holding cell, the 5'6", 135 pound twenty-seven-year-old scratched her long, wavy brown hair - hair that reached down to her 24" inch waist. Casey sighed in frustration once she realized that she'd be late for the weekly workout session with her girlfriends. Casey's looks could match those of any sexy music video model. The difference between Casey and those women is that she looked like she didn't need to work out at all. In fact, Casey's 32B-24-

Drunk In Love

38 completely natural body made her the object of envy in most women's eyes and brought lust in every man's eye that saw her.

Casey loved to party. She also had big dreams of running her own law firm one day even though she lived every day as if it were her last. Being a player and a lawyer was hard work. But some women had to treat men exactly like they had been dogging women out for eons, and Casey Cooper felt like she was the chosen candidate. In her mind, Casey knew that if she didn't do it, then no other woman in Ohio would.

Among all the days in her life, she'd never forget this one. This day she would always remember most vividly. Even Judge Nelson's non-pussy-eating, one minute-fucking little dick-having ass couldn't darken the shine of a woman who had just kicked the state's prosecuting attorney's butt in a hostile courtroom while Judge Nelson eye-fucked her throughout the second degree murder trial that seemed un-winnable.

Casey sat on the cold steel bunk, slightly angry and daydreaming about the sex she'd had just a few hours ago. She had been using Judge Nelson for over nine months now. During that time, Casey had won many trials in his courtroom without the use of a jury. She had sexed and sucked the judge off to the point where he made it his business to keep all of her cases on his docket sheet. Judge Nelson eventually fell for Casey's freaky ways. He caught feelings, falling in love with Casey to the point where he loved her just like he loved his wife.

During a long jury trial in a high profile murder case, Casey figured he wanted something from her. So she began plotting, thinking that she could get him to rule in her favor on any future cases in his courtroom if she gave him something he wanted.

With her devious thoughts mixed in with a little bit of wine and a lot of flirting conversation, one thing led to another. Later on that night, Casey had Judge Nelson's body contorting into all kinds of positions while she laid the pussy on him. Judge Nelson instantly got hooked on the pretty young thing who seemed so eager to put out. Casey noticed his addiction after the first time they had sex.

There was one problem: Casey had vowed to remain a player and dog all men. She had been winning case after case while dating the judge, which made her feel unbeatable, unstoppable, and which ultimately made her lose focus. Casey was dealing with a few other men, but Judge Nelson became exclusive in her life and Casey realized that he was monopolizing too much of her time.

Earlier that day, right after Judge Nelson called a lunch recess; Casey slipped inside his chambers and closed the door. He looked up at Casey and smiled. She always made him feel good inside, like a high school kid in love all over again.

"What can I do for you, Counselor?" he asked, looking at her thick covered thighs and the chunky camel-toe print that bulged out through her tight, cutting slacks. His erection grew instantly while starting at her hard nipples poking through the thin material of the tight pink blouse she wore.

"You can find my client not guilty." She laughed, locking the door. She walked over to his desk.

"Now why on earth would I do something like that?" he asked with a mischievous smile while standing up and moving around his desk to meet her.

"Because you're a very naughty old judge that can't get enough of this brown sugar." Casey smiled and began taking off her clothes. She took off everything except her knee-high designer boots.

"You got that right, doll. Come here," he said in a throaty whisper, reaching out for her.

"Nope! Not until you promise me that my client will go free," she said, backing away a little from his reach. She played with her perky breasts to help sway his decision.

Drunk In Love

"Okay, okay, I promise." He smiled, walking closer to her.

"Okay now, your balls and your word are all you have in this world," she said, reaching out to grab the bulge under his robe.

"And I don't break them for nobody." He grinned and kissed her.

Casey sucked on his tongue a few times then snaked her tongue inside his mouth while lifting his robe. She quickly unzipped his trousers and slid them down his hairy legs. She began stroking his stiffness in her small hands. She then pulled on his shaft and led him over to his desk. She smiled at the picture of his wife and bent over the desk. She kissed the picture of his wife and guided his thick phallus towards her love canal.

"Ssss... We only have forty minutes, Judge, so you need to handle your business," she moaned, backing up against his hard aching boner.

He quickly penetrated her tight warmness, going to work, sawing in and out, in and out very slowly to get his rhythm. Casey looked back at him over her shoulder and started gyrating her hips to match him thrust for thrust.

"Oooh, yesss, Judge...yessss!" she moaned, leaning forward, letting the tip of his curvy shaft tickle her hard clitoris before easing back onto his stabbing love muscle. The slapping sounds of his dick and balls making contact were loud and wet, followed by some slurping sounds from the mouth of her tight twat.

"Mmmm... Yes, Judge... fuck this pussy...fuc-" She gasped, taking all of his plunging love organ to the base, letting his balls slap against her slick, meaty pussy lips. She looked back again, saw his eyes rolling upward, and knew he was about to blow his rod. She really didn't want him to explode so soon, so she grabbed the base of his wood and squeezed as hard as she could as she extracted his throbbing pipe.

"Don't you even think about it, Judge! I want to enjoy this one," she said as she eased down to her knees and took him inside her humid mouth, tasting her own juices on his jabbing love pole, which drove her wild, making her climax instantly. Getting more excited by her own peachy scent, Casey took him deeper and deeper into her warm mouth, to the back of her throat, letting his dick twine against her tonsils.

"Mmmm," she moaned, coming up for air, licking all over the head and then she went back down to his balls and back around the tender head of his jabbing shaft before flicking her tongue in and out of his pee hole. As she swallowed him whole, he raised up on his tiptoes, caressing and palming the back of her bobbing head. Casey massaged his hairy balls while slathering and sucking the shit out of his dick. She continued to suck and pop while jerking his jabbing pole off at the same time.

"Oh, oh, dear Lord, Ca-Casey... AAARRRGGH, SHIT!" he groaned, exploding his load inside her wet mouth.

She continued nursing on his spewing magic stick like she was drinking a thick creamy milkshake through a straw. She sucked all the warm semen out of him, and then licked all over his throbbing muscle until he went limp.

"You know, Judge," she said, quickly getting dressed and looked at the goofy grin on his face. "I feel really bad about sneaking around like this.

Looking at her sexy body being covered, the Judge said, "What do you want to do about it, Casey? Go public and destroy both our careers?" He reached down and pulled up his trousers.

"I thought I could do this with you, Judge, but I can't, knowing that you're fucking me and making love to that bitch," Casey said, faking the jealous mistress role while pointing at the Judge's wife picture sitting on his desk. "It's up to you, Judge. It's either me or that bitch. It's your call." Casey gave him an ultimatum, hoping he chose to stay with his wife so she wouldn't have to tell him outright that it was over between them.

Casey and Judge Nelson argued for a few minutes before Casey shouted, "It's over, Judge! Why don't you get it through your thick fucking skull?" Without saying another word, Casey left his chambers and never looked back.

Later, when they returned to the courtroom, Casey got into a heated debate about a legal issue with the judge, which made him go off and slam his gavel.

"That is it, Counselor! This court now holds you in contempt! Bailiff, get her out of my sight!" Judge Nelson fumed, really in his feelings about being dumped by her.

While Casey was being escorted from the courtroom, she cursed and called Judge Nelson every derogatory name in the vulgar book she could think of.

Now I'm that bitch that nobody wants to rumble against in court. Even Judge Nelson's pink Ben Franklin-looking ass and his citation for contempt can't stop my shine. I'm that bitch, and failure isn't an option in my book, she told herself as the sounds of the cell door popping open made her stand up quickly and rush out the cell.

"Ms. Cooper!" A policewoman called her from behind the waist-high desk at the Central lock-up checkout station.

Casey's $495 knee-high Christian Dior boots clacked against the black and white tile floors as she stepped forth. Once she reached the desk, the property clerk doled out her personal possessions that she had surrendered after being taken into custody: a Lady Presidential Rolex watch, pinstripe Dior newspaper cap, a diamond ring, diamond earrings, a Dior monogrammed purse, keys, and cell phone.

The officer produced a form on which each item was listed with a line at the bottom for the former prisoner's signature to verify that their property had been returned upon release.

"Sorry for the inconvenience, Ms. Cooper. Judge Nelson can be a jerk at times. Please sign here," the lady officer said, pushing the inventory form in front of her.

Casey snatched up the ink pen and signed the form with a flourish. She looked more like a celebrity signing an autograph than someone being released from Central Booking.

Getting outta here is so much easier than coming in, she thought as the policewoman reached down and added a piece of mail to Casey's pile of valuable possessions.

"Judge Nelson sent this down to you right after his court adjourned for the day." The police lady rolled her eyes as if to say, *I really feel your pain, girl.*

A second policeman leaned lazily over the counter, observing the proceedings. He shifted his silver head a bit in an effort to be nosy and see the writing on the envelope that the property officer put down.

"Why is Judge Nelson writing you after he sent you to lock-up?" he drawled with idle interest.

Casey focused on the envelope and then opened it. She scanned the letter within for a few seconds. Her eyes flickered across the heartfelt apology from the Judge. Her stoic expression couldn't be read by the two officers, who really wanted to know what the Judge said in the letter.

"So what does it say?" both officers blurted with interest. The suspense was killing them.

Casey stared at the letter for a second and then looked up at both officers. She wanted to tell them and exposed the judge's infidelities, but that would expose her as well. She felt she got what she wanted out of the judge and now it was time to move on. She told herself that any dealings she had with the Judge in the past would die as soon as she walked out of the lock-up area.

"The letter says I'm up out of here. I'm free!" Casey grinned while stuffing the letter in her purse.

Drunk In Love

She gave the lock-up area one more glance before walking towards the exits to a new life without Judge Nelson in it.

Vanessa Jergens
Ohio University Banquet Hall

The final staging area for prepping a huge banquet dinner is comparable to persuading a man who is supposed to love you for oral sex, Vanessa thought while shouldering her wheat-brown petite frame into the banquet hall, only to ease in upon her employee's nasty conversation.

"Girl, his freaky ass ate my pussy and ass out until I cried," a woman whose looks could match the adult film star Pinky stated proudly.

Her statement drew giggles, laughter, and high fives from the crowd of women around her. Some of the men in the crowd grunted and sighed in frustration, feeling like whoever the guy was that did that set the male race back 2000 years. Now every woman in Ohio would want them to lick it before they stick it.

"You must of returned the favor? Shiiid, if that was me, it would've been sixty-eight and I owe you one." the tall, dark-skinned brother with model looks said jokingly, but he meant every word.

Vanessa couldn't believe her ears. The same thing she was complaining about at home was happening all over the world - well, at least in the world of Ohio. Being Twenty-nine years old and the owner of a lucrative catering business, Vanessa possessed a cherubic face and warm eyes, and for the life of her, she could not fathom why her husband didn't want to go downtown on her. After listening to her employee's conversation, she began wondering if her husband of ten years felt the same way as Kenny, the guy who had just made the sixty-eight statement. Lately he'd been denying her the special treats she craved. When Vanessa addressed it with him, her husband, Russell, blamed it on work, stress, and the job burning him out.

Drunk In Love

Vanessa immediately thought he was having an affair and then quickly tossed that idea out of her head. She had contemplated having an affair, but quickly shunned the idea out of respect for the man who stepped up to father their child and did his best to love her.

But boy, do I need some licky-licky so bad, she thought. She enjoyed staying in bed naked, depending on the time of day, getting her kitty-cat serviced the way she liked. *Every woman needs a good tongue job just to complete the loving, which I haven't been getting lately,* Vanessa thought, releasing a frustrated sigh.

"Shut up, Kenny!" the woman snarled, invading Vanessa's thoughts. "Your black butt probably wouldn't know how to make a pussy cum if your life depended on it, wit' cho' Bernie Mac-looking ass!"

"I bet'cha you won't wanna find out!" Kenny challenged her over a chorus of hysterical laughter. "I'll have your red-bone ass screaming my name for days and looking for me in the daytime with a flashlight after I get finish wit' dat ass!"

Vanessa saw that as her cue to intervene before things really got heated. She walked up to Kenny and shoved a silver serving pan in his hands.

"C'mon, gang, I don't pay you guys to sit around and lollygag. Now let's get things in order. Let's get it, chop-chop!" she said, clapping her hands, signaling everyone to get to work.

As they slipped into an elfin-like work force, Vanessa called her husband. Once she got the voicemail, she left him a freaky message.

"Hey, Russy, when you come home tonight, I'm going to eat you and that big dick alive! Mmm...my pussy's wet just thinking about you, daddy. See you tonight, my Big Dick Warrior. I love you."

After ending the call, Vanessa turned the reins of serving the day's banquet over to her trustworthy assistant, Amber.

"I gotcha, Ms. J!" Amber beamed, knowing she was about to run with being the head honcho for the day. Her first agenda was to make Kenny's slick mouth-talking behind feel her wrath for talking slick to her girlfriend, Jennifer.

"Make sure you call me if you need anything, okay?"

"Will do, Ms. J." Amber nodded like an opponent does before a karate match.

Vanessa smiled and twirled her wedding band around her ring finger while leaving the banquet hall. Once she got outside, Vanessa grabbed her gym bag from the trunk of her silver-hued Mercedes SLK. She got inside her car and changed into her lemon yellow spandex short set.

Seeing that she only had thirty minutes to get to the park and meet her girlfriends, Vanessa left the parking lot, dropped the top on her sporty ride, and let the humid summer air whistle through her auburn, shoulder-length mane.

While racing towards the park, Vanessa decided to be more aggressive in the bedroom. She felt that being a funny, sharp-tongued, hardworking, and loving wife just wasn't going to cut it anymore. She needed to drive Russell crazy, both good and bad. Being such a humble person inside and out, Vanessa just loved life and couldn't fathom the idea of harassing her husband about his neglect in the bedroom. She figured it would be far better to try to coach him into what she wanted tonight instead of flat out telling him.

'Cause if he thinks I'm going to settle only for the dick, then he's in for a seriously rude awakening, she told herself while taking the exit for the James H. McGee Expressway, aka The Coast.

Drunk In Love

Anitra Stamos
Gem City Sports & Apparel Headquarters

The male assistant slipped inside Anitra's office with a handful of sports equipment orders while the former track star engaged in an important telephone call. She glanced up after noticing him and signaled for him to drop the papers on her desk.

She mouthed, "Thanks, boo," after he dropped the orders on her desk.

The assistant paused, not believing his ears. Knowing the twenty-eight-year-old reddish sex-kitten had been heralded for both her numerous impressions on single men of the world during her track meets and for her seductive pussycat mannerisms, the assistant decided not to let the perfect opportunity pass him by.

"Yes, baby, I'll see you tonight and we'll tell them together. Okay... Okay, now would you please let me go? I have work to do. Uh huh...u huh... Well, I'm meeting the girls for some racquetball at four. I love you more, baby. Mwah!" She gave the caller a kiss through the phone and began laughing after the caller said something that amused her. "Okay, I'll see you later, love you, bye-bye," she said and ended the call.

"Ah, Ms. Stamos, you need anything else before I leave?"

"No, John, I'm fine, thanks," Anitra responded with a smile as she stood up.

John's mouth fell open when he saw her body being suffocated in some bright orange form-fitting hot pants and matching sports bra. He couldn't stop himself from looking at her 5'8", 142-pound thick athletic frame.

17

Damn, lil mama's fine as hell, John thought, licking his lips like LL Cool J.

Anitra assumed that the young retired drug dealer and convicted felon had the major hots for her. She remembered when he mentioned several of her track competitions that he had watched during his prison bid.

If she was still a player like her bosom buddy Casey, she would've already jumped his bones just to see how long his magic stick could hold up inside her wet, tight love zone - an addictive piece of heaven that still had plenty of brothers in Ohio and all over the world searching for her in the daytime with a flashlight.

But those days were long gone.

I'm doing the grown up thing now and settling down, she thought while looking through the sales invoices.

Business was picking up even in the recession, which meant that her bank accounts would eventually grow as well. She felt good about Barack Obama's State of the Union address speech the previous night, mainly because he talked about small businesses like hers thriving in America to become corporate empires. The first black President gave Anitra the motivation to believe that she could do and accomplish anything she set her mind on doing.

Suddenly Anitra felt John's large, pencil-brown colored hand on hers. She felt his gaze gripping her, so she looked up.

"Are you sure, Ms. Stamos? Because I really don't mind doing you - I mean, doing anything - for your fine ass, and I'll give you whatever you want. Just say the word."

Before Anitra could reply, the assistant took a gamble and kissed her so passionately, all she could do was close her eyes and accept his probing tongue.

♥ ♥ ♥

Drunk In Love

Doctor Briana Evans was finishing up a yearly examination on an older patient with hypertension while his portly nephew sat on the examination table behind him.

"Okay, Mr. Hughes, everything seems to be okay. Just take it easy on the salts and fried foods. I think you'll be just fine. You're too handsome to die on me. What will happen to our female race without you?" she joked with a smile.

"I hear you, Doc, but it's hard. Them fried pork chops be saying something, darling. Mmm mmph!" He licked his lips and began buttoning up his shirt. He reminded her of a younger-looking version of the singer Lou Rawls.

"Now Mr. Hughes, I done told you…I done told you!" she said sternly.

"Okay, okay! Oh, hey, Doc, would you like to meet my brother? He's around your age and he's a good fella that needs a sweet woman like you in his life."

"How old is he?" she asked, looking past the nice gentleman. Briana noticed that his nephew was shaking his head back and forth in a negative way as if to say, "Don't do it!"

"He's 'round 'bout twenty-seven or thirty, one of them numbers. I forget, but any whatnot, I think y'all go good together."

"Ah, Mr. Hughes, I don't think so. I'm very busy right now at this stage in my career and I'll just do be doing your brother an injustice," she said, weaseling her way out of the situation, which caused Mr. Hughes's nephew to give her the thumbs up signal.

"Okay, Doc, I'll be seeing you then," he said, grabbing his fedora. He left the examination room seconds later with his nephew in tow.

Briana gave the lad a conspiratorial nod and wink before closing the door behind them. She laughed a little behind the youngster saving her from a potential disaster. She liked the young boy. She wanted kids, but wouldn't settle for just any man being her baby daddy. She already didn't trust any men. She figured if she would've met Mr. Hughes's brother, he probably would have made it harder for her to ever open up to another man again in life. Plus she had high expectations for the guy she wanted to spend the rest of her life with.

Their stuff has to be in order. They gotta have a nice paying job, be somewhat handsome, own a car, be in fit condition, and most importantly, they have to know how to work that dick, she thought while changing into her recreational clothing. After giving it some more thought, Briana decided to bide her time and let love find her. If it didn't, so be it. As long as she could get her rocks off with her sex toys from time to time, she'd be okay - or so she thought.

After getting rid of her last patient for the day, Briana moved to her office, logged in her hours inside the Grandville Hospital's mainframe computer, and called it a day. While she walked through the hospital corridor flaunting what her mother gave her, Briana wondered if Mr. Right would be at the nightclub tonight for girl's night out, or would she meet Mr. Right Now to help clean some of the cobwebs out of her secret garden?

Drunk In Love

Girlfriends
Dayton View Park

The humid summer afternoon drew an assortment of excitement, which made many head out to find something to do. Many of Dayton's denizens decided to head out to the same place, overrunning the historical park. Here and there along the expanse of the park, several groups of men and women strode along the asphalt paths, enjoying the usual games of cat mouse that people played.

As it got hotter, a friendly game of team-doubles racquetball got very competitive. Even the Ohio players that were used to drawing huge crowds on the basketball court with their high-flying dunks and A-1 b-ball games had stopped their game just to observe the four sexy women on the racquet courts battling for the victory, supremacy, and bragging rights.

"G-G-G-Go get it, Nessa!" Briana squealed, watching her partner, Vanessa, return Casey's surefire kill shot.

"Get what? She got a partner right here! I got your back, girl!" Anitra said in a slick tone while swinging her small racquet in vintage Serena Williams's fashion.

As soon as the ball slammed against the wall, Briana took off. She sprinted towards the serving line looking like a woman possessed. She squatted quickly and sliced the ball for a soft kill shot, drawing cheers and murmurs from the crowd.

"AAAAAHHHH! We are sooo good…so, so good!" Vanessa yelled joyfully while jumping up and down and taunting her friends.

"The game ain't over yet, trick. Just shut up and serve," Casey hissed, bending over in anticipation to return Vanessa's serve.

While bending over, Casey gave all the male spectators a nice memorable view of her shapely behind. Though she was short, Casey possessed a huge ass that looked unnatural on her small frame. In an attempt to keep their muscle tone and shapely bodies from their youth in shape, racquetball had become the ladies' weekly ritual for the last six years. The sport also provided a way for them to stay close and talk trash among themselves about their lives, jobs, and the men in the world. You could relate them to that reality show *Basketball Wives* without all the extra drama and showing off for the cameras. But today, they had an unexpected audience of secret admirers and male groupies.

"Game on the wall, ladies," Vanessa stated in a taunting tone while showing her best Queen of England smile. "You know if we get this point, you guys have to treat for girls' night out tonight," she added, smacking her hip for emphasis.

Vanessa had made her original bond with Briana back in elementary school during cheerleader try-outs. As they grew up, their bond got to the point where they loved each other like sisters. Even though Briana and Anitra were first cousins, everyone among the tight-knit group knew that Briana and Vanessa loved each other dearly.

That's why I always get stuck playing with Anitra. She's an excellent sprinter and track star, but this here is my sport, Casey thought while waiting on the serve.

"Ball's in," Vanessa crooned with a silly laugh before serving the ball.

"They sure are!" Casey grunted, taking off. She attacked the serve with a sideswiping power shot that killed Vanessa's dreams of an easy victory.

"I can't hear ya now, Nessa!" Anitra and Casey teased her in unison.

"It looks like it's a win by two to us!" Anitra pointed back and forth between herself and Casey.

"And it's our serve, Miss Thang!" Casey taunted Vanessa with a hard edge in her gaze.

Drunk In Love

Vanessa gave her the finger as the team switched positions. Casey rolled her eyes playfully at Vanessa like she'd done on numerous occasions when they were younger. Anitra stuck out her tongue at Briana mockingly, making Briana roll her eyes at her.

"C'mon, Casey, let's make these hoes pay for our way into the club tonight," Anitra said, pumping up Briana and Vanessa to the point where they wanted to make Anitra eat her words.

Born the daughter of a bus driver and a mother who worked in the federal government, Anitra grew up in a middle-class neighborhood. She had attended one of the country's most prestigious high schools, Dunbar. She continued her education by attending Howard University in Washington, D.C. As a track star at the historical African American college, Anitra met Casey, whose school studies were never a priority like her studies on playing men. Casey didn't claim to be a gold-digger, but she made it a point not to mess with any broke niggas.

At twenty-two years old, Anitra graduated with a business degree and a B.A. in fashion designs, making her a double threat armed with beauty and brains. Six months later, the love for track and field competition stole Anitra's heart. Everything else became secondary until she won several gold medals and hung up her track shoes five years later.

As Anitra became one of the fastest women in the world, Casey attended every event, cheering her friend on with platinum pom-poms. After passing the bar exam, Casey took a break and traveled the world just to party. After witnessing so many minorities fail while trying to make it out of the Parkside projects - aka The Dark Side, which was one of the roughest of many hoods in Dayton - Casey welcomed the new experience of being able to practice law in her hometown with open arms. During her travels, Casey always made mental notes to return to the hood and help out her peers. After witnessing and hearing numerous stories of how the justice system treated young black indigent males and other minorities, Casey decided to study criminal law in hopes of making a change one day for the common man.

The Diplomats Capo/Jim Jones classic "Baby Girl" invaded the park and Casey's thoughts. Brought up on hip-hop, Casey had surprisingly almanac-like knowledge for a woman when it came to rap music.

"One of y'all needs to serve!" Briana snapped, the challenge rising in her tone.

"Baby boy, you tryna be down with the Clit Set, yeah... Well bruh, then you gotta get your tongue wet... What? Yeah boy, if you wanna get some bomb sex... Y'all ain't thought we was s'posed ta know..." Casey crooned, changing the chorus of the song to her liking while gyrating her wide hips, causing mouths to drool and hang open. She loved attention, and what better way to get it than in a park around a million lusting, sweaty, rock-hard men?

"Go 'head and serve, Anitra, so we can get those sluts off the court!" Casey added.

As soon as Anitra served, Briana returned it with a powerful swing. As the ball hit the ground in the corner, Briana and Vanessa began celebrating, knowing the ball was impossible to return. They began high-fiving, clapping, and jumping up and down until a blur shot past them.

Anitra hustled past them, saving the play and chopping the ball softly, causing it to hit the wall and roll back to the tip of Vanessa's yellow and black Asics boxing shoes.

"OOOOOOOHHHHHH!" The crowd of lusting men erupted while Casey and Anitra celebrated with high-fives and clapping before taking a bow and blowing kisses of appreciation to the crowd.

"Sluts!" Briana fussed in a teasing way as she backed up, preparing to defend against match point. She looked over at Casey, who was bouncing the ball in preparation to serve.

Drunk In Love

"Serve the ball, Casey, so I can get me some!" Briana said, trying to get in Casey's head.

"Get some what?" she replied and then she served with lightning speed.

"Embarrassment! YEEEYY! WOOOO!" Casey shrieked joyously after sneaking in an ace.

Staring at each other for a moment, the look of shock and disbelief registered loudly on Briana and Vanessa's faces. They couldn't believe that Casey had just pulled a stunt like that.

"All I do is win-win-win no matter what!" Casey chanted along with the DJ Khaled/T-Pain song playing somewhere in the background. "Got money on mind I can never give it up...and every time I step up on the damn court, everybody hands goes up!"

Anitra along with several men in the ground threw their hands up on cue.

"And they stay there... and they stay there!" Casey chanted, nodding her head, which infuriated Briana and Vanessa.

"You cheated!" Vanessa complained, sucking her teeth.

"No I didn't. I just saw an opportunity and took it. It's not my fault that y'all got caught sleeping on the job."

"Whatever, Casey, you just a cheater, that's all I know. I didn't know it was that serious and you would have to stoop so low to win," Briana griped as the group of men began filing out and returning to the basketball court and other areas of the park.

A few guys stuck around, trying to get the girls attention, but they ignored them. The men took the hint and walked away, cursing them out under their breaths.

"Chill, Bri-Bri, we got in y'all ass - simple as that! Don't be mad!" Anitra blurted, giving Casey another high five.

All four women gathered their bags and took a seat on the gunmetal gray benches. They began pulling out their bottled sports drinks and water, taking long swigs. After they caught their breaths, Anitra stood up and faced them.

"Guess what happened today, y'all?" Anitra asked.

Before they could answer, she filled them in on her assistant's actions.

"No he didn't, girl!" Vanessa said with a slight giggle.

"That ain't all. This little bastard had the nerve to ask me to let him eat my pussy and asshole out for an hour straight."

"And you didn't let him?" Casey blurted. "Girl, you getting soft on me...you getting soft."

Anitra looked at Casey and rolled her eyes. "Anyway, he was cute..." she said as she began describing his handsome features to her girlfriends. She even gave them the approximate size of his manhood from the memory of the excited bulge in his pants that looked like a thick tent.

"So what's the problem if he's all that and then some?" Casey asked.

"I'm a professional first, dear. I can't be having that freaky-freaky stuff going on in my place of business, so I suspended his ass for his actions. Girl, he scared the mess outta me by doing some shit like that. I spent the whole ride over here trying to figure out what would make him do such a thing, and what if he really wanted some and tried to take it?"

All of them paused, giving Anitra looks of surprise.

"Girl, you s'posed to let him get some," Casey said while taking another sip of her sports drink.

"No, I'm not! Believe me, I really wanted to, but unfortunately, for him and me, I have turned over a new leaf in life. Even for me that was hard to do, but I decided from now on I'm going to be a one-man woman."

"WHAT!" Casey spat out her drink and began coughing.

"Ah, now look at what'chu did, Anitra, you got Casey all upset over here." Vanessa giggled while tenderly patting Casey's back like she was trying to get a burp out of a newborn baby.

Drunk In Love

"Nessa, get off me, don't touch me," Casey hissed, while ice-grilling Anitra, her partner in her quest to disrupt and shatter all men's lives.

"Girl, let me be the first one to say I'm so proud of your freak behind," Briana joked. "But I thought you and Miss Casey here were vowing to be players until y'all got old and gray?"

"I was until I met this really wonderful guy. Plus the fact that he really laid the dick on me and blew my back out got me second-guessing. I have never come so much in my life," Anitra said, fanning herself, adding emphasis before continuing. "Bri-Bri, I'm talking about this stud had me trembling and climbing the walls and screaming his name. You know I don't ever scream no man's name. Ever since I met him, I've been cumming all night when we get together, and I'm talking about multiple orgasms. I'm so in love right now. I have no choice but to lock the dick down," she said. She told them how she met the guy at the grocery store, about their first date, and how they were always spending the night at each other's houses. Anitra stressed to them his countless attempts of doing things to make her happy.

Everyone listened in awe except Casey. Casey studied her friend with her chin resting on her steepled fingers. She couldn't believe Anitra had gone out and gotten whipped by the dick when they had vowed never to fall in love, regardless of how good the loving was in the bedroom.

"Mmm mmph!" Briana and Vanessa hummed loudly while Casey stood up and took over the conversation like she was in the courtroom trying to win a case.

"I don't agree with that at all. You fuck one man, you've fucked them all. Like for instance, I'm tired of all these tired-ass brothers. It's time for me to get some white meat in life."

Waving her off, Vanessa said, "How many times do we have to go through this interracial thing with you, Casey? I mean, whenever you can't get your way with the brothers, you

27

cry about wanting to run to the other side. Go ahead, there's nothing stopping you but you."

"I'm serious this time, Nessa. A so-called brother had me thrown in jail today." Casey lied a little and then informed them about her fling with the judge and the way he used his power to try and control her.

Casey's girlfriends looked at her like she was crazy for sleeping around with a judge, but they remained silent. They'd rather be quiet than argue with Casey, who never thought she was wrong about anything.

"Then this limp-dick bastard had the audacity to send me an apology card and reservations for dinner for two at Chez Pierre's."

"Oooh, girl, Chez Pierre's is a very expensive restaurant," Briana chimed in. "If I was you, I'd go just to run up a huge tab on his ass. Then I'd excuse myself to go to the ladies room before the food arrived and leave his ass right there looking stupid. That will teach him not to fuck with a lady."

"Mmph, for real though!" Vanessa added, giving Briana a high five.

"Fuck him! I got everything I needed and then some from his punk ass. I just hope I don't have to ever go through his courtroom again."

"All you have to do is open up your legs like you been doing and cheat to win, just like you did today!" Vanessa teased, throwing water on Casey.

"Ooh, you bitch!" Casey snapped, going after Vanessa. "Oh, it's on now, trick! Don't run now! What'chu running for?" Casey giggled while chasing behind Vanessa.

As soon as she caught Vanessa by her hair, Casey tackled her, causing Briana and Anitra to join them. By the time they got over there, Vanessa had sprung back to her feet and was lunging at Casey.

Drunk In Love

"Team fight! Team fight!" Briana squealed as they began bumping into each other. They started playfully throwing punches and grabbing each others hair.

After several minutes of tussling and playing, they collapsed on the ground and the benches. Once they caught their breaths, they began making plans for their girls night out - another ritual they shared to keep their bonds strong throughout the years.

"I'm serious, Casey, don't be late this time and have us waiting on you, slowpoke," Briana warned in a motherly tone.

It was an unspoken rule amongst them that Briana was the leader of the group considering her job and all the money she made, plus the fact that she always made sure to put their happiness before her own. None of them had a problem with calling Briana up at one or two o'clock in the morning to discuss the problems in their lives. She was like a big sister that all of them wanted in life, but never had until they met her.

Casey stuck out her long tongue as if she were a little school kid teasing her friend.

"Okay now, children, stop it. It's sistah-girl hug time," Vanessa announced, cutting into Casey and Briana's battle of wills and egos.

"I'm not hugging none of you fish-smelling skanks!" Anitra joked, causing them to rush her and squeeze her until she started crying with laughter.

While they shared a *Waiting 2 Exhale* moment, Anitra began wondering how they would react tonight after she revealed her surprise.

Girlfriends
Spunky's Nightclub: Ladies Night

At close to 11:15p.m., Vanessa, Briana, and Casey spotted Anitra prancing in the club, hanging all over a model-looking brother with soft features. He rocked a John Legend R&B type of curly afro. The aura covering him made all the women stare at him during his trek towards the place where Casey and the girls posted up, waiting on Anitra.

Casey, Briana, and Vanessa simultaneously rolled their eyes as the couple headed in their direction. They wanted to curse Anitra's butt out. Not only was she late, she violated their special bonding outing by bringing a date.

Lust is not supposed to be this addictive and time-consuming. In a minute, whoever that brother is will be a dominating presence in her life that will dictate her every action and eventually come between us, and I just can't sit back and allow that to happen. No, uh uh, not to me it won't, Casey thought while admiring Anitra's one-piece Prada catsuit with cut-outs and matching peach five-inch faux diamond-studded booties and the pearl choker she wore. Casey had to admit that Anitra was looking very fly that night, but she would never let Anitra know it, mainly due to the fact that she was late and with a man: the enemy!

"Hey, gang, sorry I'm late, but Nathan here had to make a quick detour to the jewelry store," Anitra squealed excitedly while flashing the seven carat diamond engagement ring in a rose gold setting.

"AAAAAHHHHH!" Briana and Vanessa screamed joyously, giving Anitra hugs of congratulations.

While they hugged, giggled, and made a fuss over who was going to be the bride's maid of honor, Casey stiffened at the realization that her girlfriend had deserted her. A look of

Drunk In Love

anger creased Casey's face as she realized that her girlfriend had changed her mind about being a bachelorette until the sun burst. Casey turned up her drink and downed it quickly, preparing herself to confront Anitra.

Just a few months ago, Anitra vowed never to get married until she was on her last leg. Now at the age of twenty-eight and in the prime of her life, she suddenly changes her mind? Uh uh, something just not right with this picture. I can feel it, Casey thought, letting her expression show her true feelings and disapproval of the whole ordeal.

"Well, Casey, are you going to congratulate my cousin?" Briana asked as Vanessa, Anitra, and Nathan stared at her, waiting for a response.

The uncomfortable silence seemed to last for an eternity, but only a few seconds passed before Casey finished off her drink and gave Anitra's milk chocolate fiancé the evil eye. Keeping her evil look glued on him, Casey gave Anitra a squeezing bear hug.

"Honestly, I'm not okay with your decision to get married, but I guess you gotta do what'chu gotta do," Casey said as she leaned in for Anitra's ear. "You ain't shit, hoe," Casey, whispered, making Anitra cringe. "You left me out here to complete our mission all alone. Some friend you are!"

Anitra's heart began pounding with disappointment as they broke their embrace. Anitra glanced at Casey who gave her a "you know you dead wrong for this shit" type of look.

Why can't she be happy for me? That mission is so juvenile. We're grown women now; we made that pact back in college. Everybody does crazy things in college and moves on with their lives. Why can't Casey follow the protocol? Well, I really don't care because I'm going through with this marriage with or without her blessing, Anitra told herself as the deejay threw on a classic from Rick Ross.

Anitra pulled her man to the side and started explaining that she needed some time alone with her girlfriends to explain the sudden surprise engagement.

"What's to explain? I love you, Anitra, and if you have to explain that to your friends, then they're really not your friends, ya feel me?" he asked, looking over her shoulder at Casey, who kept ice-grilling him like he had killed her cat or something.

"Please, Nate, just give me a minute to clear the air up about a few things with Casey, that's all."

He sighed. "Yeah, okay. Well, I'll be over by the bar checking out all the women if you need me," he joked before kissing her on the forehead.

"Nathan, don't play with me, boy! You're going to get one of these skanks hurt up in here."

"All right, all right, I'll be good," he said soothingly before walking away.

Anitra spun quickly on her heels and rushed towards the stand-up oval table that her girlfriends occupied. She didn't allow herself time to think as she shook the table, toppling their drinks. Her expression frightened them.

"Oooh, Casey, I could just kill you! I don't believe you!" she snapped. "How could you dis me like that in front of my man?"

"Now, now, cousin," Briana intervened. "I don't know about this marriage thing either. I was just fronting for ole boy over there."

"You sure he's not after your money or something?" Vanessa added, not really wanting to go against the majority. In fact, Vanessa wanted one of her girlfriends to join her in the married life so she could really share what was going on in her world.

"No!" she raged, leering at Casey, who didn't say a word – what she thought, was written all over her face. "Why y'all just can't be happy for me?"

Drunk In Love

"We just want to make sure that you're ready, that's all. Marriage is a huge step, cousin," Briana reasoned and then threw Anitra's previous statement about being single back in her face.

"And you know what else?" Casey jumped in. "Men have serious problems with commitment. A guy can have the perfect woman, but men will remain the dogs they are because being a player is just in their sneaky-ass nature. They are going to do whatever they want to do regardless. You can never really base your life on someone else, because at the end of the day, you'll never know what's going to happen. You just have to be about your business."

"For your information, Casey, Nathan treats me like a queen!" Anitra retorted. "That man worships the ground that I walk on. He's funny, caring, hardworking, spontaneous, and everything that I could possibly want in a husband. Nathan completes me, and I love him so much." Her voice cracked a little during her speech.

"Bullshit!" Casey snapped. "How long have y'all been together?" Casey asked while nursing the remnants of her Sex on the Beach cocktail. She had saved the drink when Anitra first shook the table. Now that she was sipping on her fourth drink of the night, Casey felt a little tipsy and very loose at the lips.

"Close to six months," Anitra stated timidly, quickly realizing her mistake.

"You been hiding out with some dick for close to six months and now you expect me to sit up here and believe that you're in love?" Casey grilled Anitra like a hostile witness on the stand in the courtroom. Casey really hated the fact that her road dawg had gotten dick-whipped in such a short time frame.

"Yes."

"That's it, just yes?" Casey griped, raising her voice and clenching her fists. She felt Anitra owed her more of an explanation than just a simple yes.

"You heard what I said!" Anitra rolled her eyes before continuing. "Listen to me, guys, I'm tired of chasing behind men and having them chasing behind me. I think Nathan's the one for me, and I'm going to get married with or without you guys blessing."

"So you're willing to just throw away our friendship over some man you just met and barely even know?" Casey asked, looking angry.

"Whatever you wanna do, then do it, Casey. I love you, but I'm not about to go there with you over who I love and want to be with."

"Well, since your dick-whipped butt put it that way, then I guess I have to accept it and roll with you on your decision. Congratulations, girl!" Briana smiled, giving her a loving hug.

"I'm happy for you too, girl!" Vanessa cooed, joining in on the affectionate hugging.

"I'm telling you now, Anitra, if he breaks your heart, you better believe I'm going to throw that shit all up in your face, you freak!" Casey smiled before joining them for a group hug.

"Now that we settled that, I might as well go find me some soul mate dick to take home," Briana joked, easing out of the group hug.

"She's just jealous because you're getting married before her," Vanessa said with a giggle while looking at Anitra as Briana backed up until she was surrounded by bodies on the dance floor.

After finishing off her drink, Casey slammed her glass on the table and began snapping her fingers to the "Champagne Life" song by Ne-Yo.

"Well, ladies, I have got to represent for the last of the playa bitches!" Casey announced, smacking her soft behind, making it jiggle for a few microseconds. She took off seconds later, heading for the crowded dance floor.

Drunk In Love

"Uh uh, girl, those are your friends," Vanessa joked, making Anitra laugh as they watched their friends engage in some man-hunting.

At that moment, Anitra began wondering if Casey was right. She realized that she would miss the thrill of the chase and different sizes of male love muscles that the world had to offer, but then again, Anitra figured that she had one helluva man in her life who was willing to love her through thick and thin.

But am I really, really ready to give up everything I know and have been used to in life to return that love to Nathan? Why does everything good have to be so bad? Anitra thought while watching Briana and Casey talk to two handsome men who looked like they were packing a lot of love muscles.

Briana

"Party over here! I said party over here!" Briana yelled over the loud music, trying to get some male attention on the crowded dance floor.

Briana and Casey were working their sexy bodies in the midst of the thick clam chowder-like atmosphere. Vibrating music, smoke, and a mixture of bodies saturated the air inside the nightclub. Women, including Casey and Briana, shook what their mothers gave them in conjunction with the music while men did their best to cozy up to their gyrating bodies.

Briana was really enjoying herself. She and Casey had similar taste in men. They loved some Mandingo warriors, and they were not short in supply tonight. Everywhere they looked, tall, athletic-looking men with firm, toned muscles and cute faces filled their sight.

Casey acted like a hen in an all-male rooster coop. Within an hour, Casey had already collected more than nine cell phone numbers and still politicked for more of them. *The more the merrier,* she thought, trying to stay true to her player lifestyle.

Against her will, Briana had collected two telephone numbers from two men who wouldn't take no for an answer. Being an attractive woman with sexy curves and a sex appeal out of their world, the men of Dayton, Ohio seemed to come at Briana in droves tonight. She politely turned them away.

Then she saw him - talk about sexiness personified!

I know his fine ass could do wonders on this pussy, Briana thought, watching the 6'4" lean, muscular chocolate Mandingo. The attraction for him was instantaneous, like a bear attracted to honey in a tree. Briana couldn't keep her eyes off his toned upper body, which he had covered in a dark, form-fitting T-shirt. The large print dangling in the crotch area of his slacks alerted Briana to the fact that he was definitely working with the proper plumbing tool needed to clean out her neglected love oven.

After catching Briana looking at him, the Mandingo surprisingly took the initiative and stepped to her.

"Hey, cutie," he said in a low, rough tone that reminded Briana of Barry White's sexy vocals. She wanted to find out everything about him and see where things went from there. There was no hiding her surprise by his approach as she fanned herself like she was all hot and bothered.

"Hello."

"What are you sipping on tonight?" he asked conversationally, gesturing toward the half-filled cup in her hand.

Your sweat and love juices, if you play your cards right, handsome. "Oh, this is a little Sex on the Beach…something light."

He gave her a cute Colgate smile. "So you're into sex on the beach, huh?"

What kind of lame-ass come-on line is that? "Of course, because I only drink on a weekly basis."

You know what I meant, but that was a slick brush off. "That's very admirable," he said dismissively. "I wouldn't want to see a fine sister like you hooked on the bottle."

You're losing me and this pussy fast, buddy. "Mm-hmm."

"So you want to buy me a drink?"

I know this motherfucker just didn't ask me to buy him a drink? "Now why on earth would I want to do that, sweetheart? It's L-A-D-I-E-S night," she spelled it out for him. "Which means the drinks are supposed to be on you, darling." She looked him squarely in the face to add to the embarrassment of him asking such a socially unacceptable yet personally alluring question.

Taken aback by her response, he remained quiet.

"Look, if you really want to get to know me, why don't you start by telling me your name?" Briana coached him a little and smiled at a man for the first time since leaving the appointment with her shrink earlier. Being single and lonely had truly emboldened her.

He responded cautiously because of her rebuke. "My name's Terrence. And you are...?"

Putting all hostilities aside, she extended her hand and shook his. "I'm Briana. It's nice to meet you, Terrence. Now see how easy that was?"

"Yeah, it's a pleasure to meet you too."

"Do you always come here trying to con women into buying you drinks?" she teased him playfully.

"Aw, I see you got jokes, huh?" he chuckled. "But no, on the real, I come here to expose the stingy player-hating sisters like your fine self," he said with sarcasm oozing heavily from his tone.

Terrence Warthen was twenty-five years old, the product of two African American parents that moved from Camden, New Jersey to keep their only son away from the grungy streets. Terrence managed to capitalize on the move to the Midwest by getting an associate's degree in business and telecommunications. As much as Terrence enjoyed his love for producing music - just one of the many talents in his repertoire - he currently attended graduate school at Ohio State University. He wanted to get the degrees he needed to obtain the goals he wanted in life, plus he wanted to have a backup plan just in case he didn't become a multi-million dollar record producer in four years. Terrence definitely had his stuff in order with solid plans to make it in life.

"Oooh! Flattery will get you everywhere," Briana laughed. She liked a man who could fire back on her sharp, sassy remarks. She wanted a strong man who could keep her in check.

"I'ma see if you bluffing or not too," he said with a smile.

Drunk In Love

"So what other ghetto pick-up lines you have beside the one about the drinky-drink you just used on me?"

"Why you tryna go there? That wasn't a pick-up line," he protested.

"Well, you did come over here and use it, right?" she smugly pointed out.

"I just so happened to be thirsty, but I can bounce right back over to where I came from and use it on another less stingy lady," he said with a challenging expression.

Briana eyes turned soft and sweet in a heartbeat. "But where will that get you?"

Needless to say, Terrence fell for her gaze. "Nowhere," he said grudgingly with a smirk.

"Well c'mon, Mister king of the ghetto pick-up lines. Let's go find us some seats and get to know each other a little deeper."

"I'm a freelance music producer and I'm not really looking for a woman," he blurted, shocking the hell out of Briana.

Now where did all that just come from? I hope he's not some weirdo, she thought, all the while hiding her disappointment. She had really begun warming up to him. "Well, I am a doctor, honey, and I'm definitely not looking for a man!" she fired back, feeling her love juices slither down her thigh. The thought of being rejected by any man turned her on tremendously. Now she had to get what she wanted out of him. She crossed her legs and licked her lips in a salacious manner.

"Oh yeah?" He arched his eyebrow at her response and body language. *You just my type of gal,* he thought, eyeing her breasts covered in the silk fabric of the clingy, form-fitting blouse. He could see her hard nipples poking through, looking like two pencil erasers.

"Yeah," Briana smiled, clasping her hand.

Briana pulled on his hand, and led him around the nightclub. After circling around the nightclub twice, Briana alerted her girlfriends that she was leaving with Terrence. Vanessa stopped her, trying to find out what was on Briana's mind.

"Are you okay or are you just drunk? You just can't leave with a complete stranger?" Vanessa reasoned.

"Anitra's getting married to a stranger, but I can't leave with one? You sound so hypocritical right now, Nessa!" Briana slurred, and Vanessa could tell she was a little drunk.

"He could be a mass murderer or anything."

"That's what I'm hoping for, 'cause I really need somebody to kill all these cobwebs sitting in my coochie!" she giggled, causing Vanessa to stare at her with her mouth wide open.

"Girl, you crazy!"

"I know, right! I love you. Call me tomorrow," Briana said and took off to get her late night snack for the night.

After saying her goodbyes to Vanessa, Briana found Terrence. She grabbed his hand again and led him out of the nightclub. Once they got outside, they decided that he should follow her to their nightcap destination. Thirty-five minutes later, Briana and Terrence were inside Briana's bedroom exchanging saliva during a passionate tongue kiss and trying to strip each other butt-naked.

Once they were completely naked, Terrence covered his thick boner with a Magnum condom and crawled between Briana's thick legs. He licked all over her hard nipples as he slid his thick girth up and down the mouth of her juicy love canal. Briana inched down lower under him and guided him deep inside her tight warmness.

"Aaah!" She gritted her teeth as he penetrated her deeper and deeper. "Sssss… mmm…aaah!" she gasped, biting on his shoulder while working her pelvis bone upward to meet his downward thrusting. He slid in and out, in and out, deeper and deeper, giving her one of the best sexual encounters of her life.

Drunk In Love

He watched her perky breasts shake and jiggle as he long stroked her. He gave her dark nipples soft kisses, slipping his tongue up and down her chest, while rubbing on the soft mounds of her sweet ass. She came up on her elbows, slipping her tongue in his mouth, in and out in synch with each of his hard, circular thrusts.

"Aah-Aaah-Aaah... Ooohh, baby, ooooh!" she moaned as he dug deeper and deeper, creating a painful and enjoyable slow friction within her meaty, sugary walls - a feeling that she had been missing out on for the longest. He extracted his love pump and began sliding it up and down along her shiny, throbbing slit, making sure to grind against her clitoris. She roughly grabbed his manhood and forced him back inside her.

"Fuck me, baby! Don't play with it...punish this pussy!" she commanded, completely turned on. She opened her legs wider as he plunged deeper and deeper into her with the force of a jackhammer. "Aaah...mmm, shit! Ssss!" she cried out, taking the forceful jabs of his thick organ, loving every minute of it. She let him know how much she missed getting some loving by throwing her legs on his shoulders, allowing him maximum penetration. With each punishing stroke he gave her, Briana regretted that she had waited so long to have sex. "Mmm, yeah, daddy...yessss! Gimme that dick, daddy! Give it to meeee!" she yelped, grabbing hold of his waist. She bit down on her bottom lip to distract herself from the lovely pain of taking all of the dick he was stroking her with.

Hitting her well-oiled depths harder and harder, Terrence kept pounding relentlessly inside what seemed to feel like a much smaller and tighter pussy than he was used to. Her drenched twat pulled and tugged at his plunging pole with each pulverizing stroke. "Damn, you got some good-ass pussy!" he blurted while going in deeper and deeper and deeper.

"Aaaah, aaaah, aaaah! Fuck Me, daddy...fuck - AAAAAAAAHHH!" she cried out while exploding all over his gut-churning man meat. She could feel him throbbing in her stomach as he pumped harder and harder.

"You just cum without me, huh! Huh!" He groaned, twisting her guts into a knot, making her soar. He began digging in and out of her for close to thirty minutes straight. She had two climaxes already, not letting it be known. She couldn't hold back on the third orgasm, because his loving had really hypnotized her body.

"I'm sorry, daddy," she moaned in a little girl's voice. She learned that from Casey, who had revealed that it made men go crazy and climax quickly. "Please don't punish me. I'll never, ever do it again." She felt goose bumps forming on his butt cheeks, which alerted her that he had to be on the brink of erupting. "Please forgive me, daddy, I'm sorry. Sssss… Oooooh, I'm sooo, sooo sorry!"

"You better…be! Don't let…it…happen…aga— AAARRRGGGGHH, FUCK!" he groaned in a throaty whisper as he exploded inside the condom like a hot geyser. Feeling his jerking spasms, she cried out and climaxed again for the fourth time.

"Mmm… Damn you good, baby." She grinned, winking at him, as he remained stiff inside her for another minute or so until his throbbing boner went limp. The tingling sensations rocketing through her body let her know that she couldn't let this awesome love machine out of her life so easily.

Terrence rolled over and lay on the bed beside her. She rolled over and curled up beside him. "Damn, T, where have you been hiding at all of my life?" she asked, planting soft kisses on his chest. He had done something to her that no man has done in a very long time: he rocked her world with the sex, completely blowing her mind.

"So I take it you liked what I just laid on you, huh?"

"Mmm hmm." She smiled, wrapping her hand around his limpness and starting to play with his joystick. "You think you can give me a repeat performance?" she asked, kissing him on the neck and chest.

"All you have to do is get my soldier to stand at attention and it's on like the Energizer Bunny. It just keeps going and going and going," he said, causing her to laugh.

Briana laughed and rolled over until she straddled his waist. She reached for another condom off the nightstand. After tearing open the wrapper, she wrapped him back up with latex and quickly impaled herself. They made passionate love well into the early morning hours, bringing each other to multiple leg-shaking orgasms.

Casey

"Oooohhh! I n-never had it done to me like that before!" Casey huffed, trying to squirm away from the man's darting tongue, which sent an explosive orgasm rocketing through her body.

After Briana left the nightclub, Casey decided to find a man to take home for the night—and actually, he found her!

He noticed each of Casey's smooth, alluring dance moves under the disco strobe lights that featured her flawless skin, shapely behind, and perky breasts. She was his type of female.

"Excuse me, beautiful," he said, getting her to turn around and take in his six-foot tall creamy-coated frame. He resembled one of those Guidos that Snookie always talked about on the *Jersey Shore* reality show. "I was hoping that I could get the honor of dancing with you."

"I didn't know white men could dance," Casey joked, trying to brush him off.

"You shouldn't believe everything you hear. C'mon, let me show you," he said, not giving her a chance to refuse.

"Uh uh, boy!" Casey protested as he pulled her close to him and began waltzing.

"If you keep playing hard to get, I'm going to break out with the Funky Chicken up in here and embarrass the hell out of both us. By the way, I'm Todd...Todd Lucas." He smiled and twirled her in a circle.

"Please do not do the Funky Chicken, Todd." Casey grinned, following his lead.

They had fun dancing the night away, which created unbearable sexual tension between them. Two hours later, they were in Todd's bed having sex - hot and sweaty sex. It was as if they had melted into each other's arms like cold slabs of butter in a hot skillet. And Casey took advantage of the gentle,

Drunk In Love

hot, buttery love that Todd dished out. Casey feared that she might never feel so good, wanted, and loved, by another man ever again.

Slurping up her flowing juices greedily yet slowly, the lean, freaky, muscular Guido slipped his index finger inside her slick chute and his ring finger in her anal canal for the double penetration effect. The probing fingers unlocked new portals of pleasure for Casey.

"Mmm...work your magic, Todd...mmm..." Casey moaned, enjoying the marvelous sensations of double penetration and the simultaneous nursing of her tender clitoris.

Casey positioned herself with her backside facing his nursing mouth. He heightened her sensations by giving her soft suction with side-to-side motions of his head so that different parts of his soft lips made contact with her clitoris. The threefold intensity drove Casey into wild, crazy bliss.

"Oh Gawd, I need you inside of me now...right now, dammit!" she demanded as Todd placed on a condom.

Moments later, he invaded her pulsating love oven with the huge thickness of his girth.

"Mmm! You're packing t-t-to be a white boy." She sighed, loving the feel of his plunging thrust. She humped back a little harder, anticipating his jabbing piston.

"Thanks for the compliment." He groaned, stroking faster and faster as if he was stirring something in a pot. He kept up the steady, pumping rhythm until their slapping organs became extremely loud from the moisture of Casey's leaking love nest.

They met each other stroke for stroke for a few intense moments, then stopped and enjoyed the vibrating throbbing their organs made together. Then they went back at it again, in and out, in and out for another short duration. After several minutes of hard penetration and Todd stroking her with profound pleasure, he turned her over on her back so he could look into her seductive bedroom eyes while he gave her the jackhammer in the captured tortoise position.

"Ssss... Give it to me, baby! Oooh yeah, right there...yeeaah," Casey hummed, holding her thick, shapely legs up to her breasts, allowing him total access to penetrate her deeper and deeper. "That's it right there. Bang it out, white boy! Don't be scared to bang it out!" she urged, placing her arms over her knees, cradling them as he plunged in and out, in and out of her tight warmness. Then he pulled her towards his stabbing pole, causing her excited body to twist and flip over. He followed her movements, digging deeper and deeper into her fiery tunnel, obliging her request to be banged out.

"You do know that this dick belongs solely to me now, white boy? Whenever I want it, you better come and deliver. Understand?" she said firmly, contracting her inner muscles to squeeze his invading slab of meat.

Her demanding tone of passion only excited Todd more and increased his desire to please her in every possible way he could think of. They continued enjoying the freaky voyage to ecstasy, pulling, pushing, pumping faster and faster, plowing harder and harder, trying to reach that ultimate peak of sexual bliss.

"I love t-t-the feel of your puss—AAARRRGGGGHH! Lordy...Lordy...Lordy!" he groaned, grabbing her waist tightly as his love gunk exploded into the condom.

"Keep it up, white boy. K-k-keep... it...UUPPPPPP!" Casey screamed passionately, gripping the sheets tightly while arching her back and pelvic bone upward as she climaxed and released her love juices all over the slick, coated latex of his throbbing love bone.

"Mmm...that felt sooo damn good!" Casey smiled, closing her eyes before pulling him towards her for a gentle kiss on the lips.

Drunk In Love

"I'm starving, baby. You want something to eat?" he asked her while tracing tiny little circles all over her back, causing her to have uncontrollable body spasms.

His question and tender touch surprised her, feeling and sounding like music to her ears and body. *Usually it would be the other way around whenever I deal with them so-called brothers,* she thought and then said, "Sure. I would love a good ham and cheese sandwich on rye with plenty of mustard and mayo, hold the lettuce and tomatoes."

"Anything else, Princess?" he asked before climbing out of bed.

"Yes, I want you to give me one more of those leg shaking performances you just gave me after we get through eating so I can sleep like a baby."

"You got it, beautiful." He smiled, kissed her forehead gently, and trotted out of the bedroom whistling loudly like a man who just won the lottery.

Casey stared at his firm, pale behind and giggled. There was no doubt in her mind that Todd was the cream for her coffee - well, at least the cream for the cups she was enjoying that night.

Vanessa

Like a crushing wave, Vanessa and her husband exploded together, releasing a memorable orgasm. As soon as his engorged love muscle slid out of her slippery slit, Vanessa pushed him off of her and turned her back to him.

Nessa, what are you doing? He just gave you the best sex in your life.

I know it was good, but…

But what?

He didn't lick my kitty-cat like I just did to his selfish ass. Something has to give. I can't take it no more! she argued in her head, growing angry by the touch of his hands gently rubbing on her soft behind.

"Stop!" she snapped, raising her voice. The irritation was evident in her tone as Russell tried to cuddle with her and kiss her on the shoulders and neck.

Russell gave his wife a confused and scared look as if to say, *What the hell has gotten into you?*

There's still time to get him to do it, a chance to really experience what all my girlfriends are bragging about. All I have to do is speak my mind and complain a little – no, complain a lot!

But Vanessa couldn't bring herself to do any complaining. Russell was so caring, so damn responsible in her eyes, providing for their four-year-old daughter Dejah and herself. He always put their needs and wants before his.

Why he can't put my needs before his now? she wondered, but she decided to bite her tongue for the moment. She took his arms and guided them around her in a loving embrace. Her breath caught, and then she exhaled.

"Baby, are you okay?" he asked, kissing her on the neck.

Drunk In Love

"I'm fine," she lied. "It's just the job and this thing about Anitra that's stressing me out." *It's really about your tired ass neglecting this pussy that's behind all of my stress, but I don't want to hurt your feelings.*

"Well, you know I'm here if you want to talk about it." *I'm really tired as hell, but I'll pretend to listen to keep your evil ass from fussing and complaining about other shit.*

"Anitra's getting married to some guy that she barely even knows." She turned over to face him. "They have only been together for five months and a few days, can you believe that?"

Why did I have to say something and stick my foot in my mouth? Now we're going to be up all night talking about this soap opera bullshit, he thought before giving her a simple answer. "Baby, listen, you don't have any reason to worry." He brushed a lock of her hair away from her face with his hand before continuing. "Anitra's a big girl and I'm quite sure she can look out for herself."

"You would say something like that," she hissed, climbing out of the bed. She gave his reflection an evil stare while looking in the huge bureau mirror on her way to the bathroom.

After she entered the master bathroom, she slammed the door. She felt he was as inconsiderate about her friends as he was to her in the bedroom.

"Nessa, I was just being honest with you!" he called out from the bed.

Cool it, Nessa. He knows not what he does or says, she told herself. But honestly, she couldn't control her temperature or the weird feeling that immediately made her think about the 6'3" sexy chocolate Kenny whom she employed. *He's really a cute guy, a hard worker, and probably an even better lover. I wonder, could I foolishly sample his goods and not get addicted?*

49

No, Nessa! That's adultery!
The temptation was hard to ignore. Even as she stepped into the hot shower, Vanessa thought she could still smell Kenny's Jean Paul Gaultier cologne on her skin from his touch. She began wishing she could taste him, and vice versa. She wanted to get freaky with Kenny - and all she could think about was how wrong it would be to do it.
Am I cheating on my husband right now for thinking about Kenny?
"So you're just going to ignore me, right?" Russell called again, making her cringe with irritation.
Vanessa gazed down at the water cleansing her meaty slit - a slit she felt needed some serious tongue action.
You ignore me and my pussy on a regular basis! she wanted to scream in response, but she only said, "I'm not ignoring you, honey. I was just washing up." She looked down at herself again, hoping that he'd go to sleep soon so she could concentrate on her thoughts and fantasies.
"Okay, don't say I didn't try!" he called. "I'm going to sleep now. I love you!"
You're not trying in the right areas, motherfucker! She wanted to tell his ass off, but instead she cocked her head to the side and said, "Okay, honey, I love you too. I'll be in there after I freshen up a little."
He didn't answer, which was music to her ears. The silence surprised her, though it probably shouldn't have. Vanessa began looking around the marble and granite-styled encased shower, all the more aware of the stage her life was in. She was very successful in the catering business, a proud mother of a beautiful daughter, and married to a handsome man.
But that was it. She was married, which had her unhappy and angry all the time. Vanessa closed her eyes and began thinking about Kenny again - thinking about his huge hands

Drunk In Love

caressing her body until she found herself guiding two fingers insider her warm love tunnel.

When she rubbed her pleasure principle, her hips started moving in rhythm with her touch - Kenny's touch. She began panting, moaning, and stroking and stroking, realizing that it was time for a change - time to add some sexual excitement to her ordinary and boring life.

Anitra

Anitra sprang right up from under the sheets with trembling legs, looking winded. She couldn't stop her right leg from shaking.

"Nate. I had enough. You're gonna kill me, boy!" She gasped as he eased up from nibbling on her swollen clitoris.

He rose up slowly, looked at her, and said, "I'ma give you a few more minutes to get some rest and then you know what time it is."

"What?" she pouted, enjoying the euphoric feeling surfing through her body. She had just had her eighth orgasm.

Ever since leaving the club, they had laid in each other's arms making love. Anitra didn't know that one man could have so much energy and sexual stamina. She decided to let things get wild and freaky for only one more night because she was a little drunk. Tomorrow she would put some restraints on their lovemaking. She would have to figure out some other way to be close to him without being intimate all the time - at least until after the wedding.

Yet deep down inside, she sensed what was happening. She could feel it everywhere, especially in her loins, which was the main reason why she accepted his marriage proposal. Anitra was hooked on Nathan's bedroom skills.

"It's not that late, baby, and you know it's the weekend, which means no work tomorrow for either one of us," he pointed out, invading her thoughts.

Anitra noticed his reaction, a frisky little grin that somehow managed to warm her heart and be sexy at the same time.

"Well, since you put it that way... Then I guess we can go one more round."

Drunk In Love

"That's my baby. Don't worry; I won't tire you out this time."

Now Anitra revealed a huge smile. She began giggling repeatedly, sounding like she was in attendance at a hilarious comedy show.

"What's so funny?" Nathan asked, climbing his beautifully naked frame out of the bed. He put his hands on his small waist, arched his eyebrow, waiting on her response.

"I was just thinking about everyone's reaction to our news tonight. They really gave me the third degree about you."

I hope you defended me! "Actually, I can see that happening." He took a deep breath and released it before getting back in bed. "I can see from the short exchange I had with your friends tonight babe, that they really care about you and want to make sure that you're in good hands."

"Am I?" She looked into his light brown eyes.

"There has to be a way I can slip out the back door or something without answering that." He smiled.

"Nathan, don't play with me!" she whined, playfully punching him in the chest.

The old player in Anitra didn't really have a problem with whatever his answer would be. But the new one-man woman and future Mrs. Layne had to really know how Nathan felt about her.

"Baby, you know I'm just joking." He kissed her. "You're forever my lady and definitely in safe hands with me. Whenever I touch you, I feel happy inside. Whenever I see you, I know there's a meaning to life. You have that special something that makes me want to show it out to the world just how much I love you, girl… You go guurrrlll." He smirked after mimicking a famous one-liner by comedian Martin Lawrence.

Anitra spun in bed and somehow straddled him with an eager vigor. "Now Nathan, do you promise to love, honor, and obey me as long as you live?" she asked, all the while guiding his flaccid pipe inside her torrid tunnel.

"Ain't no question...'til the day that I die. Now what about you?" he shot the question back, cupping her breasts, getting a soft moan out of her. He quickly grew hard inside her.

It didn't matter what Anitra said. Her clenching vaginal walls were already expressing how she felt. "I suppose I can do that for you, big boy," she purred.

"That's the gal I know and fell in love with." He smiled, raising his pelvic bone and tightening his butt cheeks, as she began bucking up and down on his impaling love sword.

Glancing down at their sexual organs intertwining, Anitra yelled for him to fuck her harder as she started bouncing faster and faster on top of him.

"And...it b-better...mmm...always stay th-th-that way," she moaned, coming all the way up off the dick so his helmet-shaped head could tease the nerve-endings at the mouth of her slippery love cave.

"You know it will, boooooooo...dayyum!" He huffed as she sat down slowly, gyrating her hips and impaling herself until his balls met her slit. "Baby, you got that butter love..." he moaned. Then he started singing to her with the same frisky grin on his face, all the while trying to push all his love inside her.

And you got that whip appeal, Anitra wanted to sing out loud, but she held in her thoughts and got lost in the moment of racing towards another satisfying and breathless climax.

Drunk In Love

Briana

The following morning, Briana stepped out of the shower and wiped off the fogged up mirror with her hand until she could see her reflection staring back at her. She shook her head again, and then again. She still couldn't believe she had a one-night stand with a total stranger.

Well, slut, you have really done it now.

Being single required a certain amount of room to maneuver, but last night was an act of desperation. Even though it felt really good, she knew it was all wrong. She had gone way beyond her morals and principles for one night of pleasure.

But she missed that feeling. Briana missed the feeling that warmed your heart to happiness whenever you talked about the one you love. She missed the feeling of absolute comfort and contentment experienced while watching her favorite TV sitcom or a good movie in bed with a man on any given night. She missed the feeling of making love to a man with her words days before ever making love to his body.

Briana figured that after last night, there was a strong possibility that Terrence would be the man to return that feeling she had lost and desperately yearned to get back.

From here on out, things are going to be very, very interesting, she thought, feeling excited and terrified by the possibilities of being in a new relationship.

"Yo, Bri-Bri, are you okay up there?" she heard him calling her.

Bri-Bri? Now that does have a cute little ring to it. I can get used to him calling me that, she thought with a smile. She opened the bathroom door and answered, "I'll be down in a second, T."

"Hurry up, because your food is ready!" he called. "And it's waiting on you."

"Oookaay!" she squealed, smiling from ear to ear. She closed the door and then hurried over to the sink to comb her wet hair. Moments later, she was out of the bathroom and rushing downstairs to her meal.

I can't believe he went through all of this for me! I must have really put it on his butt, she told herself while taking in the sight of the decorated table that had a single white rose, a glass of orange juice, and some sort of omelet with strawberries surrounding it in the shape of a heart. "All of this just for me?" She beamed, getting a jolt from the feeling that had been eluding her for far too long.

"You're the only Queen in this kingdom, my lady," he said before kissing her on the cheek and pulling out her chair, beckoning her to sit down.

Damn, she's even more beautiful in the morning, and most beauty queens look like sick old dope fiends. She don't need no make-up or nothing, he thought while watching the terrycloth robe hug her curvaceous frame as she gave him a thank you smile for his chef services that morning.

Briana noticed that there was only one setting at the table. She looked at Terrence, somewhat confused.

"You're not eating with me?" she asked.

Nope, because I want you to fall for me, for what I can give you and do for you. "Nah, I'm still full off of you from last night." He smiled, winking at her.

"Mmph," she said, shivering at the memory of his tongue waltzing across her body, taking her to new heights of ecstasy and euphoria that she thought didn't exist. "No, for real, why you're not eating with me?"

"I already told you, Bri-Bri. Besides, I already had something light to eat. You know I have to preserve this six pack," he said, rubbing on his tight abs, which made her pussy

Drunk In Love

pulsate. She had always been a sucker for a man in shape -
especially a man with ironing board abdominal muscles.
"They look good and felt preserved to me." She inhaled
the scent of the rose and closed her eyes. *I can really get used
to this kind of treatment. Hopefully this won't stop after today,*
she thought and opened her eyes. She gazed down at the big
fluffy western omelet.

"Thanks for the compliment," he smirked.

"Anytime, boo. Wow, this omelet sure looks good," she
said, looking at her meal. And she *was* hungry - maybe
because she had burned off dinner and several hundred calories
last night in the bedroom.

"Well, you need to dig in before it gets cold," he urged
and then he picked up her fork. He cut a piece of the omelet for
her, picked it up, and guided it inside her mouth.

"Mmmm…it's delicious." She licked her pouty lips after
easing her mouth off the fork.

"Now you wouldn't lie to me, would you?"

Now where did all that just come from? "Who, me?" she
asked with a mischievous grin.

"Yeah, you, Ms. Briana Evans," he said before leaning
over to kiss her. After the slightly passionate kiss, Terrance
began spoon-feeding her again like a baby and she loved every
minute of it. "Do you need anything else?" he asked while
helping her finish up her meal.

Just your sexy behind in bed with me every night! "Just a
glass of water. I always drink water in the morning before I do
anything."

"I almost forgot that you're a good doctor, and I must
admit you give one helluva physical," he joked while heading
over to the cabinet for a glass.

"You were a good patient," she playfully said while
continuing to chomp away her breakfast. And it was truly
delicious.

"So that should give you all the more reason to be with me again tonight," he thought out loud and she caught some of his words.

"What did you say?" she asked as he headed back over to her.

"I was saying can I see you again tonight? I mean, that's if you're not too busy."

He's giving me a way out politely. Will you take it, Briana, or go after what's behind curtain number two? Will you go after that missing feeling in your life or just be a lonely woman complaining to your shrink about finding love every week? she asked herself, glancing around her kitchen before looking back at Terrence, whose eyes waited for her answer.

"Listen, T," she sighed. "When things get serious between a man and me, sometimes I tend to freeze up when it comes to commitment. I don't know why, but it just happens. I always end up finding some lame excuse to cut the guy off," she confessed, instantly hating herself for it. She liked him, but she didn't know if he was the right guy for her right now.

"Like I told you before, Bri-Bri, I'm a producer and I'm not looking for a woman. We can just hang out and have fun…no strings attached," he stated, clarifying where he stood on the commitment issues.

She glanced at his rock-hard abs again and felt her juices flowing to the point where she wanted to feel him inside her again. *What the hell is he doing to me? I have never felt this way before about no man.* "And like I told you, Mr. Producer, I'm a doctor and I am not looking for a man, just a friend to kick it with, no strings attached." She licked her lips again and then deep throated the fork.

"So I don't see any reason to keep us from kicking it and chilling tonight," he said, rubbing the bulge in his boxer underwear.

He had a point and she wanted to admit as much, but you know women. She had foolishly sampled his goods and gotten addicted quickly. Now all she could think about was how she wanted more of him in her life. Even though she wanted to play hard to get, she was already putty in his hands.

Briana broke into a smile. "I think I can fit you into my busy schedule," she said. "Only on one condition."

"What's that?"

"You agree to take me out tonight, get to know me for me and keep that Anaconda in your pants. Pretty please?" she said, batting her eyelashes at him, causing him to laugh.

"That sounds like three conditions, but I'll see what I can do for you." He grinned and began talking to her while she sipped on her glass of water.

Casey
Bally's Gym, Trotwood, Ohio

The sounds of DMX barking rhymes blaring through the speakers around the state-of-the-art workout area made Casey pound away faster on the Stairmaster as if there was a slave master chasing her down with a whip. Working out helped her dismiss the countless men she had slept with in her life. Call it release therapy.

What was his name again? Oh, Todd. Mmph! Now he was really good in bed, but he's too much of a stalker for my taste. He keeps calling me wanting to hook up like I owe him something. Well, stalk on, loser, 'cause I don't need you. I done got what I wanted outta your ass, she thought, debating whether or not to approach the dark-skinned brother pulling away on the pull-up bar with a forty-five pound disk hanging from his slim waist.

Casey stared at him in awe, believing that his picture could be placed in any workout magazine under "athletically-fine, muscular specimen". He wore a pair of navy blue Rocawear baggy shorts, calf-high socks, and a pair of tan Timberland construction boots. He had thug written all over him. His huge, tattooed-covered arms looked like chocolate pistons of power.

Fleetingly, Casey imagined his huge biceps lifting her bare bottom up in the air and carrying her all around the house while they engaged in a passionate session of sex. Once she saw the wonderfully curved S-shape scar on his face, running from his eye down his cheek, Casey's fate was sealed. She left the Stairmaster immediately and approached him from the side.

"Hello," she said with a smile while he pulled up and down, up and down.

Drunk In Love

Casey eyes were glued to the swinging bulge in his shorts. She automatically assumed he had to be packing well in that area also. Usually most guys she dated with all the big muscles in the arm and chest areas always had little muscles in the most important groin area. She hoped that her next prospect wasn't the same. From the looks of things, Casey knew that wasn't the case.

The man glared at Casey with a quizzical look as if to say, "Can't you see I'm busy right now?"

"Okay, I can see you're getting your work-out thing on, so you don't have to talk right now. I just wanted to introduce myself and see if there's a possibility for us to talk later on and get to know each other a little better. I'm Casey." *The woman who has time enough for your fine, Mandingo-thug-looking ass.*

He released the pull-up bar and dropped to his feet. He extended his hand a bit with sweat dripping and took the end of Casey's manicured fingers, shaking them quickly. He leaned over, discarding the forty-five-pound disk, allowing all the sweat to drip from his chiseled upper body.

"How many sets do you have left? Because I really would like to talk to you." *So I can see if you're worthy enough to entertain this kitty-cat.*

The man placed the drum back on the weight rack and looked back at Casey. He looked irritated and flattered.

Are you still being a groupie? Persistent can't even describe your little hot-to-trot ass. And you're kind of cute too. And you came straight at me, instead of it being the other way around, which earns you some points for being assertive, he thought while sizing up all of her curves. They seemed to be suffocating in the lemon-yellow leotard and black spandex biker shorts.

"That was the last one," he said, degreasing his hands on the sides of his shorts before extending his hand to her. "I'm Ronzell."

You sure are! she inwardly squealed, liking the strong Afrocentric name for the sexy 6'4" 235-pound Mandingo warrior standing before her.

"So what's good?"

She blushed. "Oh, I'm sorry. I mean, I was doing my own little workout and you kind of distracted me. So I just had to come over here and meet you." *To see why you got my juices flowing and my pussy throbbing.*

"Is that so?"

"Yeah. To be honest, you have a sexy body and I figured that...well, I wanted to find out what you do to get in such splendid shape and maybe see if you could be my workout partner sometimes?" *You can work on this pussy and I can work on your dick!*

'You sure this isn't a come-on line?" he asked impishly with mock despair. "I mean, you're too fine to be looking for any man to work out with. Now what's really good?"

Busted! Enough of this cat and mouse bullshit. "Look, Ronzell, don't make this any harder than it has to be. Are you going to give me your cell phone number or what?" Casey asked with a devious smile, trying to downplay the way she was controlling the mood of the conversation. She hated playing games. She felt it was a colossal waste of time.

"Only if you want it and will use it, 'cause I don't like to play games," he said with a smile.

"C'mon, Ronzell. Do I look like the type of woman who plays games?" she asked meaningfully with a playful smile.

Hell yeah! But I have to give your sexy ass the benefit of doubt for now. "Nah, you don't, but looks can be very deceiving."

Nice comeback! And you're real smooth with it too. I like that...I like that a lot, she thought, licking her lips discreetly. "I get that from guys all the time, but I'm a really good girl." *Until I get bored with your ass, and then all the bitch comes out.*

Drunk In Love

"Since you put it like that, then I guess you can come over to the counter with me and get that number, Ms. Good Girl," he said and then he grabbed her hand to lead her over to the counter.

Once they reached the check-in counter, Ronzell wrote his phone number down for her on the back of a Bally's flier. Casey took the flier and studied the number for a moment before plucking the flier with flair.

"So, do you live 'round these parts, Casey?"

"Yeah, I'm a ten minute drive away from here. Why you ask?" she questioned, studying his physique. Plenty of carnal things flashed through her mind about what she wanted to do to him.

"Because we're friends now and I just wanted to make sure that you get home safely."

Damn, you smooth. I wonder if your dick game is the same way? she thought, giving him a flirtatious smile.

Vanessa

Vanessa sat alone on a stool in the corner, facing the vast greenish-blue walls of the hotel's banquet hall. For Vanessa, her sitting position was downright normal with only a mild hint of authority. Regardless, it troubled her, swathing her in emotions and a tug of war with herself about cheating on her husband.

Vanessa's staff, along with Kenny, regarded her with curiosity. They all wondered why such an assertive, hands-on, and hardworking boss was sitting down on a major job just watching them do all the work. No matter. Vanessa was too distracted and emotionally detached to care what they thought about her.

All day, she had been shouting orders and cursing at her staff like a drunken sailor, which shocked everyone. Vanessa had taken her home life problems to work with her, exposing herself little by little to her staff. In the back of her mind, Vanessa knew that she was dead wrong, but her drained soul and stubborn pride wouldn't allow her to admit it and apologize to everyone she took her anger out on.

"Mrs. Jergens," Kenny called out to her after walking up on her.

"What do you want?" she snapped, staring at him with evil eyes, giving him the kind of look that would make a person think twice before asking her anything.

Dear Lord, why does he have to be so damn cute, tall, and sexy with his fine ass? He's obviously my type of man, she thought while trying to keep her angry stare going on. She hated him instantly, and then she loathed herself.

Vanessa wanted him. She wanted to do things with him like go roller skating and dancing. She wanted to share all the sexuality and freakiness inside of her with someone who would return her passion with the same amount of passion and maybe more. She wanted someone to buy her flowers, shower her with baby kisses, and freak her out in the bedroom at 2 a.m. just to express how much he craved her and loved her. She wanted everything that her husband, Russell, used to give her in the beginning of their marriage. She figured Kenny could be that guy to give it to her, but she didn't want to destroy her marriage to get it.

There has to be another way!

"I just wanted to find out why you're so upset today?" Kenny asked, invading her thoughts. "I mean, you're so upbeat every day. Now you come through here like the wickedest witch in Dayton. What's wrong?"

"You just wouldn't understand, Kenneth," she spoke blandly.

"Wait a minute… Just wait a damn minute, Boss Lady!" he said, his urgency grabbing her full attention. "When did you start calling me Kenneth? Now I know something is definitely wrong. What, you and the hubby ain't getting along or something?"

His question stung her. She didn't feel like telling him anything about her personal life. She wanted to show him how neglectful her husband was being to her without spilling the beans. "That is none of your business, Kenny. I suggest you get back to work," she stated sternly.

"Sorry, Boss Lady, but it is my business when you come in here fussing at us for no damn reason. I -"

"Kenny, you're out of line and I think you need to just -"

"Talk some sense into you," he cut her off. "Yeah, I'm the sacrificial lamb that's been sent over here by the troops to talk to you. You know we're family here, Boss Lady. When you're hurting, we all hurting, so I suggest you start leaving whatever problems you got at home, right at home. Don't bring that shit in here and make all of us miserable. From here on out, you need to come to work all smiles and bring that sexiness that most of us guys secretly talk about. You're too beautiful to be acting all ugly and shit...real talk," Kenny said. He left before she could say anything.

She watched him head back to work in silence. She gave his back a look as if to say, *Who the hell does he think he's talking to? I'm the boss, not him. I should fire his ass for talking to me like that. But if I do that, I can't secretly lust off his fine tail no more,* she told herself as their eyes locked in on each other. He gave her a wink before returning to his duties.

From then on, their eyes locked in on each other on several occasions, lingering there for a moment, apparently evaluating one another with their eyes. His pink gums held a full set of perfect white teeth, which made Vanessa grin inside. She felt like a high school cheerleader who had spotted the cutest football quarterback she'd ever laid eyes on. During that moment of their intense staring match, Vanessa told herself that she wouldn't mind letting him score.

Drunk In Love

Briana

The need for that missing feeling had Briana doing more than enough to get closer to Terrence. She even invited Terrance over to her father's house for a college send-off party they were giving her baby brother, Benjamin. Although it was their first official date after their one night stand, Terrence still felt it was too soon to meet the relatives, especially Briana's father. After her father grilled him about his intentions for Briana, Terrence knew he was right about meeting her pops.

Despite Briana's father offering Terrence his version of a police interrogation about his daughter and wanting to know Terrence's intentions for her, Briana felt good about their first date. Actually, she hoped Terrence would stand up under her father's probing questions so she could continue dating him. She loved a man who didn't take no mess from anyone - including her.

The home of Briana's father was like every other stucco two-level home in Dayton that Terrence had seen. The semi-big house walled with odd and character artifacts could be easily forgotten after one visit, yet, for some inexplicable reason, the house made Terrence feel very comfortable and right at home.

The diverse crowd outside in the backyard was stepping joyfully, owning the dance floor. African Americans, Caucasians, and Latino brothers and sisters joined forces in a memorable Electric Slide routine to the sounds of R-Kelly's classic "Step in the Name of Love."

While the deejay got busy spinning on the turntables, Briana and Terrence shared a lawn table with Casey, Anitra, and Briana's brother, Benjamin. Once Vanessa arrived with the drinks and began handing them out, Benjamin lit up a cigar and looked at Terrence.

"So, you're the nigga that's fuckin' my sister now?" Benjamin spoke with the big fat stogie poking out of his mouth like he was trying to imitate some mob boss.

"Benji!" Briana gasped, after spitting out her drink, causing Anitra and Casey to giggle behind her embarrassment.

"What I say, Sis?" Benji laughed. "I'm just saying we all grown folks here, Sis. Ain't that right, Terrence?"

"Of course," Terrence answered, hating the stench of the damn cigar and Benji's offensive line of questioning. Terrence figured that Briana had loose lips and all of her girlfriends probably knew about their intimate sexcapades, which didn't sit too well with him. Being a romantic at heart, the whole ordeal of meeting the family so soon and enduring all these interrogations was killing Terrence. He just wanted to be alone somewhere with Briana, enjoying her company and relaxing, not being grilled by her little brother in front of her all of her girlfriends. Refusing to let the family and touchy situation get under his skin, Terrence just smiled at the awful day he was having. He began reflecting on the fact that Briana could possibly be someone he wanted to fall in love with.

She's gorgeous, and she's a doctor with the best pussy I ever had and she could be a potential soul mate, despite her ignorant brother and pops drilling me with questions. I see no other odds stacked against me in making her all mines, he thought with a smile. A microsecond later, Terrence's smile quickly faded into a hard frown.

Damn, I spoke too soon, he thought, watching the swarthy woman enter the backyard, waving in their direction. Her looks could match First Lady Michelle Obama's.

"Hey, Superstar! Come here and give your mama some sugar!" the woman said, getting Benji's attention.

"We'll rap a little later, Terrence," Benji said while standing and taking a sip of the bubbly. "If you guys will excuse me, I have to go see my mama."

Drunk In Love

As Benji rushed over to the woman, Terrence kept his eyes locked on them. He watched as Benji kissed and hugged the woman. When their eyes met and locked in on each other, Terrence looked like he had seen a ghost, but he played it off smoothly. Benji's mother returned Terrence's gaze with a smile and she headed over in the direction of the table with Benji in tow.

Fuck! Not now! This is some bullshit here, Terrence thought, and then he realized that finding love with Briana would be hopeless. He was in a totally different setting dating the daughter of the woman he had once called his own.

I bet you're really thinking about me now, ain't chu', Evelyn? he wondered, standing up and extending his hand to greet Briana's mother. He did it so smoothly that one would have never thought they met until today. She did the same, acting as if it was the first time they ever met.

"It's a pleasure to meet you, Terrence," she said with a smile, giving him an intense stare like she wanted to change him into stone. And in her mind, Terrence did turn into stone, backed by the strength of her pride. She turned to her daughter and gave her a hug.

"Hey baby, I see you have good taste in men just like your mama. Here, I want you meet my friend Darryl," she said with emphasis as if she was trying to throw her new man up in Terrence's face.

A much taller and much older man who could pass for the rapper LL Cool J's father stepped up and started shaking everybody's hands. Terrence felt hatred towards him instantly, but he kept his feelings close to his chest. He couldn't believe what he had stepped into today. He knew Dayton was a small town, but not that damn small.

"Evelyn, you didn't tell me your daughter was as cute as you are. I see why Brah-Man here has the hots for her," Darryl joked, drawing a few giggles and laughs from everyone except Terrence.

Evelyn leaned back against her date and laughed harder than she normally would have in an attempt to rile up Terrence. Although she was completely over Terrence, Evelyn wanted to show him what he was missing out on. In her mind, Evelyn thought that Terrence was still trying to be with her by dating her daughter.

He's definitely not prepared to make my daughter happy. Hell, he couldn't even make me happy, so I know it's a lost cause for them. But Briana's grown and has to live and learn on her own. Until then, I might as well make him sweat a little, because I'm quite sure he thinks I'm going to spill the beans to Briana about our past. She began making a show of everything she did to keep Terrence's attention focused on her. Evelyn wanted Terrence to continue checking her out and sweating over the fact that their secret could ruin any chances of a future relationship for him and her daughter.

"Yep, she's my baby. I went through seven painful hours of labor with that chile before I spat her ass out." Evelyn chuckled, keeping her eyes on Terrence, who kept looking around like he was nervous about something and only she knew the reason behind his sudden jitters.

"It was well worth it, because you brought a good doctor into this world who loves helping others," Briana's father spoke while walking up behind Evelyn.

"Hey Roscoe!" Evelyn beamed and gave him a kiss on the cheek. "How have you been treating my baby boy?" she asked, nodding in Benji's direction.

"Like a man. I'm so glad his ass is going off to college in the fall."

"Stop frontin', Pops, you know you're gonna miss me," Benji said with a smile.

"Miss catching a new case over your hard headed ass!" he snapped. "Evelyn, you need to talk some sense into that damn boy's head and warn him about all them little chicken heads running around here just looking for a NBA prospect.

70

Drunk In Love

They going to trap him with a baby the first chance they get and all he's thinking about is getting his little dick wet," Roscoe vented, embarrassing Benji.

"Aww Pops!" Benji whined, hating how his father had just exposed him in front of his mother.

"Pops, my ass!" Roscoe snarled. "You grown now, so don't Pops me. You heading off into the real world now, go on and fuck it up, I bet chu' I won't be there to help you pick up the pieces," he said before kissing Briana on the cheek and storming off.

"I'ma go check on Daddy real quick," Briana said, giving Terrence a look first as if waiting on his approval.

He gave her a nod.

"I'll be right back, y'all," Briana said as she hurried off after her father.

When Briana left, Evelyn pulled a Mercedes Benz car key from her Coach purse and gave it to Benji. "You know your father's right, knucklehead. But if you want to be hardheaded, then you will have to live and learn for yourself. Now don't be speeding to much in that thing, or you won't make it to the NBA, you hear me?"

"Yeah Mama, thanks!" Benji said, giving her a kiss on the cheek before he rushed out of the backyard.

"C'mon, everybody!" Casey yelled. "Let's go check out Benji's new pussy-mobile!"

"Girl, you is too much." Anitra giggled as everyone began leaving the backyard except Terrence and Evelyn.

"Evelyn, baby, you coming?" Darryl asked while backpedaling out of the yard.

"Yeah, Darryl," she said over her shoulder while looking into Terrence's eyes. "I just have a few questions I want to ask this young man who is dating my daughter. I'll be out there in second after I find out what his real intentions are for my baby."

Darryl left without saying another word. As soon as her date left, Evelyn walked up to Terrence and shoved him hard. When he didn't bulge, she pushed him again and again until he fell backwards in his chair. She leaned over him, causing her cleavage to be right in his face as she talked to him like she was scolding a child.

"Now you listen to me and you listen up good, Terrence. I don't care about you or what you did to me!" she raged, sticking her slender finger in his face. "But if you ever hurt my baby, I swear to God, I will cut your fucking dick off and kill you, understand?"

Right then and there in the backyard of Roscoe's house, Terrence began thinking about Evelyn and her threats. Now he knew he had fucked up by having sex with Briana. He thought he was on to something special until today - until he found out the identity of Briana's mother.

Of all the women in Dayton, I just had to meet Briana and make love to her, the daughter of this deranged-ass woman that's staring down my throat like I'm the one who fucked up our relationship. She's definitely a loony-bird and her daughter may have the same traits, he thought, trying to tell if she was serious about her threats.

This much Terrence did know: Evelyn was like a tropical storm that would eventually turn into a ferocious hurricane and destroy his life with Briana. And the more he withheld his past dealing with Evelyn from Briana, the more the secret could keep him away from loving Briana, which was something that he didn't want to happen.

He had to admit this whole situation was crazy and he had to figure out a way to deal with it so he could keep Briana in his life.

Drunk In Love

Casey

Casey's mother, Nora Cooper, walked into her home after a long day at work. She headed to her bedroom, where she knew her nice soft bed awaited her tired bones. As she got near her bedroom, she heard something funny coming from her youngest daughter's bedroom. She walked lightly, just enough to hear what was going on the other side, but not enough to interfere with the wickedness that her baby girl was involved in. She walked up to the door and turned the doorknob slowly, making sure to be as quiet as possible. When she opened the door and she walked into the bedroom, Ms. Cooper's heart stopped, catching right there in her mouth at the sight of the pornographic sight before her, starring her youngest daughter.

Two naked young men had her daughter sandwiched. She gave one boy a blowjob, sucking greedily, while he rapidly fucked her opened mouth. The other boy was sawing in and out of her love oven from the back, slapping her sweet ass with each pounding stroke.

"Yeah, lil mama, take dis dick!" he groaned, digging inside her love canal harder and harder, making her butt cheeks jiggle as his balls slapped rapidly against her swollen pussy lips.

They were completely lost in the threesome and never even noticed the bedroom door opening. Gagging a little on the boy's impaling pipe buried in her mouth, Ms. Cooper's daughter, Justine, gripped his meaty boner and eased her lips off him, turning her head only to see her mother barging in the room, yelling up a storm.

"What in the hell! Get the hell outta my house! Now!" Ms. Cooper went off, chasing the naked young men around the bedroom as they ducked and dodged her wild blows while trying to retrieve their clothes. "I said now, goddammit!" she

73

yelled, managing to smack one of them in the back of the head as they ran from the bedroom butt naked, bent low at the waist.

While Ms. Cooper chased the youngsters from her house, Justine grabbed some clothes and ran to the bathroom to lock herself in and away from her mother's fury. Seconds later, Justine heard her mother banging on the bathroom door.

"Justine, open this damn door right now!"

"No!" Justine yelled back, making her mother lose it and try to break down the door.

"You little nasty heifer! I'ma beat the black off your ass! Now open up this door! Fuck is wrong with you having sex in my damn house like you pay the bills round' here!"

Justine ignored the banging and her mother's screaming while going for her cell phone to call her big sister Casey, the only one that could get her out of the mess she was in.

At the same time, Casey had walked up to the double doors of Ronzell's oversized brownstone. She reached inside her purse for her ringing cell phone. With anticipation building up inside her loins for a sweaty night in bed with Ronzell, the little voice in her head whispered, *Don't answer the phone, Casey.*

"Hello?" She answered the phone on the fourth ring as she stepped closer to the door and began knocking. "What? I can't believe her. Just give me a few minutes, okay? I'll be right over there." Casey frowned before hanging up just as Ronzell's front door opened.

"Hey, gorgeous," Ronzell greeted her, holding up two wine flutes and a bottle of Don Perignon 1985 that he had chilled in anticipation of her visit.

Casey stood there, listening to the distant sounds of Phyllis Hyman and her magnificent voice trickling out from his

Drunk In Love

stereo. She bit down on her tongue, hating herself, her mother and little sister for what she was about to do.

"Don't keep me waiting. Come on in here, girl." He smiled, opening the door wider and looking good in his cut-off Dockers shorts and white stretch polo shirt.

"I'm sorry, Ronzell," Casey sighed. "But I'm going to have to take a rain check. Something just came up," she muttered, blinking a few times.

With a completely stunned look on his face, Ronzell sat the champagne bottle and glasses down. Disappointment and anger were evident in his chinky eyes. "Is this your idea of a joke? I'm being pranked, right? Okay, okay, you got me; you can bring the cameras out now!" He raised his voice a little, looking around for a hidden camera crew that didn't exist.

"No, Ronzell, it's no joke," Casey sighed. "Honestly, I was looking forward to spending some time with you tonight, but unfortunately a family emergency just came up. My sister and mom got into a huge fight, so now I have to go play referee. I hope you understand?"

The hell I do! This supposed to be booty call time, not this bullshit-ass rain check shit!" "I understand," he lied as he picked the champagne bottle back up. Moments later, he popped the cork and poured two glasses of champagne. After filling the glasses, Ronzell passed one to Casey and raised his glass high for a toast. "To wonderful first dates," he said, the sarcasm evident in his tone.

"Don't be that way," Casey said, instantly feeling bad about leaving him hanging tonight. "I promise I'll make it up to you on the next one," she said before they clinked glasses. They took a few sips of the bubbly and held hands at his front door.

Ronzell wanted her to come inside so badly that he felt himself growing an erection. He released her hand and backed up a little to contain his lust. Madly overwhelmed with guilt, Casey stepped closer to him and gave him a hug. She moved in for a kiss, which felt so natural to her that she didn't mind when he slid his probing tongue deep inside her mouth. Casey tried to avoid kissing any of her male conquest because she felt kissing was personal. But what the hell, he looked so sad; she felt he deserved some form of affection. After the passionate kiss, Casey backed away slowly and wiped his lips with her thumb.

She gave him a warm smile and said, "I'ma call you late-"

Casey's blaring cell phone cut her off. She looked at the phone and saw that her sister was calling again. She gulped down her drink quickly and began backing away from him. He waved as she made it to her car. Moments later, Casey was calling out to Ronzell as she started pulling away from the curb.

"I'll be back to see you soon. So keep whatever you had planned for us on the stove, lover boy!"

Ronzell gave her a weak nod and slammed his door. She could tell he was upset, but she couldn't dwell on his feelings right now. Her family came first over everything—even getting laid. Casey sped away and spent a moment making minor adjustments on the iPod stereo system. Once she found a tune to her liking, Casey put on her shades and sped towards the Germantown Parkway.

During the drive to her mother's house, Casey thoughts were on the fight between her little sister and her mother, but mainly on the fact of how their fight had a domino effect that made her cancel a surefire booty call with Mr. Mandingo.

Somebody has a lot of explaining to do for making me miss some dick, Casey told herself, as she got closer to her mother's house.

Drunk In Love

Casey

A tall glass of water and some aspirin - a little preventative medicine in the wake of the booty call she had to miss because of the drama with her family. Casey was furious that she had to come over and quell the spat that her peeps were engaged in, but thanks to the sad and disappointed look on Ronzell's face and the dried cream in her panties, Casey was heated at them like a volcano ready to erupt.

No, I need two glasses of water and six aspirin, she told herself before popping the pills and drinking down the water to calm her anger and nerves. Casey exited the bathroom and headed into the living room, where her mother and sister were facing off like two prizefighters before round one took place.

Closing her eyes, Casey stepped between them, creating enough space between them so they wouldn't come to blows. Casey knew her little sister was different from her and wouldn't hesitate to defend herself - even against her mother.

Kids today, she thought before turning on her mother. "Now what's all the fuss about, Ma?"

"She's always try -"

"Justine!" Casey snapped holding up her hand to silence her. "Girl, not right now. Please not right now. I'm talking to Ma. Matter of fact, go sit in my car while we talk. I'll get your version later."

"But Casey," Justine whined.

"No buts! Go, Justine, now!" Casey stated sternly, and the buxom French-vanilla hued teenager with grown womanly curves lowered her auburn-hued mane and began walking out of the house, obeying her big sister's orders.

Justine knew her limits when it came to getting smart out the mouth with Casey. The fifteen-year-old knew all of her designer clothes and money that came from her big sister would halt immediately if she went too far and got on Casey's bad side. With that in mind, Justine left the house quietly without looking back.

As soon as Justine left, Casey took a seat on the sofa and released a sigh while starting into her mother's tired eyes. Casey could sense that something was troubling her mother, who resembled an older version of talk show billionaire Oprah Winfrey.

"Ma, before you even start, why don't you just let Justine come and live with me? I can -"

"No, don't even think it!" Ms. Nora snapped in a harsh tone.

"Why not, Ma?" Casey sucked her teeth, taking her turn to whine like she did when she was younger whenever she couldn't get her way. "All you do is treat her like a child. Justine is a young lady now and she needs some type of freedom."

"Just like the freedom your fast tail had growing up, huh?"

"Ma, this is not about me and you know it. With all due respect, Ma, I'm a grown woman. I have finished school, finished college, and have a good-paying job, and I have never gotten pregnant, so there's no reason for you to be mad at me about nothing."

"Well, your sister is hot in the ass and she's not like you!" Ms. Nora said, raising her voice as tears began welling up in her eyes. "Did you know that chile was having sex?"

"No," Casey lied quickly, looking away from her mother to hide her guilt. Casey had known about Justine's promiscuity for over six months now. She didn't scold her like she knew her mother would. She just tried to instill in Justine to have safe sex and not to have too many various sexual partners. She also stressed the importance of not getting pregnant, because she wasn't paying for any abortions. "Ma, when did this start?

Drunk In Love

I'm going to wring her little neck," Casey said, faking like she was upset behind the news that she already knew about.

"I don't know, but I came home from work earlier tonight and caught her in the act in my house – my house where I pay the bills, not her ass!"

"Whaaat!" Casey whistled, not believing the nerve of Justine. *Kids today!*

"Casey, she had not one, but two boys in her room. I mean, they were going at it, doing things that you only see in porn movies," Ms. Nora said before filing Casey in on every detail about what she had witnessed Justine and the two boys doing.

"Mmph! I didn't know it was that bad," Casey muttered, saying to herself, *My little sister's a ho'!*

"Casey, I wanted to kill that little hussy!" Ms. Nora vented, breaking Casey's train of thought.

I'm going to kick her ass! Who the fuck she think she is disrespecting Ma's house and herself like that? No, calm down, Casey and just talk to her and show her that she's not supposed to do things that way, Casey thought before responding to her mother. "See Ma, that's why you should let her come live with me. I can keep a better eye on her than you because I don't work all day and night like you. Besides, Justine knows I will beat the life outta her ass - excuse the French, Ma - but she knows I won't tolerate her pulling any stunts like that."

"You call that a stunt!" Ms. Nora went off. "A stunt! Casey, that was immoral, sick, perverted, dangerous, and just downright nasty! Neither one of them boys had on any condoms. They could have had AIDS or anything, Casey, and you call what she did a stunt? Now I know I'm making the right decision by not letting her ass come live with you. And furthermore, how in hell you going to be able to watch that chile twenty-four hours a day? You can't! Nope, uh uh, her fast ass is staying right here under this roof even if I have to kill her ass. And she's grounded for three months. You go tell her what I said and make sure you tell her fast ass that if I ever catch her doing some sick, perverted shit like that again under my roof, you will be representing your mother for the murder of your sister." Ms. Nora spoke her mind before turning on Casey and heading upstairs.

"But Ma," Casey called, trying to talk.

"Casey, I done said what I said; now I'm done with it!" She waved her hand, letting Casey know that she didn't want to hear no more on the subject.

Casey just looked defeated while watching her mother head upstairs. Casey felt like a failure. Here she was some big-time defense lawyer that had won many high profile cases and she couldn't even win an argument in her mother's home.

Ms. Nora paused at the top of the stairs. "You go out there and do what I say, you hear me? And keep that little heifer away from me for a few days until I calm down, then you can bring her back home."

"Okay, Ma," Casey pouted, knowing her mother's decision was final. No superior argument or appeal could sway her judgment, which Casey hated.

As Casey headed out to the car to give her sister the bad news, she began compiling a mental checklist, orderly and concise, with all the things that she liked about being with one guy versus the other: Todd versus Ronzell.

Both of them were so much fun to be with. Even though she didn't get to have sex with Ronzell yet, he gained cool points by making her laugh and feel special like he was really after her heart, which made her decision that much harder about who she was going to dump first.

Drunk In Love

Briana

Briana looked at her Lady Rolex, wondering where the hell Terrence was. They had agreed to meet at the spot at 7 p.m. and it was now thirty minutes after the hour. She began wondering if he was trying to stand her up. She hoped that wasn't the case because she was really feeling him. Plus his sex game had the recipe that could melt any pussy he put it on.

Terrence rounded the corner on his motorcycle and noticed Briana standing outside the restaurant, looking even sexier than the first time he laid eyes on her. He could tell that she had picked out the tight but not revealing outfit solely for him. The red-painted toes peeking from her peep-toe sandals made him want to suck them. Her ample cleavage on display in the silk floral print blouse she sported made her look downright irresistible. Terrence noticed several men stopping what they were doing to watch Briana. They couldn't help it. Briana was polished femininity dressed provocatively yet tastefully with a beauty that shone like sunlight and raw sexuality that lingered just beneath.

Terrence was glad that he met her and even gladder that he was tapping that ass. He pulled up next to her. Briana rested her hand on the right handlebar of his Kawasaki motorcycle that had the Incredible Hulk paint job on it.

"T, what in the hell? I know you don't expect me to ride on that thing, do you?"

He shook his head. "No, baby, I'm the only thing that you should be riding," he joked, causing her to playfully punch him.

"Whatever, you silly man." She giggled. "Now where's your car?"

"At the crib. I felt like doing my Ruff Ryder thang today."

"Okay," she said giving him a funny look. "So are you ready to eat?"

"You know I can't eat chu' up in public, woman." He kissed her quickly. "What'chu tryna do, get us thrown in jail?"

"Boy, you know what the hell I'm talking - oh, never mind, silly." She smiled as he got off the bike and put it on a kickstand.

"Hey, whatever you want to eat is on me," he mentioned with a wide grin. "You know I'm a producer, so money ain't a thang," he capped.

"So you balling like that?" Briana raised an eyebrow in question. "You know this is Chez Pierre's?"

"So what? If you want it, I'll buy it for you," he said, squeezing her hand while they held hands and headed inside the four-star restaurant.

"So what do you do when you're not producing records?" she asked him after they were seated at their table.

"Think about you and spending more time with the sexiest woman in Dayton."

Smooth...real smooth, she thought, giving him a nod. She gave him a warm smile, taking in the ambience of Chez Pierre's.

The small, quiet restaurant was the epitome of romance. Nestled in downtown Dayton, the place had a seating arrangement of thirty, for fifteen couples only. Slow jams played softly from the speakers inside the restaurant. The lamps on the dining tables had that dim candle lit feel to them, reflecting off the framed oil paintings of abstract couples in various intimate poses, from hugging to making love, that hung on the plaster-covered walls. There was even a miniature version of the Eiffel Tower sitting in the corner of the restaurant with a "Welcome to France" sign on it. Replica street signs from regions all over France were posted at each table and all over the restaurant. White-jacketed waiters and waitresses moved back and forth around the restaurant,

Drunk In Love

providing guests with swift and superb service. Terrence and Briana sat right next to the Eiffel Tower in the rear corner of the restaurant on the Gascony region.

"What will you be drinking tonight?" asked a waiter with a heavy French accent.

"Get me a bottle of your finest wine, please?" Terrence ordered.

"Very well, sir," the waiter replied while writing down the order on his notepad. "May I suggest the aged Pinot Gigi?"

"Sounds like a winner," Terrence told the waiter while Briana looked over the menu.

"I'm ready to order, T," Briana smiled, closing the menu.

"Oh, okay then. We're ready to order," Terrence repeated and the waiter opened his tiny notepad back up.

"Very well, sir, and what will ze madam be having tonight?"

"I'd like the Lebanese broiled fish with a side order of Mediterranean creamy rice and noodles, and for starters, you can bring me a basket of French bread and a chef salad."

"And you can give me ze French fries with ze French dressing and a double shot of ze French fried chicken!" Terrence told him, making fun of his accent, which caused Briana to giggle.

"And for dessert, madam?" the waiter asked, trying to remain professional. It wasn't his fault that he was a Frenchman. He just looked at Terrence as an ignorant fool and kept it moving.

Glancing at Terrence for a moment, she thought, *I want all of him with some whipped cream, strawberries, and syrup dripping off his sexy ass.* "Hmm, I'll let my date decide after dinner," she threw it out there with a sexy smile, and Terrence caught on immediately.

"Very well, madam." The waiter bowed slightly and then walked off towards the kitchen to fill their orders.

"Boy, you're so silly. Why did you make fun of him and his accent like that?"

"C'mon, Bri-Bri, when have you ever known a person from France living in little old Dayton and working in a so-called French spot... That's too much of a coinky-dink." He grinned.

Briana giggled. "I suppose you're right, but that still gives you no right to rain on his parade."

"He'll live. But enough about ole' boy. I thought we came here to enjoy each other's company?"

"We did, but can I ask you what made you choose Chez Pierre's?"

"Oh, this spot is supposed to impress all the ladies." He smiled. "This is my first time eating here though."

"I can tell by the way you ordered your food."

"What?" he asked. "You mean to tell me that this French restaurant don't specialize in French fries? I am shocked and appalled!" He sucked his teeth, giving her a wide-eyed look of disgust that tickled her pink inside.

She laughed her butt off. "Stop it, T, before you make me pee on myself with your silly self. I like a man who can make me laugh. You're really stockpiling some cool points."

Terrence leaned back in his chair, letting the smooth sounds of Michael Jackson's love ballad "One More Chance" do a little talking for him. She had him out of his element after telling him to cool it on the jokes. He was a jokester at heart and loved making people laugh. Now he had to impress her another way, which had him thinking a millions thought per millisecond. "Well hey, I love having fun, Bri-Bri, especially when I'm with a beautiful woman like you."

She blushed. "So tell me, T, why is it that a handsome man like yourself doesn't have a woman in his life?"

"Cause I'm a producer and -"

"You're not looking for one," she finished his statement. "Yeah, I already heard that one, but seriously, you never think

Drunk In Love

about being with someone to escape those lonely rainy nights?"

He sighed, thinking about all his attempts at finding love. His failure still hurt deeply. He looked at Briana as if he wanted to confess his whole life to her about all the pain and heartache he'd been through. Figuring it was too soon, he declined to act impulsively. "I think about it…I think about it a lot. But I guess I'll find that special lady when I least expect it, you know."

She gave him a warm smile, liking his answer - simple and honest. Briana peered up in time to see the waiter returning with the champagne. Prince's "Adore You" blared softly from the speakers, setting the mood.

"Until the end of time, I truly adore you…
You are my heart and mind, I truly adore you…
From the first moment I saw you, I knew you were the one…
That night I had to call you, we were rapping
'til the sun came up…"

The waiter set the chilled bottle of champagne down along with the French bread and salad on the table. He quickly filled their champagne flutes and stood at attention.

"Your orders will be arriving shortly, madam," he said with a slight bow before heading to another table.

Terrence lifted his glass in the air and Briana did the same. "Here's to new beginnings, new friendships, and new possibilities," he told her.

"To new possibilities," she smiled, clinking her glass against his.

New possibilities sounded good to her - especially if those possibilities had anything to do with her and Terrence being together as a couple. She had virtually made herself a hermit to the dating scene. Now that she was out and about again, Briana knew anything was possible for them. Despite the sex, she realized that she might have found a gentle soul brother in Terrence, a man of another kind, a man who offered her new possibilities. She couldn't believe that her one night stand turned out to be a blessing in disguise.

Briana really wanted things to work out between them. She wanted him to love her; she wanted to be in love again. She wanted to share her world and everything in it with someone again. Briana convinced herself that Terrence could turn all of her wishes into reality if he played his cards right.

Taking a few sips of the bubbly, Briana lifted her glass in the air to propose another toast. "To no more lonely, rainy nights and to happiness and having fun. May those guidelines be the cornerstone of our friendship and lives from this day forward."

"I'll drink to that." Terrence smiled. "Spoken like a woman who knows what she knows."

They drank up the bubbly as Keith Sweat's Classic, "I'll Give All My Love to You," invaded their ears, really setting the mood.

"I've always wanted to love you...
You can make all my dreams come true...
I know you're the one for me, baby...
Yeah, I know you're the one for me, baby...
Yeah-Ay-Yeah... Yeah-Ay-Yeah... Ay-Yeah-Ay-Yeah-Yeah-
Yeah... Whoa-Oooh...
I will never do anything to hurt you...
I'll give all my love to you...
And I'm gonna give you every bit of my love tonight, girl..."

Briana hummed along with the song, staring deeply into Terrence's eyes. She wanted him to pick up on the hint. She wanted to re-create that magic they had shared the first night they met. She wanted to do and experience things with him that she had never thought of doing with another man. Terrence examined the look in her eyes briefly before reaching out to

Drunk In Love

clasp her hand. He turned it over and kissed it tenderly. Briana instantly creamed in her panties.

To new possibilities, she thought, giving her new beau a seductive smile.

Anitra

Anitra and Briana sat at a corner table inside a downtown Starbucks. Just about every table was in use by slackers and moochers, but the environment felt safe and secure, probably because of the numerous hang-arounds and moochers.

Hell, for three dollars and some change, you should be able to get something extra for free with your coffee, some added benefit, Anitra thought before addressing Briana. "Tell your mother - I mean, Auntie Evelyn - that I appreciate her for letting us use her crib for the bachelorette shindig. Girl, it is going to be so off the chain."

Briana began taking a sip of her frozen cappuccino and then suddenly stopped. She slightly turned to see the handsome man trying to get their attention from the next table over. His wavy dyed blue and black hair totally turned her off to his looks. Briana would never think of giving him the time of day because of his stupid-looking blue hair. Briana kicked Anitra's foot under the table. "Girl, look at the freak at the next table," Briana said through clenched teeth while smiling.

Anitra gave him a quick glance over her shoulder and couldn't help but laugh. "Girl he has blue hair." Anitra giggled.

"I know, right? He's such a lame. I'm about to have a little fun," Briana said and finally looked his way.

"You know the old joke. I could show you what's underneath my skirt, but then I'd have to kill you."

The man smiled, loving Briana's frame that was being concealed in an olive green one strap ruffled curve-hugging mini-dress. Her look was tasteful and very enticing to the eyes. "What about the joke, you show me yours and I'll show you mines?" the man came back, making both women laugh a little.

Drunk In Love

"Girl, no he didn't!" Anitra gasped, giving Briana an idea.

"Ah, I don't think my girlfriend here would like that. Besides you don't have what I like to suck on...sorry," Briana said with a shrug before sipping her cappuccino.

"It's your loss." The man shrugged and got up from the table. He began walking away and stopped. He looked at Briana again. "You're too cute to be such an asshole lesbo!" he said, loud enough to cause people to stare.

"Get a new hairdo, you fucking queer!" Briana called out, making Anitra laugh as the man walked away with a chip on his shoulder.

"Girl, you wild! I can't take your ass nowhere." Anitra giggled.

"Yes, you can, you know I'm such a lady." Briana smiled. She waited a moment and told Anitra that she thought Terrence might be her soul mate.

"How can you tell so quickly? I mean, what makes you feel that way?" Anitra asked, while sipping on her chestnut and vanilla double latte.

"Girl, he makes me laugh so much. You know he just makes me feel special. And there's certainly no denying his wonderful skills in the bedroom and wherever else we choose to make love. And he always wants to be around me. You don't find that too much in this day and time when it comes to men."

"Tell me about it! All the good ones are either locked up or caught up on them white women."

"Okaaay!" Briana agreed, giving her cousin a high five across the table.

Anitra took another sip of cappuccino. "All I can tell you, girl, is to go for it. If you think he's really the one for you, go for it. I will make sure that I toss the bouquet right at your behind after the wedding, just to give lover boy a hint-hint, okaaay? Hopefully I can persuade Nathan to toss the garter to Terrence."

"Slow down there, cousin. I just said I think Terrence is my soul mate for right now, not until death do us part. That's a pretty big step and I still have to feel him out some more."

"Well, you definitely have that dick in your life type of glow again and you need to figure out if you want to continue having that glow. Any which way you look at things, you're definitely in the loop now, even if you wished to hell that you weren't."

"Anitra, I'm a big girl. I got this." Briana smiled.

"You better, because I would hate to have to pull out my blade and get to cuttin' on Terrence's fine ass."

For the rest of the lunch hour rush, Briana and Anitra talked about love, life, and relationships. They shared a few laughs while planning Anitra's bachelorette party.

♥ ♥ ♥

After leaving Anitra, Briana met up with Terrence later that day at the mall. They went into a few stores, flirting and joking as usual. One thing led to another and Briana found herself in a dressing room with her mini-dress hiked up over her waist and Terrence's head buried between her thick thighs.

"Ssss…mmm…" she moaned, feeling really good. She massaged his head while he went to work, sucking and nibbling on her love button. "Baby…mmm…we gonna get caught," she moaned, turning him on even more.

He used one hand to undo his pants while using the other hand to rub her clitoris in circular motions while he slurped from her dripping wet ocean of love. Overwhelmed with lust, he lapped up her juices, ravenously devouring her.

"Aaah, aaah! Sssss…ooooh shit!" she gasped, unleashing a thunderous climax all over his lapping tongue and face.

Drunk In Love

He raised his face to look at her. Her eyes were glassy as she bit down on her bottom lip. He took that as a signal to continue. He kissed her passionately, allowing her vaginal fluids to saturate their wrestling tongues. Feeling her pulsating pussy throbbing in anticipation, she wasted no time in guiding his rock-hard meat inside her wetness. Right there in the department store's dressing room, they went at each other, making love as passionately as they'd done the first night they met.

Stroking her with powerful yet slow grinding thrusts, he wanted her to know how much he loved being deep inside her and how he never wanted their fling to end.

"Sssss...mmm, baby... Sssss... I'm going to cum... You making me cuuuuummmm!" she cried, biting into his neck as he plunged steadily inside her, getting lost in the land of her honey.

"Aww...aww....Fuurrrgghhhgadaaaa!" he exclaimed, exploding deep inside. He grabbed her by the waist and held her tightly while draining his love rod into her canal.

"Boy, stop! What are you tryna do, get me pregnant?" She moved from under him, getting herself together. She pulled her dress down and left the dressing room, only to catch several people gawking and looking at her like she just committed murder. Briana rushed from the department store with tears welling up in her eyes. After Terrence exited the store and caught up to her, Briana yanked away from him and began cursing him out something terrible.

"Bri-Bri, I'm sorry, I just got caught up in the moment," he explained, but she didn't want to hear any of his excuses.

She read him the riot act. Briana felt pretty sure that he had tried to impregnate her. Even though she started taking birth control shots after she met him, Briana didn't appreciate the stunt he just pulled.

"Bri-Bri, for the last time, it was an accident," he lied. "I didn't mean it." Terrence did want her to have his child. He didn't know why, but he felt that she would be the best mother for his child, maybe because she was a doctor.

"Whatever, just take me home," she hissed, getting in his car and slamming the door.

Briana remained silent, not speaking to him during the long ride to her home, which made it really uncomfortable between them. The mind-boggling sex he just had with her had him reflecting on all of her moans and beautiful, ugly sex faces. Her being pissed off at him was the furthest thing from his mind. He pulled up in front of her house and he got a scary feeling. He didn't want them to part on bad terms.

Damn, you stupid, he scolded himself, knowing he had to do something quick to get her to talk to him. Nothing good would come of their day if she left him feeling a certain kind of way.

He put the car in park and gave her a funny look. She kept looking straight ahead, knowing he was trying to make her laugh.

"So you just gonna act childish? Damnit, I said I was sorry! What more do you want from me?" he snapped, causing her to turn her head and give him an evil look.

"I want you to be more responsible!" she fired back with tears in her eyes.

She kissed him on the lips before getting out of the car and dashing to her house. She ran into the bathroom to wash the traces of their sex away. Her cell phone rang an hour later. It took everything Briana had not to ignore Terrence's call. But she figured it was an accident after how much he kept apologizing before she left him in the car. She answered calmly as possible considering the circumstances.

She could hear his deep baritone asking, "So we cool or what?"

"Yes. I'm sorry, Terrence. I mean…just don't do that to me again. I'm just not cool with you nutting inside me. We haven't talked about children yet and I don't want to have any

Drunk In Love

right now," she said, still feeling hurt by him in some strange way, even though she enjoyed every minute of the sex.

"I know, I know, and I promise it will never happen again," he said. He smoothly made more conversation with her until he got around to the memorable and spontaneous sex they just had. Before she knew it, Briana became lost in the conversation. She looked up and noticed that it was a little after 10 p.m.

Briana took a deep breath and said, "Well, it's getting late, T. I have to get my beauty rest."

"Okay, beautiful, I'll see you soon."

"Okay," she said before ending the call, smiling like a teenager smitten by her first crush.

Vanessa

The following morning on Friday, Vanessa decided to go into the office early. The weatherman on TV had promised clear blue skies and sunny temperatures that would reach a high of 88 degrees. With that in mind, Vanessa drove to work with the top down on her convertible BMW.

Vanessa parked under the towering oak and maple trees that lined Main Street in front of her office building. As soon as she went to reach for her purse, another car caught her attention.

What the hell? she thought before exiting her car.

Several spaces away from her office building she spotted Kenny's black Dodge Magnum, the same car she had seen him driving on many occasions. She saw him sitting in the driver's seat with his eyes closed - her fantasy man!

Why is he here so early? Only one sure way to find out, she told herself while walking straight for his car.

She reflected back on the conversation they had before when she was upset about her husband. She thought he had been friendly when she was upset the other day. *But now this...waiting for me to arrive at work in his car. It seems a little creepy, or worse, a little suspicious.* She cautioned herself not to overreact.

After reaching his car, Vanessa tapped on the glass lightly, waking him. Kenny saw her standing there and quickly pulled out a gun and aimed it at her.

"AAAAAAHHH!" Vanessa shrieked, turning on her heels and bolting for her car.

"Aw shit!" Kenny gasped before springing from his car. He started chasing behind her in his blue Nike summer-weight suit. The material flapped in the wind, looking like he was free falling from an airplane and the airwaves were making the

Drunk In Love

tracksuit flap. He finally caught up to her just as she reached her car.

Vanessa turned on him and quickly lifted her knee, belting his family jewels. Kenny doubled over and started coughing violently.

"If I didn't know any better, I'd say you were trying to damage my hardware for life." He winced, massaging his groin area.

"Kenny, why do you have a gun? And why are you here so early?" She asked in a stern tone while pulling out her cell phone, preparing to call the police on him. "And why did you aim that thing at me? You could have killed me, boy!"

Straightening himself, Kenny tilted his head and smiled. Even though she was mad at him for startling her, his smile melted her heart. "I'm very sorry, Boss Lady. It's not what it looks like. Actually, you can blame yourself for all this."

"And why would I blame myself for anything you have done?"

"You just scared the hell outta me. I was sleeping good and you came up and messed that up. I didn't know who the fuck you was until you took off running like a bat outta hell."

Vanessa gave him a blank look. "Kenny, you still haven't explained why you have a gun and why you're here so early?"

"The gun is for protection. I used to live in the streets before this gig I got with you. So I guess some old habits are hard to break. The reason I was here so early, I wanted to ask you for the day off."

She nodded. "I see," she said, figuring either he was telling the truth or he was a born liar. "You couldn't have called in and asked for the day off?"

"Naw, I handle all my business face to face like a real man supposed to do. So you not going to ask me why I want the day off?" He smiled, figuring he had her undivided attention.

95

"Excuse me?" she muttered, glancing at her wedding ring. She figured that he already had a solid excuse to play hooky from work on this beautiful day.

"I wanted the day off so I could take you out today. Are you available or what, Boss Lady?"

Vanessa stared him right in the eyes without blinking. As far as assertiveness went, she had to give him a few points for originality. "Well, that depends."

"Depends on what?"

"On the fact that I'm married, Kenny! Are you out of your damn mind?"

"Yep," he answered, leaning in far enough to pin her against the car. He could hear her erratic breathing. "I'm outta my mind about you. I see the way you look at me. I've been attracted to you for quite some time."

"Is that supposed to be a compliment?" she muttered, watching his slightly long tongue slide across his big lips.

"For me it is."

She smiled. Although her husband was better looking, Kenny certainly was more attentive, more charming, and definitely after her goodies. It was reason enough to accept his offer of going out for the day and keep the flirting going for a while.

Drunk In Love

Casey

Ten minutes past 11 p.m. on a festive Saturday, Casey sat at the bar having drinks with Todd. Their date had been phenomenal, but she didn't care. She closed her eyes and let them wander, thinking about Ronzell, and then she blinked.

She had escaped all of Todd's inquiries about sex, claiming that she was on her period. She had her eyes on something better, which automatically X'ed Todd out of her life. Casey didn't feel the need to dump him so she could move on with life. She'd just move on and hope he'd eventually take the hint. Besides, she didn't want to dump him now and have to hear all of his questions about what and why she wanted to end things.

Four days of constant and careful deliberations of being with Todd brought her to this point: the final date. She sat in a dark bar with drink in hand waiting for it to be over. At the stroke of midnight, which would be arriving soon, she would get on with her life and close the chapter with Todd out of it.

The bar was an Irish pub in Dayton's wealthy Irish neighborhood - Todd's stomping grounds. Outside, distant traffic hummed like a swarm of insects. Little shamrocks hung everywhere inside the pub while Irish folk tunes warbled from speakers. The sounds muffled were by the many patrons watching and cheering for the basketball game. The Boston Celtics had rallied from a thirteen-point deficit that helped to send the game into overtime against the feisty Chicago Bulls.

At a table near them on the right, Casey heard an Irish woman complaining to her husky date, clearly making it known that she wanted Casey to hear her. "Inconsiderate bastard, always bringing niggers here."

Yes, I am here, bitch! Please call me a nigger one more time, Casey thought, ready to kick some Irish ass.

Tonight Todd was trying to show Casey his culture and roots. The bar belonged to his uncle, who had vested interest in a weakened neighborhood to ultimately provide a fun, secure location for his Irish friends to relieve stress and be entertained.

Another couple at a nearby table behind Casey chatted loudly enough for Casey to hear them. They gossiped back and forth about interracial dating and sex as though their conversation was not demeaning to the black race.

Casey had heard enough, which only made her feel good about her decision. At first, she felt a little bad about stringing him along, knowing she'd never have sex with him again. After this experience among his racist friends tonight, she couldn't wait to leave and use the racism as the reason for breaking up with him.

Checking her Lady Rolex, Casey noticed it was approaching midnight. She had other plans. One of her male friends told her in a whispered phone call that he wanted to see her tonight—at a hotel a few miles away from his sleeping wife. Frantic that she'd miss out on his good oral skills, Casey prayed for Todd to get restless. Plus she was going out with Ronzell in two days and if she got Todd out of her hair tonight, she would be back to normal in no time to focus on Ronzell.

The basketball game went into the final minutes and Todd still didn't move. They watched the Celtics win the game and then the TV screen switched to Mel Gibson's "Braveheart" film. Casey finished off her drink. The racist couples began to get louder with their heckling, causing Casey's head to feel fuzzy from anger.

This was a bad idea. What made you date this white guy anyway? she wondered, gritting her jaw in cold fury.

Todd noticed the disturbed look on her face. "What?" he asked with genuine concern. "Casey, what's wrong?"

Drunk In Love

Casey said nothing until her cell phone rang. She sent the call to voicemail and then glanced at both couples and rolled her eyes. "I'm not feeling too well."

"Oh, okay."

"Todd, it's not you. I just have to get home. I wanted to hang out with you to get to know you more, but these cramps are killing me," she lied, punking out on ending things with him. She just wanted to get out of there and go get ready for her booty call.

"Yeah, okay, well, I'll walk you out to your car and -"

"No, I'll be fine. You stay here with your peeps and I'll call you when I get home."

When she left the bar, Casey headed straight to the hotel for her booty call. She erased Todd's phone number from her cell phone along with every memory of him and the things they did together. Casey was on to the next one.

Briana

Driving along the coast, Briana took another look in the rearview mirror, not believing what she was about to do. Terrence had done something to her, maybe turned her out. If that's what it was, Briana assured herself that it was merely the long absence without sex in her life, which only added to the weird feeling in the pit of her stomach, the feeling she'd been yearning to recapture since her last relationship: the "I'm in love" feeling. After arriving on Terrence's doorstep, the feeling seemed to intensify.

She put on some MAC lip-gloss while walking up to his door, wearing a tan Burberry trench coat and Manolo Blahnik sling-back heels. She dug in her pocket and pulled out her cell phone to call him. Seconds later, she heard the phone ringing inside Terrence's house.

Terrence finally answered after the fourth ring. "What's good?"

"Hey baby, it's me." Briana smiled, looking at his door.

"What's going on?"

She giggled. "You wouldn't believe where I am right now with a flat tire?"

"Where are you?" he asked, sounding concerned. "I'm coming to get you right now."

"I'm a few miles from your house."

"Don't move. I'll be there in a sec. Bye." He ended the call.

It took Terrence only a minute to bolt out the front door half dressed. As soon as the front door opened, Briana opened her trench coat and let it fall to the ground.

"Surprise!" she said with a devious smile.

Drunk In Love

"Damn, girl!" he bellowed, his strong jaws dropping. He took a minute to view her naked hourglass shape before closing his mouth and licking his lips.

"See anything you like, Big Boy?"

"I see a whole lot that I like! Get cho' ass in here," he said, pulling her inside his house.

Whatever the record was for a man shedding his clothes, Terrence quickly broke it. After getting naked, he gently laid Briana down on the carpet in his foyer and slowly crawled between her spread legs. Digging his hands deep into her soft flesh, he wrapped his muscular arms around her thick thighs as she grabbed hold of his rigid pipe. He sucked on her hard nipples as she stroked on his rigid manhood.

"You bet' not lose control this time," she said, squeezing his pecker, reminding him about the dressing room incident.

"I won't," he huffed, pushing his tongue inside her mouth and pushing himself forward until he penetrated her wet center.

She arched her back, pulling him towards her, taking him into the depths of her love until she swallowed every thick inch of his love sword. She closed her eyes, keeping them shut the entire time they made love, completely caught up in the moment. She wanted to ignore the dangerous risks she was taking by having unprotected sex with him for a second time. Even though the sex felt far better without the latex barrier, Briana just couldn't ignore the dangers they were partaking in.

C'mon, Briana. You know what's has to be done. You have to be the responsible one here.

I know, but it feels too good.

And it felt good to a lot of those HIV and AIDS patients you see at the hospital on a daily basis too.

"Unnghk...mmm," she grunted, moving back to meet his thick slamming beef stick, which plowed deeper and deeper inside her love tunnel.

The way he stroked her made her feel good and wanted. His loving also made the little voice inside of her sound like an unwelcome stranger, someone she almost didn't know. She tried to ignore it as Terrence plowed away, going in and out, in and out of her pulsating nookie.

"Get all...of it...in meeee! Harder, T...HARDER!" she moaned, feeling his pounding muscle stretching her wet, sugary walls as he stroked deeper and deeper, but it was no use. That only made the voice inside grow louder and louder, more insistent, more controlling.

"Ssss...stop it, T! We have to get a condom."

"A what? Nah, I'm almost there Bri-Bri," he huffed, continuing to pump faster and faster. "C'mon, girl, I'ma pull out this time, I swear." He slammed inside her harder, making her gasp for air.

"Aaahh...NO! T, we have to sto-" She gasped as he extracted his slick-coated love stick and exploded warm semen all over her flat stomach and heaving breasts. He rolled off of her, out of breath.

Bitch, you better curse his ass out right now! He just disrespected you to the tenth power!

She wanted to obey the voice inside, but she knew it would just be a waste of time and make her lose the feeling that Terrence gave her. There was only one thing to do and she knew it.

"Where are you going, babe?" he asked, watching her get up from the floor and walk off.

She didn't say a word on her way down the hallway, heading to the bathroom.

"Bri-Bri, what's good?" he called out as he got up off the floor.

"I'm going to the bathroom to wash up," she said over her shoulder. "Then I am going to find some condoms and get ready for round two, round three, round four, and round five and six," she said, trying to sound sexy, but deep inside she felt dirty and violated.

.

Drunk In Love

Casey

"Yeah, I really like that color for the bride maid's dresses," Anitra encouraged Casey's selection of the Baltic Blue Vera Wang dresses while they chatted on the telephone.

"I knew you would. Oh My God, they're so hot! I know I'ma catch me some dick wearing that thing," Casey stressed tauntingly.

"Look, I'm not planning a thing or planning what dresses y'all going to wear. Just hook up with Briana and get her take on things. If she likes the dresses, then it's a go."

"But it's your wedding, Anitra. Don't be letting Briana have all that control over the best day in your life."

"It's cool. I'm fine with her decision and I trust whatever she's going with. Plus you know she loves doing things like this 'cause she already thinks she's our mother."

"I know, right?" Casey grinned. "Hold on, girl, I got another call," Casey said before hitting the flash button to click over to the other line. "Hello?"

"What's up, stranger?"

It's Ronzell! "Nothing much," she responded. "How have you been doing?"

"Wondering what's up with you?" He said. "What'cha doing?"

"Nothing, just talking to my girl about her wedding," she answered. "What are you up to?"

"Calling to see if you'd like to hang out with me again, being as though you forgot all about our rain check."

"I did not forget," she muttered. "It's just that a lot of stuff came up at the wrong time and bad timing play a major part in things," she explained, feeling her heart quicken after knowing he wanted to see her again.

103

All of a sudden, Casey felt her juices stirring in her love nest. She hadn't had sex in close to two weeks and here was a man who she wanted to give her body to calling her up on a Friday afternoon to see about her. What better timing? She couldn't ask for anything more to look forward to for the weekend.

"So you busy like that now, huh?"

"Not really, I just had some family stuff to handle that's all, but I'm free now."

"That's good."

"You said that like you miss me or something?"

"I didn't say all that, Casey." He chuckled, being a hard-ass, which she enjoyed.

It was the challenge she loved the challenge of turning hard-asses into putty in her hands. After giving them a taste of her goodies, she loved making them cry and beg to get a second chance at hitting the golden treat resting between her thighs. "You don't have to." *I can hear it all in your voice, Mr. Confident.* "Your phone call says it all, Ronzell, and while we on the subject, why are you so scared?"

"Scared of what?"

"To ask me to come over to your house?"

"For what?" he asked, playing hardball. He really wanted her to come over, but he didn't want to seem hard-pressed.

Casey sensed that much, which made her combine a socially acceptable answer with a sexually inviting one without offending him or seeming too easy. "You know, to just chill and hang out with you."

"To chill, huh?" he stated in a nonchalant tone.

"Yeah. Unless you want to take me out and let me run up your credit card bills. But since I know you don't want that - because I wouldn't want to be a financial burden to you - why don't you just rent a few movies and let me come over there and spend a little time with you?"

"You're not going to take another rain check on me, are you?"

Damn, he's killing the mood. I have already taken a risk by pushing the envelope on the slow, getting-to-know-each-other process. By advancing the prospect of a third in-home date, where the chances of romance are much greater, he should be mature enough to know that something is bound to happen, which is what I wanted from the moment I saw him in the gym.

"Whaddya want to watch?" he asked, sensing he was losing her by the uncomfortable silence he heard in response to his last question.

"Um, you pick something out for us. I'm quite sure your choices will be good."

"So, I'll see you around what time?"

"Give me about an hour."

"That's a bet. See you then."

"Buh-bye." Casey chuckled and clicked back over to Anitra. "Hello?"

"Bitch, why the hell you kept me waiting on the line so long? I was about to hang up on your ass."

"My bad, gurl, check it out though. I'm about to make another hit and run on some dick."

"Damn, freak, you still at it, huh? Who's the latest victim?"

"Some stud I met at Bally's over in Trotwood. I never mentioned him to you?"

"Maybe one or twice, but I probably didn't pay much attention. I've been so focused on this wedding and running away from that life that you're still living."

"Gurl, you don't know what you're missing...you really don't." Casey giggled. "You know just as well as I do that you need a variety of meat in your life. It's impossible to get used to one," Casey said.

"Well, I did used to think like that before I met Nathan. I'm on some grown folk stuff now and all I need is Nathan's meat."

"Yeah, right, tell that bullshit to somebody else dat don't know your ass." Casey laughed. "Once a ho', always a ho'. One piece of dick ain't never gonna change that craving for more and more. Well, this ho' gotta go. I have an appointment with a dick doctor."

"Have fun, slut," Anitra quipped. "My dick doctor stays on call twenty-four hours a day, seven days a week. I don't need to make no appointments. Now tell me how you love that?"

"You ain't shit, bitch!" Casey spat playfully. "But I'll talk to you later and maybe I'll give you some of the freaky details."

"Umm-hmm… Get at me, gurl, I love you."

"Love you too, holla," Casey said before ending the call.

She headed for the bathroom to take a nice hot bubble bath. She wanted to soak her coochie and add her favorite douche products so her punanny would be nice and tight for what she wanted to do with Ronzell.

After handling her business in the hot bathtub, Casey put on a pair of dark blue Christian Dior stretch pants minus the panties. She tossed on a white form-fitting tank top minus the bra, which made her perky breasts sit up high, revealing a lot of cleavage. The open-toe sandals she wore made her look taller than her real height. She pulled her hair back into a ponytail and put a pink hair tie around it.

After putting a box of condoms inside her purse, Casey grabbed her car keys and flew out of the house. While walking to her car, her cell phone began ringing. She hurried to get inside her car, thinking that Ronzell was calling her back to see what was taking her so long. She started the engine and answered the phone, all the while applying a light coat of lip-gloss to her lips. "Hello?"

Drunk In Love

"Hey, Casey! What's going on?"

"Oh, h-hey Todd. What a pleasant surprise," Casey said, attempting to disguise her astonishment. It had been going on three weeks since their last date at the bar.

With a subtle edge of sarcasm, Casey said, "So you finally fed up with the wife and kids. That's why I get the honor of hearing from you?"

"Look, Casey, I know I haven't been attentive lately, but I have been swamped with work," he lied. The truth of the matter was that he had allowed peer pressure and harsh words from people he knew about dating a black woman get to him. After she left him at the bar, everyone that knew Todd and his uncle told him that he could do better than Casey, stressing the point that he could do better than betraying his race with some black woman.

"It figures." Casey pulled out of her parking spot and drove off.

"Listen, sweetheart," Todd began. "I want to make it up to you, really I do."

"Unfortunately, Todd, you can't," she said. "It's too late. Just as I was beginning to catch feelings for you, you pulled a disappearing act on me, and that hurt me really bad," she lied.

"How did I disappear?" he protested. "I sent you flowers every day, explaining where I would be at any time if you needed me."

"What!" Casey snapped. She didn't have time for this. *This motherfucker acting and sounding like I'm his woman or something, he's already putty. I have no more use for this clown anymore. He's too weak.* "Todd, why did you really call me?"

He sighed. "I was just wondering…what, are you busy or something?"

"Yeah, I'm on my way to meet somebody, Todd."

"Who?"

"I don't have to answer to you. You psychoanalyzing me and shit. But if you must know, I found some black dick and decided to stick with my own race just like your peeps were stressing to me in your face the last time we went out together."

"Why you didn't tell me?"

"I shouldn't have to," she sighed. "Look, Todd, I think it's best that we just part ways."

"So that's how you really feel?"

"Something like that, white boy. That's how I felt hanging out with you at that racist bar. I wasn't physically sick. I was mentally sick and tired of hearing your people throw racial slurs at me like it was cool. But I thank them 'cause they made me go black, and guess what, honey? I can never go back to you." She laughed and hung up on him.

Casey felt glad to be getting rid of Todd. It never occurred to her that she would miss Todd's efforts to love her. Ronzell, noticeably taller and cuter, presented a nice change of pace for her.

But for how long? she wondered while speeding on the expressway, heading towards that nice change of pace.

After reaching Ronzell's home, they watched both movies he rented. Casey was really feeling him. She liked the way he snuggled up with her under a blanket on the couch like they were some kind of loving couple. She went right along with the flow, rubbing up and down on his chest until she went lower and lower, making contact with his nature. Once that happened and she squeezed him, he began kissing all over her neck and rubbing on her titties while the second film was playing. Their friction and touching made the sexual tension between them boil over to a point where they needed release.

Drunk In Love

Casey threw her leg over his lap and straddled him. She kissed him all over his face, pressing her body up against the bulge in his sweats. She wanted some of what he had, and his teasing foreplay just guaranteed that he was worthy of one romp in the sack.

Continuing to kiss all over his face, she moved lower to his neck and ears, inching lower down his chest until she made contact with his right nipple. She bit it gently through the fabric of his T-shirt before helping him raise the shirt over his head. As she licked the smooth skin on his chest, he palmed her soft behind, aching to slam his throbbing meat deep inside her.

"Casey, you know what you're doing, right?" he said, staring into her eyes.

"Yeah," she moaned before sliding her tongue in his mouth.

She began tugging on the strings of his sweats, urging him to get his manhood out. He pulled down his sweats and quickly helped her come out of her jeans. Casey's eyes zoomed in on his smooth, rock-hard piston with thick crooked veins, easily standing up to an impressive size for her. He grabbed at the base and guided it towards her slick dripping slit. She stopped him.

"I want the dick, but I don't wanna die for it, you feel me?" she said before reaching for her purse and pulling out the box of condoms. She opened one and slowly rolled it on him, then guided him inside her warm, wet lagoon of love. She started riding his girth inch by inch until her stomach felt the penetration of his granite pole. Her hands gripped his neck as she gyrated her pelvis and bounced up and down on his upstanding boner.

"Mmmph, shit!" he groaned as she made her contracting opening suck in the last inch of his wood down to the base. She tightened her muscles on him and darted her tongue in and out of his mouth to match the slow rhythm of their union.

They started humping faster and faster, making their own rhythm. Moaning and sweating, as he raised up off the couch, he still kept his joystick buried deep inside her tight wetness. He went from short, tight strokes to straight all out slamming her on his jabbing piston. The more he slammed her on his pecker, the more Casey screamed out his name.

"Aaaah! Yessss! Yessss! Fuck me! Fuck meeeeee!" she shrieked, bouncing up and down faster and faster, loving the way his love pump was bringing her to the ultimate peak.

He laid her on the floor still buried inside her. He gave her a goofy smile before putting one of her legs over his shoulder. She put her arm around his waist and pulled him deeper inside her wet garden. Her body was boiling and his pounding muscle had her gasping for air. She arched her back, shivering on his sawing piston until her milky white love juices oozed all over him. He kept punishing her love tunnel like he wanted to make a new exit. A few moments later, he was hitting her so hard; all she could do was hold on for the ride. He laid it on her so good, she thought she was dreaming until he slowed down a little and gave her a deep, guttural churning rhythm.

"Ssss...oh my Gawd! Stop! No, don't...stop! I'm cuuummmmmiiing, boy, I'm Cuuummmmmiiing!" she screamed, racing towards that good place.

"Take dis dick! Cum for me, lil mama. Cum for dis dick!" he urged with pounding strokes while reaching between them, massaging her puffy clitoris until she climaxed over and over. Seconds later, he finally exploded, filling up the condom.

Casey's heart stopped when he pulled out of her and she saw the little split in the condom.

"Don't trip, Casey, it tore when I was almost all the way out." He kissed her and then got up and went to the bathroom.

Still under his spell, Casey got up and followed him into the bathroom, ripping open another condom. Once in the

Drunk In Love

bathroom with him, they took a quick shower and went at it again and again and again.

Vanessa

It had been a fun day for Vanessa while hanging out with Kenny. First, Kenny took her to the zoo for a very memorable and flirtatious tour at the lion's den and then they went to dine out at a romantic restaurant for lunch. After that, it was off to the movies and finally they took a long walk through the park near the lake. The day had been so much fun for them both that they began dating on the sly.

After two months of dating, Vanessa found herself at Kenny's place gazing at the spacious apartment. Up until now, they had avoided all the sexual tension building between them, trying to keep it on a strictly harmless buddy-buddy thing of just hanging out and having fun. Kenny beamed, watching her short body walk towards the couch. Noticing the bubble raised beneath her blazer, Kenny began wringing his hands at his good fortune.

"Here you go, let me take that for you," he said, removing her blazer, revealing a pair of tight, form-fitting stretch pants and a snug-fitting T-shirt with a designer's name noticeably pasted across her protruding chest. Her strong, lightly-defined arms alerted him that she worked out, which he loved: a healthy, strong, and independent woman.

"You have a nice place here."

"Do you want a quick tour?" he asked politely while hanging up her jacket in the closet.

"Just make sure it's quick," she said, emitting a radiant smile, ignoring the little voice within.

"You got it. Just follow me." Kenny smiled, holding out his hand, until she grabbed it.

A quick tour of Kenny's two-level town house left Vanessa duly impressed. Now she knew she paid well, but the apartment screamed for some decoration. Kenny's yellow-painted walls needed some color.

"Kenny, I'm going to have to give you the day off one day and drag your butt down to the Home Depot and help you spice this place up a little bit," she commented lightly.

"So you got jokes, huh?" he asked, getting on the defensive in a playful way. "Why you crackin' on my spot? I think it's cool for me. It could use a lady's touch, but until I find the right woman, I'ma just do me."

"That sounds good, but until you do find the right woman, your place could look a little more lived in, you know?"

"I feel you," he replied. "But I be too busy for all that stuff. I mean, between work, working out, going to school, and hanging out with you, I haven't found any time to get it together yet."

Vanessa blushed. "What do you do when you get home?" she asked.

"What do you do?" he asked back with a smile that made her turn away from him.

She felt herself falling for him, but she knew it was wrong. She tried her hardest not to go over the ledge. Right now, she just looked at herself as being on the brink of diving over into his arms of lust, love, and adultery.

"Let's see, what to do… I start off by feeding my family. Once that's done, I relax a little and then take a long, hot bubble bath and throw on some Luther Vandross."

"Well, for me, that's too much stuff to do. I be so tired, I fall straight out right there," he said, pointing towards the love seat. "Hey, but I'm always up for new experiences. C'mon and have a seat with me. Let's relax."

They sank down on the love seat, leaving a little bit of space between them.

"Nessa, I really enjoyed spending time with you tonight and for the last sixty-two days, twelve hours and…" He trailed off, glancing at his watch. "Thirty-eight minutes and seventeen seconds," he said, stretching out his arm along the top of the love seat, relaxing in the process. "You're really a fun chick to hang out with," he added, making her blush again.

Damn, he's so smooth!

DON'T DO IT, VANESSA!

But he's waiting for me to lean back. There's no harm in leaning back.

DON'T DO IT!

"You're pretty chill your damn self, Kenny." She smiled and leaned back, resting her neck in the crook of his arm.

They talked well into the night, connecting quite similarly to the way they had done the first day they went out together. Vanessa was a huge fan of good, stimulating conversation, and Kenny threw plenty at her. But what their conversation had brought up again was just how different their lives truly were.

"I am appalled that you have never considered getting married."

Why? So my wife can cheat on me with another man like you're doing to your husband at this very moment because you're not happy with him or bored with your life? I don't think so! "Why you appalled? Yo, don't even go there," he ridiculed.

"Why not? Kenny you're such a prize catch. You're smart, a very hard worker, and very handsome. What woman in her right mind wouldn't want you in their life?"

"The one that's sitting right next to me, for one," he stated sarcastically, mocking her, which really caught her attention.

"Excuse me?" she asked, shooting him a look of disbelief as he stretched his body out lengthwise.

His move forced Vanessa to adjust her body, making her lean back against his chest. Looking up at him, her brown eyes

Drunk In Love

shimmered like brand new copper pennies at the bottom of a fountain.

Kenny smiled and made a wish. "You talk the talk, Nessa, but you're scared to walk the walk," he said, tentatively testing the waters with a slight caress of her neck here and a brush of her breast there, trying to bait a genuine response from her.

She never rejected any of his advances. "I'm not scared at all," she whispered, encouraging him by slightly shifting her weight in suggestive and enticing ways.

"Then what's holding you back? We've been seeing each other for over sixty days now. I know what I want and I think you know what you want, because if you didn't, you wouldn't be here," he pointed out, making a move to wrap his arms around her stomach.

She allowed him to do so. "True, I do know what I want, but you know what's holding me back, Kenny," she replied as she lazily held up her ring finger, giving him the answer. She leaned back against his frame comfortably. "Now what?" she asked impishly.

He turned her over so she could face him - a bold move, for sure. She followed, giving him a daring stare to do something, to be a take-charge kind of guy. Kenny's eyes challenged her to close the distance between their lips. It became a true battle of wills. Vanessa knew it would be easy to lose, especially with his aggressive nature, but she didn't want to lose.

NOT THIS TIME!

If she were going to fool around, it would begin on her terms only.

DAMMIT, GIVE IT UP! she howled silently

I want you bad! his eyes retorted.

GIVE IT UP, KENNY! I'M MARRIED! her eyes expressed vigorously.

Stop being scared of me...of us! I got you! his eyes countered.

You're right. I am scared. You win, okay? her eyes conceded as she broke eye contact with him. She was competitive and hated to lose.

Before Vanessa's body made a move to get up, Kenny's huge lips swooped up and engaged hers.

Houston, we have lift off! WE HAVE LIFT OFF!

Feeling consumed by the warmth of his mouth and body, a small moan escaped from her lips before she could gain control of herself.

From there, things went fast for them. Having been neglected by her husband over the past several months and being aggressively pursued by Kenny all that time, Vanessa's mind went into autopilot along with her body as Kenny's strong hands took control, roaming freely, caressing places that were only meant for her husband to caress.

At that moment, Vanessa's husband was the furthest thing from her, and a certain hardened muscle inside Kenny's jeans that poked her in the belly was the only thing she could feel and think of, which drove her to reach for it like a nympho on a mission to please.

"I can't let you do that," he whispered, grabbing her hand while easing from under her. "Please, let me please you like you deserved to be pleased," he said, pulling her up gently from the love seat by her arms.

As soon as she got to her feet, he covered her mouth with his, parting her lips with his darting tongue. She moaned, pressing against him, feeling her nipples hardening against his chest. His fingers traced the thick curves of her soft buttocks. He felt good that he had finally gotten her to this point because he'd been wanted to sample her goodies, but she kept playing hard to get. During the passionate kissing, Kenny led her to his bedroom while they helped each other strip out of their clothes.

Drunk In Love

Vanessa turned around slowly, modeling her sexy, firm birthday suit for him like he'd just opened a sex toy.

"Damn," he managed to say while licking his lips, looking at her stretched out on his queen-sized bed with its purple satin sheets.

He lay on top of her, taking one of her breasts into his mouth, sucking on her nipple like it was a baby's bottle. He then rolled it around on his lips until several moans escaped her lips.

"Mmm..." she moaned, gasping for air when he moved down her body, kissing and licking gently, all the while sliding his fingers down her belly.

He quickly dipped one of his fingers inside her wet opening, working it there for a while before he added another finger. She began humping on his probing fingers. While she humped back on his penetrating fingers, Kenny went lower and started licking her clitoris.

JACKPOT! she thought, arching her back, shivering on his probing tongue as he made tiny circles all over her throbbing clit.

Kenny moved lower, forcing his tongue deep inside her love tunnel. He lapped up her love juices hungrily and gently nibbled on her outer pussy lips until her shiny, sweet tasting cum oozed out of her, flooding his tongue and chin. She could tell by the way that he devoured her flesh that he'd been wanting to do it for a while.

"Ssss...Ken... Sssss...slow down... It feels sooo good," she huffed between his forceful nibbling on her clitoris and outer lips.

Ignoring her screams of passion, Kenny pushed her legs up higher until they rested on his shoulder blades. She bit down on her bottom lip, feeling his snaking wet tongue licking the rim of her asshole, which caused her to flop around on the bed like a fish fresh out of water. The feeling of his tongue penetrating her back door made her lightheaded with euphoria.

It wasn't long before she felt him sliding his tongue back inside her wet twat with gentle strokes.

"AAAHH... Mmmmm... Kenny, OMIGAWD! Boy!" she cried, which only urged him on to suck and eat her love nest even more. She began climaxing over and over again, as he fingered her tight anal canal.

"St-Stop, Ken, hold up, I can't take no more!" she cried passionately. "Please put it in me! I need to feel you inside me now."

Kenny moved upward swiftly after hearing her cries to fill her up with his manhood. Sliding between her legs, he rubbed his boner up and down the slit, driving her wild with lust.

"Hold on," she said, pushing on his hips to keep him from penetrating her pulsating love oven. "You do have condoms, right?"

She hadn't used a condom in years because she only had sex with her husband. She wasn't about to endanger her life or her husband's life for just a few moments of sexual bliss. She didn't know Kenny's sexual background as far as being clean of any STD's, so she decided to make him wrap it up.

"Yeah, I got some. I always wrap mines up," he said, and then he kissed her and rushed over to his bureau to grab one.

A few seconds later, he returned and she rolled the condom over his stiffness, making sure that it was on securely. She then felt his thick, meaty bone shoving up inside her wetness with brute force, causing her to scoot back on impact.

"Daaaamn, Kenny! You deformed!" she shrieked, exciting him more and more.

He locked one of her legs over his shoulder and started thrusting harder and harder, banging violently against her tight walls.

"Ugh...ugh... Sssss... it's in my stomach, Ken - KENNY! You're being too rough, baby! Sssss... Sl-slow down!" she pleaded as he banged away wildly in the missionary position.

The sight of her eyes and titties shaking with every powerful thrust only made him speed up the rhythm, slamming his pipe in her really hard. The thought of the mind-blowing oral sex he had just given her was the only thing keeping her from literally fighting him off as her body jerked back and forth under his brute pounding. She was on the verge of tears as he continued slamming his thick, long erection inside her relentlessly.

"Aaaah, fuck! AAH-AAH-AAH!" she groaned in pain as the violent sensations ripped through her womb.

"Ken-KENNY! You're hurting me!" she yelled, trying to scoot away, but he had her locked under him.

After several more minutes of violent banging, he extracted his throbbing boner and she relaxed a little, only to find herself being turned roughly onto her stomach.

"Kenny, take it easy, boy! I'm sore from that big ole thang," she said timidly, feeling him climb on top of her and pushing her legs into a split.

In response, Kenny slid back up in her tightness from the back and commenced to stroking her gently, letting her get into the groove. As soon as she began throwing her love back on him, he started slamming his hulking wood deeper and deeper into her with brute force, causing the bed to squeak loudly and bang violently against the wall. Her cries echoed throughout his townhouse as he got more into the ruthless penetration. He wanted her to walk funny after he was done. The thoughts of fucking his boss - a married woman - made every stroke more pleasurable than the last. The smacking of flesh was the only sound heard along with her screams of passion and pain.

"Kenny, stop, dammit! I said – UGH!" she growled, trying to fight him off, which only excited him more, making him hold her down and pummel her insides with his hard muscle.

"It's there, Boss Lady. Got-dayyum, it's almost theeeerree!" he groaned, drilling away savagely at her jiggling ass cheeks, which jumped with every ferocious thrust.

All Vanessa could do was bury her face into the mattress and grip the sheets, taking the pain as he smacked her ass cheeks and drilled away. She squirmed and jerked beneath him as he gripped her waist and gave her one final hard thrust.

"AAAAAAAHHHH!" she yelled as he erupted, spewing his large load inside the condom.

"Aw shit...aw shit...that was the bomb...that was he bomb," he gasped, kissing all over the back, shoulders, and neck of her trembling body.

"Get offa me, Kenny!" she finally managed to get out, looking over her shoulder with red eyes that welled up with tears. Vanessa felt used and abused by him as her frame continued rocking involuntarily beneath him, still lost in the violent moment.

"Boss Lady, I didn't mean to hurt you, I swear. Your shit was sooo good, I just got caught up in the moment, and I just lost control. Let me make it up to you," he said, slipping out of her throbbing and sore melting pot.

He quickly placed his face between the crack of her tender ass cheeks and snaked his tongue around her puckered back door, bringing it back down to the slit of her swollen pussy. He began circling his wet tongue around her clitoris and massaging her twat gently, and even though it still tingled in pain, it started to feel exhilarating. The slight pain mixed with the oral pleasure he currently provided drove her wild with lust, forcing her to grind her ass against his darting tongue and face.

She rose up on her knees, giving him a better access to provide the hottest sensations of pleasure to her kitty-cat. Vanessa was a sucker for oral stimulation, and due to Kenny serving up the right feathery tongue strokes of infinite lightness, she forgot all about his brutal assault on her pussy.

Drunk In Love

She figured that he got a little carried away because it was their first time.

"Ssssss...mmm... Yessss, Kenny! Eat this pussy up! It needs all of your tongue. OH GAWD!" she yelped, climaxing all over his rotating tongue.

She moaned into the pillow over and over, backing wildly into his face as her love juices oozed out of her blood-boiling flesh, releasing a hard, intense orgasm that had been long overdue.

Casey

The following day, Ronzell invited Casey over to watch some more movies. Casey agreed to the invite, knowing what he really wanted. As soon as she got to his house and got inside, he began hungrily slurping up a good portion of her neck after greeting her at the door with a passionate kiss.

"Mmmmm…" She exhaled heavily, feeling his huge hands palming her butt.

As their bodies titled towards the edge of the door, they nearly fell to the floor.

"Mmmm, that was a nice hello." She smirked mischievously.

"Shut up!" he huffed and heroically swept her off her feet and then carried her upstairs to his bedroom.

Ronzell made good work of devouring her lips while she pressed up against his body, enjoying the ride up the stairs. Overwhelmed with lust, Casey began unbuttoning his crème polo shirt as he carried her over to the bed and laid her down.

"Whatever happened to the movie?" she giggled, peeling off her blouse and wriggling free of her boy shorts.

"You're the star of it." He smiled, stepping out of his clothes. "Lights, camera… action!"

Trying to please her, Ronzell convinced Casey to let him taste her virgin milky way. Her anal muscles contracted sporadically, accepting the feel of his long, wet tongue invading her dark chute. His probing fingers were intoxicating on her body as he massaged her budding hypersensitive clitoris, but she wanted more. She wanted the huge python dangling between his thighs that stiffened to attention quickly, just waiting to slither deep insider her secret garden.

"Ooooohh… That feels soooo nice, Ronzell!" she moaned, flipping around on the bed until she was totally

Drunk In Love

smelling the scent of the pre-cum dripping from his hard anaconda.

Casey couldn't take it anymore. Before long, she began ravishing his love rod until it tickled her tonsils. Lollipop licking the underside of his boner, she nibbled on his dangling balls a few times, causing him to have uncontrollable spasms. She slapped herself in the face with his thickness before taking him back deep inside her warm mouth.

"Aaah, shit! Damn, you sucking it good...oh so good!" he groaned, caressing her breasts while vacuuming up the pleasure bud of her love. As he feasted on her love button, he added a little generous G-spot fingering against the top of her vaginal walls.

"AAAAHHH! Ooooh boy! Oooooh shit!" She started howling with pleasure as he began applying small circles mixed with up and down strokes, evoking the kind of orgasm that brought along female ejaculate, baptizing him with her love juices.

"Oh shit... oh shit...oh shit..." she mumbled over his penetrating snake, unable to control the seismic orgasm ripping through her body.

Before they knew it, they were caught up in a very intense match of sweaty, animalistic sex for a full two hours. When they climaxed together, they both collapsed into a rewarding slumber.

Vanessa

Vanessa's alarm clock went off at 5:30 a.m., but she was already wide-awake. She had been thinking about a lot of things, mainly about how to find more ways to spend time with Kenny without making her husband suspicious. She still had to give him a good excuse about why she stayed out late, damn near all night.

She had stumbled home after four a.m., intoxicated off Kenny's lovemaking and his long and very attentive tongue. She enjoyed every minute of feeling his long tongue taste every nook and cranny on her body, especially her neglected love oven. Between the two of them, they had released more than a five-ounce cup of sexual fluids and close to a quart of sweat.

Exiting the shower, Vanessa's body still tingled, remembering all of the lustful, freaky, violent, and passionate things she'd done hours ago with Kenny. When she entered the bedroom naked, Vanessa was surprise to see an empty bed and a note sprawled on a yellow memo pad on Russell's side of the bed.

Hey Mrs. Irresponsible,
Thanks for worrying me half to death last night and not picking up the baby. We really need to talk about this tonight. Call Me...

Love,
Russ!!!!

Vanessa stared at the note in utter amazement, thinking, *What can he possibly want to talk to me about?*

Even though she had quite a freaky night committing adultery, she never seemed to be able to cut off the mental ticker tape that was her to-do list! They needed more groceries, kid's Crest for the baby, toiletries, and one of those little bulbs for the refrigerator. Anitra had wedding rehearsals today at five o'clock, which started the same time as her daughter's piano recital, which was forty miles away from wedding rehearsals.

Now figure that one out, Super Freak?

Kenny's flirting advances could have gone either way last night. Vanessa could have rebuked his advances, but she took a chance to see where he'd take her because she really wanted some much-needed oral attention to her love nest. Speaking of which, she needed to send Kenny a text message, thanking him for taking her to heaven. Even though he rough-housed her a little, she still loved the way he laid down his pipe and tongue on her, giving her something that she wasn't getting at home.

And that was the quiet part of her day. It wasn't long before she was at the stove, calling out orders and fielding the usual spate of morning-time needs.

"Dejah, help your Mommy by tying your shoes, please! Dejah, I know you hear me talking to you!"

"Mommy, why Daddy can't help me? My hands feel icky!"

"Because Daddy left early for work, baby, and you have to start being a big girl and doing things on your own!"

"Can I take my Beyoncé Barbie doll to school? Can I please? Please, Mommy? Please!"

"Yes, but you'll have to leave her in the car. Now do as I say and get dressed," Vanessa called, expertly flipping a perfectly fluffed pancake onto each of their plates just as Dejah stumbled into the kitchen with her dress covering her head.

"Mommy! Mommy! I can't see! Help me!"

"Aw, baby, c'mere," she said softly, holding back a laugh.

Vanessa picked her up and pulled the dress from over her head. While their breakfast cooled down, Vanessa took Dejah back to her bedroom and dressed her in a cute little pink Baby

Phat tracksuit and a baby tee that had *Daddy's Little Girl* on the front. "I'm so proud of you, baby. Yes, you did try to dress yourself. That's Mommy's big girl!" Vanessa cooed to Dejah as she carried her back out to her seat in the kitchen. "Who's the sexiest model in all of Dayton? Who's my lil angel?" she asked, tickling Dejah under her chubby chin.

"Stop, Mommy!" Dejah squealed. "You're going to make me tinkle on myself!"

While Dejah dug into her breakfast, Vanessa started feeling guilty about what she'd done last night. She felt worse than Casey, whose M.O. was to hit it then quit it with every man she met.

"Your cooking's the best, Mommy," Dejah said, breaking into her thoughts.

"Thanks, baby. Now c'mon, we have to get going. It's time to hit your chops."

"Okay," Dejah said delightedly, marching back down the hallway to brush her teeth while Vanessa cleared the table.

After washing the dishes, she texted Kenny with an ego-boosting thank you and then alerted him that they should forget about engaging in any more sexual activity. She got a text back within seconds.

You ain't like Big Daddy's lovin'?

She texted: *Kenny, leave it alone. It was a very good one-night stand, but I can't keep going like this!*

Going like what? You loved the dick, so what's the problem? Kenny texted back.

Vanessa ignored him and called her husband. After he answered, she gave him a solid excuse for being out late. He accepted her excuse without arguing, which puzzled her. She felt so guilty about cheating on him that she began thinking that he was having an affair because he didn't argue with her about staying out late.

Drunk In Love

"So will you be going to Dejah's recital or do you have to work late again?" she asked him in a nasty tone like she wanted to start a fight.

"No, I'll be there," he replied, picking up on her vibe. "I wouldn't miss it for the world. I'll just meet you there, okay?"

"Okay," she said as an uncomfortable moment of silence passed between them.

"Nessa, I love you, baby, I'll see you later on tonight, all right?" he said, hoping to ease the tension between them. He knew something was pulling them apart in their marriage and he blamed himself for working so much.

"Okay," she said and ended the call.

Vanessa looked at the phone for a minute and wondered if her husband knew that she had broken every vow they made at the altar to love, honor, and obey. She wondered if he even cared she was out committing adultery while he was swamped with work at the office.

Vanessa took Dejah's lunch bag, which she packed around ten minutes after getting home from last night's carnal rendezvous with Kenny, and then she grabbed her car keys.

So you just going to ignore me now? That ain't ladylike, Boss Lady! Kenny texted her right as she was headed out the kitchen. She turned her phone off.

"Let's go, baby girl! Your limo awaits!" she called out.

"I'm coming, Mommy!"

Vanessa could hear her daughter half laughing, reminding her of the joy and love she had created with Russell.

Oh God, why did I do that last night?

'Cause it felt good, remember!

Oh shut up! Now you want to throw the shit up in my face when you could have stopped me from the jump.

I tried to warn you, but your freaky ass ignored me. Only you can fuck up a perfect life, Vanessa. You so damn stupid! I told you not to lean back in his arms, but you did it anyway. Now look where it got you.

I know, I know, but I was weak and vulnerable at the time, she debated with herself as Dejah came running down the hallway and they were off.

As she strapped Dejah in the car seat, Vanessa tried to remember what evil thing her husband had done in the first place to make her stray away from home to find love - to find attention in another man's arms and now endure the guilt after gaining it - all of which seemed to blur together in a jumble of cooking, to do list making, baby dressing, constant texting from Kenny, and driving and more driving. Dayton definitely had its major league disadvantages. It seemed as if she spent half of her life in a car, stalled in traffic.

Looking at her watch, Vanessa noticed that somehow, ten minutes had elapsed - ten precious minutes, the same amount of time it had taken her to betray her husband's trust, to violate the vows of marriage and break one of the Ten Command-ments: ***THOU SHALL NOT COMMIT ADULTERY!***

How did I let all of that happen in a matter of minutes? Why does being so wrong always feel soooo good? she thought while running to her side of the car. She jumped inside and started the engine.

"We're going to be a little late, Dejah-baby. I wish your Daddy was here to help us."

"Me too, Mommy. I'm really sad that I didn't get to see and kiss Daddy this morning," she said, bouncing her Beyoncé doll up and down on her lap, making rich, warm sounds.

Dejah was a heavyset girl for her age with a striking resemblance to her father. Vanessa gave her daughter a quick glance as she rocked in her car seat, beaming at her Beyoncé doll. Vanessa wondered if Russell would accept her if she revealed what she had done last night with another man. She wondered if he'd ever forgive her and love her the same way he currently did?

"Mommy's sad too, baby. Very sad." She sighed, feeling very ashamed at how easily she had allowed a man she

Drunk In Love

employed to use her last night, all because she wanted the attention she thought was gone. But it always awaited her at home; she was just too blinded by lust to see it.

Briana

"Where we going?" she asked when Terrence drove off, heading towards the Tremont Theater.

The sparkling lights of downtown Dayton were shining brightly ahead in the distant sky as he took the highway.

"I can't tell you, or I'll ruin the surprise," he told her. "Don't mess up the mood, woman."

Briana sat back and relaxed and they listened to a few songs he'd been working on in the studio. They had been seeing each other for a good little while now and things were starting to get deep between them. Terrence treated her like no other man had ever treated her, always attentive to her every need and want. They had the most intense sexcapades she'd ever experienced and he beat up her kitty-cat at least three times a week, which she loved.

Terrence was really a romantic at heart and he had decided to show her just how he felt about her.

"Okay, now what?" she asked after he parked in front of a dark, historical theater in Trotwood that looked closed. "Did you drive all the way out here on the wrong day?" she teased him.

"Nooo, just come on." He grinned before exiting the car. Before she could open the door, he reached her side of the car and opened the door for her. "Bri-Bri, everything I do for you is for a reason and it's not just about the sex," he said while helping her out of the car.

He held her hand for a moment while they walked up to the closed musical theater. As they got a few steps away from the theater, the outside lights came on suddenly and a young white woman opened up the door.

Drunk In Love

"Glad you could make it, Mr. Warthen," she said with a smile, stepping back as they walked inside. "Everything is set up, Sir."

"You ain't gotta overdo it, Amy," he said, shaking her hand. "Everything's already been paid for."

Briana looked confused, staring around the lit lobby area of the theater that looked empty, as if shut down to the public. She opened her mouth to question him, but he shushed her with a finger to her lips and ushered her into the dimly-lit theater.

"Bri-Bri, I just wanted you to see this play that really expresses how you make me feel."

Blushing and at a loss for words, Briana gave him a kiss as he sat her down in the front row. Nothing could have prepared her for what followed. All the actors came out on stage and greeted Terrence and Briana.

"The play you will be seeing tonight is a hip hop musical written by Mr. Warthen solely for you, Ms. Briana Evans," an Asian woman told her before all the cast left the stage.

As soon as they left the stage, the lights went out and the cast of actors re-appeared on the stage, giving a superb performance of their rendition of "When Terrence Met Briana—A Hip Hop Love Story". They acted out; re-creating every scene Terrence and Briana shared since the first night the met in the club. They toned down the sexually explicit portions of their union. The argument they had at the mall about unprotected sex had been thrown in the acts, showing how Terrence stood outside Briana's house crying for hours until she answered his phone call. They even put the cookout scene in there when Terrence met her parents, minus the details about him really-really knowing Briana's mother on an intimate level. They played out how Briana visited him butt naked in a trench coat, causing her to playfully punch him in the arm.

Shedding tears of joy, Briana watched the actors act out their relationship, making it in the form of rap lyrics and heartfelt poetry. For the finale, a huge question mark was lowered from the ceiling of the stage area with a huge picture of Terrence and Briana over it. Briana couldn't believe he went through so much just for her, and she knew that the sex they'd been putting on each other didn't have a thing to do with it.

"That was so special, T," she said, wiping away her tears after the curtains closed and the lights came on. "Thank you sooo much, baby! I will never ever forget this night for as long as I live."

He just smiled and pulled her into his big, strong arms for a hug, sensing that the play had done its job. Terrence figured that impressing her in the future might be hard to do after tonight, but he was up for the challenge. What started out as a mission to sex her a few times turned into something more serious. Terrence had caught feelings for her and he wanted to have her in his life forever.

After viewing their private play, they rode down the Mississippi River on a ferryboat, dancing the night away to the oldies but goodies warbling from the DJ's speakers. He had the mature partygoers crowding the dance floor. After their date that night, Briana couldn't believe that for all this time, she had been missing out on all the joys of having a man in her life.

Later on that night in his bedroom, she tried to suck the skin off his manhood in an effort to show him just how grateful she was for the wonderful time he showed her. Terrence enjoyed every slurping, toe-curling minute of the fellatio. He couldn't control the feeling; he had definitely fallen hard for Briana.

Little did he know she was doing the same. The fact still remained that there was a huge problem that could shake up their future together. He still hadn't revealed to Briana the past relationship he shared with her mother.

Drunk In Love

Anitra

Whatever the thing she had seen in getting married in the shameless pursuit of happiness, Anitra had lost it now. Really, having Nathan's smothering love, affection, and attention made her notice all kinds of things - especially the handsome Mandingos roaming around the city of Dayton. Right now, those sexy men were loud as hell, saying, *"Come and talk to me...I really wanna meet you...can I talk to you? I really wanna know your name!"*

While Nathan and Anitra were in the grocery store, her eyes were lingering on a few people, scanning the crowds to see who was watching her. She peeked at several Mandingos who didn't give her an ounce of contact.

Why they ain't checking me out anymore? she wondered and then caught Nathan staring at her with googly eyes in a loving way, which gave her the answer.

She felt like he was cramping her style. She really couldn't complain, because Nathan made her climax more than any man she'd ever had sex with. He made a little over $87,000 a year with an established, solid banking institution, which offered to pay his way through graduate school so he could get a higher degree, and he loved everything about her.

So what's the problem dummy? she thought as he grabbed her hand and kissed it.

"You know every time I look at you, I just wanna make love to you," Nathan said, making her tingle inside. He hugged her tightly and gave her a sensual kiss on the lips. "I almost died after you started crying on me after you came," he added.

"Shoo', boy, that stuff felt too good. You just don't know."

"Just imagine how it will feel as we get better with time?" he said before heading to the checkout counter.

Anitra kept her excitement in check. She remembered what Casey always stressed to her: *"Don't ever act like you're in love, even when you are...especially in front of a man. They'll crush you like a cockroach."*

I wonder how Casey would feel if she could see me now? she thought, accepting the fact that she was in love with a man who really loved her and she was ready to leave that old life of being a player behind her.

Anitra and Nathan finished up their grocery shopping and dined out a TGI Friday's for lunch. Over their meal, they made a few plans, trying to figure out how to get through the expensive wedding without burning a hole in their savings. They stopped at an art gallery long enough to purchase several paintings for their home. They saw everything: gay couples holding hands, bodies with pierced tongues, eye rings, tattoos, and dyed hair. For a minute, Anitra thought she was in the streets of Soho and East Village in New York. The only difference was that they were in the Midwest where people were friendlier.

They stopped at Space Erotica, an adult store that had everything in supply that one could imagine to enhance the pleasures of sex. While Anitra checked out a variety of flavored vibrators, tickler dildos, and crazy 18" inch rubber cocks with lifelike crooked veins in them, a tall, dark-skinned brother with a bald head and a mulatto brother with golden-hued braids walked into the store.

They saw Nathan holding Anitra's hand while they checked out the lingerie section. The mulatto brother shook his head in disgust, making a funky sound before tapping his buddy. Anitra's stomach began knotting as the men drifted into her comfort zone. Then the mulatto brother snapped loudly enough for Anitra and Nathan to hear, "Ole boy needs to check himself. He don't know that you can never turn a hoe into a housewife."

Drunk In Love

"Um, excuse me, brah." Nathan turned on him quickly. "Can I help you with something?"

"C'mon, baby, let's just go," Anitra said, trying to pull him away from the confrontation. She hadn't heard the insult in a while, yet she refused to let the past fling with the mulatto brother ruin her future.

"Naw, naw bump that. I think this cat owes you an apology," Nathan said, jerking away from her hold on his arm.

"I don't owe her shit, or you either, for that matter. I'm just tryna put you up on game, brah, wit' yo' sucker for love ass."

Anitra watched Nathan's face turn red from anger. She glared right at the jerk she had once dated and rolled her eyes. At first glance, she grimaced and growled like it was feeding time at the zoo. Now all she could do was laugh and shake her head like what he was trying to do was pathetic.

"Nigga, who -"

"Baby, don't waste your time," she said, cutting Nathan off. "That's Eric. We used to date back in the day and I guess he's still bitter because he couldn't measure up to the man that I wanted and found in you. I dropped his ass like a bad habit and I guess he's still salty about it."

"Bitch, I ain't never salty about shit! You just another slut I got off on fucking! I just don't wanna see you treat another brother like your boy toy."

"C'mon, E, that's enough, dog," Eric's dark-skinned friend intervened, playing the peacemaker.

Something in Eric's scoff made Nathan's face etch hard in anger, because when he leaned back and pushed Anitra out of the way, his calm demeanor switched gears. "For the last time, playboy, I think you owe my fiancée an apology."

"Apology for what?" Eric snapped, getting loud, drawing stares from the patrons. Several people left the store out of fear that the argument would lead to a deadly gun battle. Guys were known for shooting it out in the mall over disputes.

"Nigga, I was putting your ass up on game!" Eric raged. Then he added, "If anything, I think the bitch owes me -"

Nathan hit him hard and then eased into the mulatto brother's mouth with another sharp two-piece combination that would have made any prizefighter proud. Blood stained Nathan's hands as he began tussling with Eric. The dark-skinned bald guy made a move to break them apart.

"Yo, break that shit up!!" he yelled, grabbing for Nathan.

"Stay the hell out of it!" Anitra shouted. She struck him with her purse as he tried to stop the fight. "His punk ass is getting what he deserves for calling me a bitch!" she raged. She continued hitting him with her purse until he backed down from the battle.

Before anyone else could intervene, Nathan had wrestled Eric down to the ground and sat on top of his chest as he started punching his lights out.

"That's enough, baby! You showed his punk ass! C'mon, baby, let's go. I think somebody called the cops on us!" she informed him, pulling Nathan off the badly beaten and bloody man.

They bolted from the store and out of the mall, rushing to his car like they had just robbed a bank. Before Anitra and Nathan could make it out of the mall's parking lot, mall security and numerous police cars surrounded them. Rushing to Nathan's car with guns drawn, the cop began shouting demands for them to exit the car with the hands in the air.

"I must really love your ass," Nathan sighed, easing the car door open. "I just risked losing an eighty thousand dollar gig to defend your honor. You owe me big on this one," he told her before getting out the car.

"I got you, baby. For better or for worse, until death do us apart," Anitra said, mumbling to herself before climbing out of the car.

"What seems to be the problem, officers?" Nathan asked, changing his voice back into the business tone he had when he first met Anitra in the bank when she came to open up a business account.

The officer pulled out a pair of handcuffs. "Nothing worth talking about. You're under arrest for assault, buddy."

Anitra's chest rose with a harsh breath. She stared in the direction of the crowd and spotted Eric holding a bloody towel over his face. Then she looked back at Nathan. Without a word, she pulled out her cell phone and called Casey. Anitra didn't look back when the cops put the handcuffs on Nathan. Before Casey could answer her phone, the cops were driving away and taking her man off to jail.

"That's why you got fucked up! Bitch!" she yelled at Eric out of frustration while waiting for Casey to answer the phone. "C'mon...c'mon...pick up the phone," she mumbled, nervously tapping her Jimmy Choo heel on the ground.

When Casey answered, Anitra massaged her temples and said, "Nathan's in jail. I'll explain everything to you later down at the courthouse. Be there in ten minutes."

Anitra hung up the phone without giving Casey a chance to respond. Anitra walked over to an officer on the scene and got the details on where they were taking Nathan. After she got the information, she jumped back into Nathan's car and drove away in hopes of rescuing her man and saving her future.

Girlfriends

When Anitra arrived at the Montgomery County Jail and sprang from the car, she couldn't believe it when Vanessa along with Briana and Casey suddenly rushed over to her side and hugged her. A few loose curls fell over Anitra's eyes and into her mouth. She quickly pulled the curls back behind her ears, trying to figure out why Casey had put Vanessa and Briana all up in her business.

"Gurl, I'm so sorry to hear about what happened. Are you okay?" Briana asked after disengaging from the hug.

"I'm fine," Anitra said, looking directly in Casey's eyes, showing her displeasure for Casey's actions.

The intimidating glare didn't seem to work on Casey for some reason. "Don't look at me like that!" Casey retorted before finishing the last of her bottled water. "I know you didn't expect for me to keep something like this from the girls? You may not think it, but we're family. Anyway, you can take your man home, but they want you to post the $50,000 bail he has."

"What!" Anitra bellowed. "Can they make us pay such a high bail for a little assault?" she questioned, ignorant as to how the law really worked. Anitra felt stoned as if she'd just smoked a good marijuana joint. But she hadn't. She felt drugged after hearing it would cost $50,000 to get her man out of jail. The revelation had pushed her shoulders down heavily while what felt like helium continued seeping from inside her head. She couldn't move. She was sinking and floating - feeling heavy, then light - and it really scared her. She tried to get her feet to move, to turn and walk towards the jail, but they buckled. She collapsed against her car.

"Gurl, don't fall out!" Vanessa blurted, grabbing her. "Everything will be all right."

Drunk In Love

"She's right," Casey added. "You only have to pay ten percent of fifty grand and also present them with some form of collateral so they'll feel comfortable that Nathan will come to court whenever he's scheduled to appear."

Anitra glanced over at Briana, who gave her a warm, comforting smile while listening to the conversation. "Anitra, whatever the case may be, we got your back if you're short on the cash right now," Briana finally spoke. "You must have some dangerous coochie. I mean, you got motherfuckers all around Dayton fighting and catching cases over your stuff."

They all cracked up with laughter at Briana's comment.

"Chile," Anitra nodded. "I never saw it coming. That was some Twilight Zone type shit." She gave them the run down on what happened from the beginning of entering the sex shop until the time they were trying to escape like the new millennium Bonnie and Clyde.

"He had every right to beat his ass then," Briana said.

"I agree," Vanessa nodded.

"I agree also, but now it's going to cost y'all more money for nothing," Casey said. "This thing may go to trial if the guy presses charges. Hopefully he won't, but you have to expect the worse in this situation, Nitra."

"How much time is he facing in jail if he loses?" Anitra asked, feeling a little nervous and scared.

"Depending, but for the category 2 assault he's being charged with, the penalty is at least two to seven years prison time or probation. It's all up to the sentencing judge."

Anitra felt lightheaded again. She couldn't see herself spending years without Nathan in her life. At that moment, she realized how much she really loved him. She felt bad that her past had gotten him into this situation.

If it comes down to it, I'ma go beg that punk bitch Eric to drop the charges, she thought before thanking her friends for coming out to support her.

After they shared another Sistah-gurl hug, Anitra turned and made the long trek towards the Montgomery County Jail to bail out her man.

Drunk In Love

Girlfriends

"Hey baby, I'm glad you came for me when you did. I almost had to fuck something up in there again," Nathan said in an uptight tone as Anitra walked across the small room and stepped into his open arms.

She gave him a strong squeeze but received nothing in return. Not that she expected to - Anitra figured that he was still angry with her for the traumatizing ordeal of being arrested for defending her honor.

Even after they left the precinct, Nathan continued looking over his shoulder every two minutes or so like someone was chasing him. He remained silent with a glassy stare.

"So what's up, jail bird?" Casey joked, watching for reaction from him as Anitra and Nathan slowly turned towards her.

"That's not funny!" Anitra and Nathan spat in unison.

"Well, excuse the hell outta me, my bad. I was just trying to find some type of humor outta all this bullshit!" Casey retorted as she reached into her purse and pulled out her keys. "You see, this is the thanks I get for helping y'all ungrateful asses. I sure can take a hint. I'm outta here. Bri, call me later. Nessa, I'll see you later, girl."

"Girl, don't act like that!" Vanessa called out to her, but Casey pretended not to hear. Casey began walking fast towards her car.

"Oh, she'll get over it. She's just being Casey," Briana sighed, forcing a smile.

These were the moments that hurt the most, when it seemed that they were being torn apart by a man. Briana knew better though. Inevitably, almost self-destructively, Briana tested Anitra to make sure.

"Do you know what day and time the party is?"

"Of course I do, Bri. It's on Saturday at eight o'clock sharp, Mother," she said sarcastically. "Why'd you just ask me that?"

"Just bring your spoiled ass to the party and we'll bring the rest," Briana said.

"Strippers included!" Vanessa added with delightful glee and then she quickly regretted saying it.

"Aw, you didn't say anything to me about any strippers, Nitra," Nathan spoke, staring at Anitra as if he'd just caught her trying to steal from the cookie jar.

"Because, baby," she grinned nervously, "you didn't ask me. You know I don't have nothing to hide." She smiled, batting her long eyelashes at him, looking innocent.

Nathan put his arm around her small waist, accepting her explanation without a fuss. He wanted her to have all the fun she wanted to have before their big day at the altar because he had already made up his mind to have a ball before he got married.

"Well, I have to head on outta here," Vanessa said. "You know Dejah has her little recital thingy tonight."

"It's a busy time for me also," Briana added. "I still have to plan this party, which is two days away." She put emphasis on two while looking at Anitra, who looked away casually.

Once they left the precinct, Nathan walked over to the car and got in. Anitra stood behind for a second to talk to Vanessa and Briana for a minute. Moments later, when everyone got quiet, Vanessa confessed her infidelities.

"Gurl, no you didn't!" Briana and Anitra gasped in unison, displaying surprised looks. They just stared at Vanessa like she had something to do with the collapse of the Twin Towers in NYC.

"Yes, I did." Vanessa's voice dropped to a solicitous whisper as she peered over to the car. She wanted to make sure that Nathan was out of earshot before continuing. "I don't know what the hell I was thinking. It kinda just happened. I guess I just lost control. But trust me; it was the first and last time, for real."

"Does Kenny know about this?" Briana probed with a raised eyebrow.

"Yes. I ended things with him the following morning."

Anitra sighed. "Well, it's good that you can recognize your faults and bounce back. Are you going to tell Russell?"

"I would, except for one thing." Vanessa bit down on her bottom lip. "I want to live long enough to see my baby girl graduate from college."

Vanessa

Vanessa left Dejah's recital, all bright smiles, and full of pep. She had the hots for her husband all over again - the likes of which even she couldn't believe. If Russell had missed out on Dejah's recital for another work-filled night at the office, Vanessa would simply die and give up on their marriage.

In the auditorium, Vanessa couldn't pay full attention to the recital due to Russell's probing, strong hands slithering between her thighs. His hands didn't stop probing until he reached her love button and started rubbing it slowly in circular motions.

"Sssss…" she moaned, trying to keep a straight face while listening to the recital.

Russell glanced over, saw the look on her face, and applied a little more pressure, pinching her clitoris gently, causing her to sit upright. She licked her lips and spread her legs a little wider, allowing him full access to her love nest. Russell slid two fingers inside her wet love oven and began sliding them back and forth along the meaty fold of her slit.

"Aaah," she caught the moan in her throat, looking over at him. She then looked around to see if somebody was watching her as she tried to grab his wrist and stop him, but he kept driving his fingers in and out, in and out of her pulsating love canal. Russell kept a steady rhythm, rotating his fingers back on her clitoris and then back inside her wetness during the entire recital, causing Vanessa to shudder with a titillating climax -simultaneously with the clapping crowd.

During the walk to the car, Russell made funny faces that alerted Vanessa that he wanted her soon as possible. Vanessa got wet and very horny while envisioning what they would do tonight. She made up her mind then and there that Russell was all she needed in life and her secret affair would just have to go to the grave with her. She wasn't about to spend another minute with a stranger between her legs. She had enough of that mess two days ago to last her a lifetime. Vanessa wanted her Russy back and the happiness he gave her, and she wasn't going to settle for anything less.

"Sure do miss spending time with you."

"I miss you too, Daddy!" Dejah beamed, breaking Vanessa's thoughts and Russell's affectionate move for intimacy.

"I was talking to your mom, baby girl," he said, pinching Dejah's nose. "But I'll take you over Mommy any day because she acts like she doesn't miss me at all," he said, staring at Vanessa, waiting for a reply.

"You know I miss you terribly, Russ." She smiled. "How did things go with the Belle and Welch merger?"

"Spectacular. I told you it wouldn't take long to close the account. Now I'm all to the good. *We're* all good. You can't possibly believe how all good I am."

"I sure felt glimpses of it back at Dejah's recital." Vanessa winked. "I hope you get to show me how good you really are."

"Oh, you poor thing," Russell teased her playfully. "I know I've been neglecting you, but believe me, baby, I've been working so hard just so I can spend some time with you and be the man you fell in love with."

"Stop all the mushy stuff, guys." Dejah grinned as Russell put the car in drive and took a spin.

"You need to close your ears then, Ms. Growny Pants." Vanessa rolled her eyes and made funny faces that warmed her daughter's heart and made her hard to resist to her husband.

"Daddy, where are we going?"

Russell turned on the radio. "Just chill out, baby girl. I've got this under control. It's a surprise for my two favorite girls."

Nathan Welch

Russell took them to a five star restaurant in town called Guito's. Dejah jumped up and down with excitement after they got out of the car. She jumped up and gave her father a kiss on the cheek and lips. Vanessa mimicked Dejah's routine, winning over Russell's heart. He felt re-connected to his family, which he loved more than life itself.

"Order whatever you want, girls." Russell smiled as they were seated at a dimly-candlelit table. "From now on, the sky's the limit, and it's only the best for you two."

"Yaaaaay!" Dejah clapped excitedly before they ordered their food.

They ordered a small feast: pepper steaks, a pasta salad, a cheeseburger and French fries for Dejah, some French bread and various cheeses with steamed broccoli. After they ate dinner, Russell took Dejah to Toys-R-Us.

"How about we buy anything you want outta there, angel?" Russell said with a smile.

"Yip-peee! Yay, Daddy, yay! Let's go, Mommy!" Dejah squealed and ran off towards the store.

While walking through the toy store, Vanessa asked Russell if they could afford the sporadic spending.

"Just chill out, baby. I just made partner in the firm, so there's nothing to worry about. It's all about the Benjamins, baby," he joked with a snicker, causing Vanessa to smile.

Dejah picked out over $1,275 worth of toys and gadgets. After paying for the items with his credit card, Russell loaded everything into the car. He made sure his two favorite girls were happy and all set for the trip back home.

Russell drove slowly to give Dejah time to fall asleep. His plan worked. By the time he pulled into the driveway of their home, Dejah was snoring lightly like a tattoo machine gun.

"I'll take her up to bed while you grab all the toys and stuff," Vanessa whispered, before easing out of the car.

Drunk In Love

"I'll meet you in the bedroom," Russell whispered back before he kissed her hard on the lips and eased out of the car.

Minutes later, Vanessa was backing out of Dejah's bedroom when Russell grabbed her from behind. As soon as she felt his rigid nature poking her backside, her panties got very wet in anticipation of what would happen next.

"Mmmm… Oh, Russy… It's very rare that I get the chance to be alone with you like this and see this side of you."

"You know I've been working real hard, baby. Now it's time I work real hard on you and your needs."

"Lead the way, my King."

As Russell swept Vanessa off her feet like a knight in shining armor saving a damsel in distress, Vanessa's cell phone started ringing and she answered it. Russell looked at her for a second while she listened to the caller on the other end. She hung up a second later and gave her husband a weak smile.

"Sorry, hon, somebody had the wrong number. I'm all yours now."

"I know that's right." He grinned while carrying her to their bedroom.

Once inside the bedroom, he laid her on the bed and Vanessa quickly stripped out of her Vera Wang summer dress. Her skimpy halter barely covered the eraser-sized nipples on her grapefruit-sized breasts. Her matching thong revealed a few strands of pussy hairs peeking out the sides of the crotch area, making it look like she had a bushy camel toe.

"Damn, I've missed you so much," he said, licking his lips. He couldn't help but stare at her chunky crotch, which made blood start pumping into his love organ, making him realize all the good things his job was keeping him away from.

Vanessa gazed at him with a kinky smile as he stripped out of his clothes. When he stood before her completely naked, she let out a mischievous giggle. "I can see that you're really happy to see me." She leaned over the bed and gave his dick a soft, sensual kiss right on the helmet-shaped head.

"Just let me show you." He exhaled a moan of appreciation before diving between her legs headfirst.

The next thing she felt was his lips kissing all over her clitoris, then he took her slick clitoris into his hot mouth. There was no mistaking the urgency in his tongue that gave her pussy some much-needed and long overdue attention from him. She nearly climaxed from the thought of it.

"Yesssss, baby, yessss! Mmm…mmm…mmm… Mmph!" She squealed with delight as his tongue and mouth devoured her honey.

Burying his nose in her pubic hairs, he stabbed his tongue rapidly into her gaping gash. He made a few swipes with it, swirling it around and around until her gyrating hips and pelvis caught up to his lustful rhythm.

"Oh my God! Don't Stop… don't stop!" she huffed, feeling his hands reaching under her to cup both of her tender ass cheeks.

She watched him inhale deeply like he was smelling a rose. When the aroma of her juices aroused him, Russell pressed his mouth firmly onto her slit and began kissing and licking her pussy with loving enthusiasm - exactly the way he'd done the first time they'd made love together. She felt her soul being lifted with each touch of his tender lips and tongue. She wanted to scream for joy, but she held back, enjoying the moment. Then he hit her spot and it was a wrap.

"Right there, baby! R-right th-there! It's almost there!" she cried out as she started humping her pussy frantically against his stabbing tongue. "Don't you ever neglect your pussy again! It n-n-needs you, boy!" She howled as his oral skills drove her over the edge.

He pressed his nose against her clit like he couldn't get enough of her to eat. He rubbed his nose back and forth, back and forth against her swollen love button until he had her sailing through one orgasm after another.

Drunk In Love

"Puhleeeassssse, baby, stick it in me!" she cried while the fifth climax rocked her, sending fabulous sensations of pleasure coursing through her body. She bathed her husband's face with all of the love juices oozing from her gaping gash. "I can't take it no more, baby! Puhleeeassse f-fuck me... C'mon!" she begged, shuddering legs resting over his shoulders.

"I thought you'd never ask," he groaned and climbed between her open legs, while keeping them over his shoulders.

Vanessa placed her hand on his granite tool and spread his leaky love juices all over the head with her thumb. She slipped her thumb around and around the crown of his head until it became thoroughly wet and ready to plunge inside her ocean. Her fingers tightened around his stiff shaft and she gave it a quick squeeze before guiding his big hard bone deep inside her pulsating tunnel of love.

"Aaahh shit! Give it to me, baby! I want it rough." She humped back as hard as she could while demanding what she wanted. "I want it hard and fast." She humped back even harder with a mean look on her face as his stiff girth invaded her passage and drove deeper and deeper until he hit the bottom.

"Oh my God...oh my God...oh my God! I love dis big-ass dick! Fuck me harder! Fuck me harder, dammit! HARDER!" she demanded, pushing up with her hips as much as his slamming dick shoved downward, drilling into her well-oiled depths.

He began driving into her with animalistic urgency, causing her to match his thrust. They went at it as if they only had minutes to get it done before the world ended. They made passionate, wild love like they wanted to kill each other with their sex organs, trying to fuck the life out of one another without the thought of leaving another for later.

Encouraged by the way she tightly wrapped her arms around his neck and braced her legs on both sides of him all the while moving her ass underneath him, Russell pulled back to give himself a good length of dick to work with. Then he let loose with another powerful, deep-thrusting plunge, following it with another and another and another and another after that.

"C'mon, daddy...don't stop... Fuck dis pussy...it's all yours... Tear it up...tear dis pussy up! Make it cum for you, baby! Fuck me good and hard! Fuck meeeee!" she moaned, humping him back until they began fucking at breakneck speed, both of them feeling close to getting off.

"Cum with me!" she shrieked, biting down on her bottom lips, trying to take all of the meat that he kept shoving inside her. "YOU BETTER C-C-CUM WITH MEEEEEE!"

"Baby, I wa-wa-want ta-AAARRRRRGGGGGHHHH!" he huffed as his hot semen exploded from his love rod, gushing up inside her, causing her climax to sweep over her like a Mack truck.

Together they made the bed shake. Then they rolled over into a tangled heap with their arms and legs about each other, gasping and panting for breath. After her climatic sensations subsided, she gradually became aware that Russell was snoring softly. She closed her eyes, conjuring up the good loving he just gave her. Her body had an involuntary spasm at the thoughts. Moments later, her eyes popped open.

She eased out of bed to get her purse hanging over the chair. She grabbed the ringing cell phone from her purse and checked the number to see what she already knew.

It was Kenny!

Vanessa couldn't blow him off twice, could she? *No, he'll just keep calling you,* she thought while glancing over at the bed to make sure her husband was still sleeping.

Just be yourself, Nessa.

"Hello?" she whispered, giving her husband another peek.

Drunk In Love

"Why are you whispering?" Kenny asked. "And why did you hang up on me earlier?" It was more of a demand than a question.

"First and foremost, I don't owe you any explanations, Kenny," she whispered, looking over her shoulder again at her husband before deciding to ease into the hallway for some privacy. "Secondly, I sent you a text message the other day explaining to you that there is no more of us. It just won't work," she stated with an undertone of finality.

"Why not?"

"Kenny, in case you forgot, I'm married, and the other night with you was a big mistake on my part."

"Ha-ha!" he laughed loudly. "No, seriously, why I can't tap dat ass again? You mean to tell me that you ain't like the dick or the way I ate your pussy?"

"Yeah – boy, no!" She sighed. "Kenny, I just can't do it no more with you. Please respect my wishes on this, okay?"

"So you saying you used me for your little amusement, huh?"

"No, Kenny. Listen, I really can't talk right now."

"I believe that even less."

"Kenny, please don't do this."

"Do what? Look, Vanessa, I don't know what type of games you're playing, but either way, I will get to the bottom of the bullshit. Either you talk to me now, or I'll keep calling you all night if I have to - or until your husband picks up the phone and then I'll just tell him what we did."

His verbal threat felt like deathblow that turned her body into helpless rag doll. Unfortunately, Vanessa didn't have a corner to throw in the towel, nor a referee to break up the fight and declare a TKO. She eased down the wall in silence as several tears streamed down her face until they coated her breasts. It sickened her to know the man she shared her body with was now threatening to destroy her marriage and the love that she just had rekindled moments ago in the bedroom.

You can't fault nobody but yourself, Nessa

"So what's it going to be, Vanessa?" he demanded, ejecting her from her thoughts.

"Kenny, please, I can't talk to you tonight," she pleaded. "I promise I'll meet you somewhere tomorrow to talk...anywhere you want to meet, okay? We'll talk about things then, all right?"

"You better keep your word too, Vanessa!" he hissed. "Or next time I won't be so fucking caring." He hung up on her.

She sighed, seeming relieved to be rid of him. She closed her phone and went back to her bedroom. She cut her phone off, put it up, and crawled back into bed with her thoughts on Kenny and the potential destruction of what he could do to her life.

She stared at the ceiling. Now she hated what she'd done to her husband, but she felt weak at the time. Now she began wondering if her weakness would die tomorrow or become more like a violent tornado upending her world?

Kenny was one of the most understanding people Vanessa knew and had ever met. That's why his phone call scared her to death.

Drunk In Love

Briana

Briana woke up just in time to feel Terrence's love rod easing into her honey pot. As he penetrated her with slow and tender strokes, she closed her eyes, enjoying the feeling of his thick, long man meat stretching her fiery center. For the first couple of weeks after meeting, all they'd done was make love every day, which wasn't a problem for Briana. Being independent and lonely, Briana had gotten used to entertaining herself sexually. Now that she had Terrence, Briana felt like a naughty kid with a new sex toy. She easily found ways to occupy Terrence in the bedroom. She was able to do all things she loved: various positions, trying out Greek sex, and making two videotapes that would put Kim Kardashian and Ray-J's sex tape in the G-rated porn section.

When they weren't exploring each other sexually, they dined out on the town, went to plays, musicals, movies, art shows, and explored each other mentally. About four days ago, Briana had discovered during some after-sex pillow talk that Terrence had been hurt emotionally by an older woman. At that moment, Briana decided to do everything in her power to see that he'd never get hurt or heartbroken again. Every minute she spent away from Terrence, the butterflies began fluttering. She felt she would lose him to a younger woman if she wasn't around him. She felt grateful to be swept off her feet by someone as sweet and caring as Terrence. Briana loved his personality, his intelligence, and the way he genuinely tried to rip her coochie walls down. That in itself was enough - more than enough - to give all that she needed in life.

"Bri-Bri, you know I'm all the way in love with you," he groaned while deepening his rapid thrusts, bringing her back from memory lane.

Still half asleep, Briana's coochie was roused by the sensation of his stabbing tube steak. Once she woke up fully, she began arching her back and putting her legs over his shoulders to accept all of his manly girth, love, and maximum penetration.

"I have been in love with you ever since you met my family at the cook out, T," she confessed, humping back faster and faster, urging him on to give her all the best that he had in him. "Anyone that stands around them long enough without spazzing out deserves to be… Ssssss…loved," she moaned right before their tongues merged.

Their bodies started slapping together in a blissful rhythm until an hour passed, sending them into climatic oblivion.

"You sure know how to keep a girl from getting her beauty sleep." She grinned, leaning over to cut on the night lamp. Then she leaned back into bed and gave him a kiss.

"You're always beautiful in my eyes," He stretched his naked body across hers. Amusedly, Terrence noted that their skin tones nearly matched. *Maybe she's the reward for all the drama I've endured with her crazy Moms over the past year,* he thought while smiling at her. "How did you do it?"

"Mmmm… Do what, babe?" she purred.

"Make me fall in love with you? I mean, before you, I was just a music producer not trying to find a woman."

She released a slight laugh. "The funny thing is, I didn't even know I did anything until you confessed it a few strokes ago."

"Oh, so you got jokes now?"

"Yeah, just a few." She giggled.

"So where do we go from here?"

"Meaning?" she prompted.

"You know, about us?" he blurted, making eye contact.

Briana avoided eye contact with him. "What about us?"

Drunk In Love

"Bri-Bri, stop playing with me! I'm for real now. This is the point where we get the answers to the question mark from our play," he reminded her.

"Okay, baby, damn!" She sighed, moved by his honesty about wanting to take their relationship to the next plateau. "So how long have you been thinking about us going to the next phase?" she probed.

"Since the first time I made love to you. I ain't gon' front, I ain't want nobody else but me getting that good-good," he smiled.

"Boy, stop lying!" she stated disbelievingly, putting her hands over her face to grimace into them.

"Bri-Bri, I'm dead serious!" he verified. "I always want to be near you, under you, on top of you, loving you, being inside you, and being your best friend and man. I love you, girl. You're a wonderful human being and I only want the best for you, and I truly believe deep in my heart that I can give you the best and then some."

Briana couldn't believe her ears. *Such honesty and warmth coming from a man to you. He might just be the one, girl!* "I like the sound of that, you giving me the best."

"Ain't no question." He kissed her. "I'm not about to let you get away from me, especially when you're a cold freak in the bedroom."

"Boy, you stupid! So that's all you want me for?" she probed playfully, but she meant every word.

"Hell to da nizzall!" he dismissed in a playful tone. "I want you for you because of your personality, your playfulness, the way you keep me grounded, and the way you give me something to look forward to every day. Whatever stupid guy let you slip through his hands, I thank him, because his loss is definitely my gain."

"But will you still feel the same way about me when I'm old and gray and a little bit fatter?" she questioned, a little puzzled.

"I think – naw, naw, I know - I will love you," he assured her. "All I want is for you to be happy, Bri-Bri. And if I can make you happy right now and whenever I'm with you, then that's it - that's all. Nothing else in life matters to me but making you happy. If we can make each other happy until the sun bursts, then I see no need in looking any further, you feel me?"

She gazed at him full of admiration. "I love you, Terrence, and I'll always be here for you."

"And that's all I need to hear. So I guess that makes us exclusive, correct?" he asked with a smile as he gave her a kiss.

"If you let me breathe long enough to answer you, maybe I can say yes with your freak -"

He kissed her again, silencing her. As their tongues merged in a mating dance, their bodies strained against each other, radiating the heat of passion, urging them to become intertwined into another memorable lovemaking moment.

The feeling was unlike any other feeling she'd ever felt before. It felt like being in a marriage without all the legal bonds of a ring on her finger and the suffocation of carrying his last name. The feeling of love had finally caught up to Briana again and she didn't ever want to let Terrence or that feeling go under any circumstances.

Drunk In Love

Casey

On Thursday, Casey found herself reluctantly walking through the mall with Ronzell. She had been unprepared for the random date outside his home. She just thought she was hooking up with him for another booty call. When he persuaded her to go to the mall with him, Casey got a little scared because she feared she might jeopardize all of her training and sacrifice of being a player in that one little decision.

She walked close to him, holding hands, trying to determine how she got to this point and how she can break the spell he had on her. Even though she felt that his sex game was far better than the norm, the world was still thriving with lust-starved men, dazed on their arrogance and their little thoughts of being God's gift to women. Casey felt that those men still needed a rude awakening. She felt that it was her duty to represent for the ladies and deliver those wake-up calls. She knew that she couldn't do that by hanging out with one man all the time.

Halfway through their date, Casey saw someone she Todd. She remembered their last conversation over the telephone and how he had begged for another chance to try and get back in her panties. After spotting him, she sighed, wishing that he would be somewhere hard at work and moving on with life.

But no, here he is, walking with a duo of tall, dark, and handsome white guys. They all look like some actors who could play on the soap operas and be models for some clothing commercials, she thought, noticing that they all wore blue denims, and yellow and blue polo shirts. Casey couldn't help but notice how good Todd looked walking with his buddies, rubbing his fingers through his dark hair. She glanced at Todd twice - once in shock and surprise, then a second time to be sure that it was him. She turned her head a second too late. *I hope he don't recognize my ass*, she thought, ducking her head, turning to Ronzell abruptly to wipe some imaginary lint off his Ed Hardy T-shirt.

"Casey?" she heard Todd's voice calling, rising in surprise.

Shit! Busted! she thought while turning and trying to lead Ronzell into a shoe store.

"Casey!" Todd called out again more loudly, forcing Ronzell to stop and turn in his direction.

"You know that guy?" Ronzell asked while staring at Todd approaching them.

Casey glanced back at Todd and then at Ronzell. She nodded as Todd walked up to her.

"Hey there, Casey. How you been?"

"I been doing fine," Casey said cordially as Ronzell backed away to let them talk. Casey kept her game face on and began talking through clenched teeth while smiling. "Todd, why are you doing this? I thought we discussed this over the telephone?" The words felt wooly in her mouth.

"We did, but I was telling my friends over there that I don't know what happened between us," he said, gesturing back at his friends who looked at Casey and waved. "And look at you, showing up at the perfect time. This has to be fate, Casey. Can we at least try again?"

"Ah," she paused, watching Ronzell, who didn't even try to hide his frustration from her - the frustration of watching her talk to another man while they were on a date. Casey wondered what this would do to their rising and steamy relationship. Casey suddenly got the urge to run.

"What do I have to do to prove how I feel about you?"

You're doing it by making a complete fool of yourself.
"Ah, listen, Todd..." She sighed. "My life has moved on. I'm dating someone else right now. Ronzell is giving me all the

happiness that I need right now." Her explanation rang hollow to her, but she forced a smile behind the explanation and gestured at Ronzell's expense, who looked up at the ceiling, pinching the bridge of his nose - clearly being over dramatic about his frustration.

"I guess I have bad timing, huh?" Todd asked.

"Pretty much," she said, glancing over at Ronzell, who began tapping his foot rapidly.

Todd smacked himself in the forehead pretty hard. "Fuck me! I'm sorry, Casey." He looked over at Ronzell. "Dude, I'm so sorry, dude. Like, for real."

Ronzell laughed. "Well, it's a little late for all that, dude!" He turned and walked away and didn't look back.

Casey couldn't believe his hasty exit. Her outing, her date, her chance at getting more good dick had just been ruined.

Todd gave her a bright smile. "Well, it was nice seeing you again, Casey. You know, if things don't work out…"

"Kiss my ass, white boy!" Casey snapped out of anger and then walked off, taking refuge in the moving crowd.

Several steps later, she glanced back. Todd and his friends were following her, pointing and laughing. Casey found the arrows of direction pointing towards the nearest ladies rest room. She headed that way fast, ducking her head and turned abruptly to dip inside the ladies restroom.

After she made it home later on, Ronzell called her and questioned her thoroughly about her involvement with Todd. She explained how she had once dated Todd and told him things were meaningless between them.

"But you was talking to him like he meant something to you, and by the way you was ignoring me, I kinda figured that y'all had some type of history," Ronzell said. "What if you run into him again somewhere? What's going to happen then?"

"Nothing, Ronzell. You making a big deal out of nothing," she said, not bringing up the fact that he left her at the mall without a ride home. She felt like she was the one who was supposed to be pissed.

Ronzell laughed, not because what she said was funny. He had to laugh to keep from going off on her. Casey, on the other hand, held high hopes of him telling her that everything was cool between them and that he had jumped the gun. But he gave her no such reassurance.

"What should I have done, Ronzell?"

"You don't disrespect me like that by talking to that ma'fucka. You was out on a date with me, your ass was supposed to act like it."

"But he knew it was me. To ignore him would've started something between y'all."

"So what!"

Coldness touched her heart. This was not how things were supposed to be. She usually had guys begging and trying to make peace after getting caught in situations like today, making it easier for her to dump them. "So what's it going to be, Ronzell? 'Cause I'm not about to sit up here and explain my past to you. You want to end this now?" she finally said, trying to get back to her old self.

His end of the phone grew silent for a long moment. "Look, just don't let the shit happen again, 'cause if it does, then, well...you know what's up. You need to get yourself together, Casey," he told her as though she was a child fresh from getting a beating.

Casey felt sure that he was pissed with her. She also figured that he wasn't going anywhere anytime soon because he would've ended things today. "So are we going to kiss and make up?" she asked, in a rush to feel him inside her again.

"No!" he said. "Let this be a lesson that you never forget."

Casey swallowed hard. "I understand," she whined in a little girl voice.

"Do you really?"

Drunk In Love

"Yes, you hate me and don't ever want none of this pussy again." She played on his little head. "I just need to get myself together. I understand clearly."

"I didn't say all that, Casey, so stop twisting things up like I never want to have sex with you no more," he said, having a sudden fear that he might lose more than his leverage if he let her stay home alone. He thought about it for a long while, saying nothing.

"Hello? Ronzell, I have to go now."

"Wait, wait. We still friends, right?"

"Well, I thought we were a little more than friends, but it's whatever you want." She composed herself, making up her mind not to sweat him any further. She felt that she had to be strong now and return to the old Casey. His good loving had been clouding her vision.

"Casey, I want to kiss and make up." He gave in to the pressure he felt about losing her.

Casey nearly collapsed in relief, but she didn't voice her emotion over the telephone. "Give me a minute. I'll swing by in thirty minutes, okay?"

"I'll be here," he said.

"Okay, buh-bye," she said and ended the call, feeling more eager than ever to have sex with Ronzell.

She took a quick shower and got dressed in a loose dress with no panties and no bra. She checked her purse a second time for the condoms she had already placed in there before going over his house earlier. Once she had everything she needed, Casey headed on out the door en route to her booty call.

Casey made it over to Ronzell's house quickly and began putting intense sexual moves on him soon as he opened the door. She reached for his hardness as he picked her up. He rushed over to the couch and dropped her gently. She pulled his sweats down, freeing his thick-loaded love gun. She stroked him a few times slowly and cautiously as if she were handling a loaded weapon.

Casey got up on her knees facing his beautiful boner. His knees buckled after she leaned forward and kissed his bulbous head and took him deep inside her warm mouth. He palmed her bobbing head and began sawing in and out of her mouth slowly and cautiously as if he were penetrating some virgin pussy.

She swallowed him down to his balls and then came back up, teasing his dick head with her flicking tongue. While she gave him deep soul kisses and licks up and down his shaft, his hands expertly removed her dress. Her nipples were as hard as bullets and tingled from his touch. She felt her pussy pulsate, releasing juices that oozed from her tight gash.

When he pinched her nipples tenderly, Casey opened her mouth, stuffing as much dick into her mouth as she could take. Then she backed off and sucked the shiny head, keeping her tongue teasing his pee hole. After teasing the sensitive spot under the head, she rose up and took the head back in her mouth. She sucked on it lovingly, allowing her cheek to collapse deeply. Then she slid her stretched lips down the shaft and began to saw up and down, up and down. She used her fingers to pump his shaft in and out of her juicy mouth.

He pushed her away from his hardness and knelt on the floor between her legs. She leaned back, spreading her legs wide. She played with her clitoris as he opened up her meaty gash with dick head.

"Mmmm… Hold up, boo. Condom's in my purse…hurry!" She smiled, licking her lips as he grabbed her purse from the floor. He ripped open the Magnum wrapper and quickly slipped on the condom and returned to her side, resuming the position.

"Now where were we?" she asked, inching closer to force his thick rod inside her.

Drunk In Love

"You tell me!" he retorted as she squeezed his pole with her hand and guided him deeper inside her tightness.

"Fuck me," she demanded, pulling on his waist, forcing him to fill her up.

"Say pretty please!" he teased, inching back out until just the tip of his boner teased the mouth of her love tunnel.

"Please...pretty, pretty please, fuck me!" she begged while he slithered his dick up and down the fold of her pussy lips.

"That's all I wanted to hear," he said, easing his hardness between the dripping flaps of her pussy lips gently. When he got all the way inside, she wrapped her legs around his waist urging him on to penetrate her deep and hard -just how she loved it.

"Yesss, baby, yessss! Gimme that dick!" she cried out joyously as he sank his magic stick inside her until his balls ground against her groin and drove deeper and deeper.

With each thrust, each release of leg shaking, spine-tingling orgasm, Casey felt in control again. She felt like she had Ronzell right where she wanted him: at the mercy of the power between her legs.

Casey & Anitra

Two days later and hours before the bachelorette party, Casey and Anitra relaxed in a beauty spa, glistening like chickens in a deep fryer. They had just finished getting a full body massage by two muscular, model-looking guys that flirted openly with them the entire time. Casey took a little longer with her massages after asking the guy for a tongue massage.

"What?" he asked in disbelief.

"You heard me! What, you don't do that or something?" Casey asked, spreading her legs to reveal her meaty kitty-cat.

The masseuse just stepped back and stared at Casey like she'd lost her mind. He thought Casey was trying to set him up, so he politely declined her aggressive offer. Casey still gave him her cell phone number and told him to call her if he ever had a change of heart.

Briana had to finish setting things up at her mother's house for the party, so she couldn't join them at the spa. Vanessa called Casey at the last minute and took a rain check, claiming she had to meet with somebody very important.

"Who the hell is more important than your girlfriends?" Anitra pressed after getting the phone away from Casey.

"Listen to me, Nitra, damn!" She sighed. "Nobody is more important than you guys. I just have to do something that came up suddenly."

"Well okay, I guess if you gotta go handle your B.I., then I guess you have to handle that first. So I'ma see you at the party tonight, right?"

"Yes."

"Okay, girl, love you."

"Love you too, bye."

Drunk In Love

"Bye," Anitra said ending the call. She gave Casey back her phone and told her about Vanessa's rain check.

"So I guess it's just me and you together again, just like old times, huh? We'll just do the damn thang then. We don't need nobody else," Casey said, giving her a conspiratorial wink.

Before the trip to the beauty spa, Anitra and Casey spent most of the day at Dayton View Park. Casey had rented a motorized golf cart for them at a shop near the 18-hole golf course. Then they drove all around the park chasing down men and flirting, acting like silly school kids without a care in the world, just enjoying the bonds of sisterhood - and the thrill of chasing behind the opposite sex.

It felt like old times to Anitra, giving her serious doubts about getting married, but she kept her emotions inside. Anitra knew if she revealed her doubts to Casey, Casey would stop at nothing trying to persuade her to follow her gut instincts.

Just the fact that Casey hadn't settled down yet and still played the field was another testimonial of what her life would be like if she didn't get married soon. Casey was so independent and hell-bent on being a player that she was going to make some man's life a living hell one of these days if she ever decided to get married.

"Gurl, I can't wait to see all those big dick strippers at the party tonight," Casey blurted as they reclined nude in the steaming sauna - a casual stop-over to relax the nerves before leaving the spa.

"Me too. I've been waiting patiently for two months now." Anitra mopped her neck and breasts with a towel. "Gurl, this is my last night to see some goodies...my last hurrah!"

"Then I'd advise you to make tonight a night to remember. Once Nathan put that ball and chain on your finger, that's it. No more goodies for you, no more choices in different flavors of men and what they packing, you feel me? Huh, if you know what I know, you'll reconsider marriage right now."

Normally Casey's smart innuendos would've been ignored. But Anitra, in all her second doubting in the last few days, had taken Casey's statement into serious consideration. "I can always look, but as long as I don't touch, I'm cool." Anitra smiled mischievously.

"Bitch, whatever! I know I'ma do a whole bunch of touching, sucking, and fucking," Casey quipped without looking up.

If Casey would've looked up, she would have seen that Anitra had that scheming look in her eyes - a look Casey had seen on numerous occasions when they used to go dick hunting together.

Drunk In Love

Vanessa

The episode with Kenny was closed. Her marriage life seemed to be right back on track and there was no hint of suspicion from Russell that he knew about her cheating on him. The phone calls from Kenny went ignored after she canceled their planned meeting. After a few days, Kenny suddenly stopped pursuing the issue over the phone, but work was different all together.

Kenny would hound Vanessa at work as she tried to keep busy to avoid him. It got to a point where she'd show up for a job and then turn the reins over to her top assistant just so she wouldn't have to deal with Kenny. She didn't want to outright fire him for sweating her out of fear that he'd file a sexual harassment lawsuit against her.

Other than that, all in all, Vanessa knew she should have been pleased with the way things were going. While she drove to meet her girlfriends, Vanessa felt that everything was all wrong. As soon as she had the thought, her phone started ringing. She looked at the number. It was Kenny!

Vanessa paused a few seconds before reaching for her cell phone. She cautioned herself, *I can't let him ruin my life. I have to put an end to this once and for all.* She hooked the Bluetooth contraption to her phone. Finally, she answered on the fifth ring.

"Yes, Kenneth, what do you want?" she stated harshly.

"Is this how you really want to play? After all we did together, this how you gon' play it, huh?"

In spite of everything and the seriousness of his tone, she laughed. "You know, you're being really immature about this, Kenneth. We had a fling. Get over it, because I sure did."

"That why your ass didn't show up when you said you would, huh? You also got over keeping your word to a

167

ma'fucka, huh? Why is that, Vanessa? Oh, let me guess, you was too busy, right?"

"I'm sorry, Kenny." She softened her tone after hearing him raise his voice. "My daughter got really sick," she lied. "I got caught up at the doctor with her all that afternoon. Then I had to run around and get her medicine and take care of her. I honestly forgot about you."

"Sorry to hear that. So why have you been ignoring me at work? What's up with that?"

"Kenny, you know how much business has picked up. I'm out securing more work for guys so you can have a check to keep on living comfortably. You just want me to stop what I'm doing to talk to you because you feel some type of way. Get over it, Kenny. It's over."

"Listen, that's cool and all, but I really need to see you now. It's very important."

"Kenny, I'm out to meet someone right now."

"Who?"

"My husband. Look, Kenny, I -"

"Stop lying to me, Vanessa!" he interrupted her. "I can see your ass right now. You're pulling up in front of some fucking beauty spa. It don't look like no place to be meeting a man to me, so cut the bullshit!"

Vanessa froze in fear. "What the...?"

"Look in your rearview mirror Vanessa," he instructed and her eyes followed cautiously. "You see the black old model Cadillac? You see the fly nigga that fucked your brains out sitting in the driver's seat? Yeah, it's me, the same nigga that's been following your ass ever since last week. Now you see the gun I'm holding? I have it aimed directly at you. Hi there, sexy!"

Gripped by fear, Vanessa watched helplessly as Kenney pulled up to her bumper, looking crazier than he sounded over the telephone.

Drunk In Love

"What do you want from me?" Her nervous question was barely a whisper coming out. She was sick with fear that he'd do something to her.

"I just want to let you know that you're a terrible liar, Vanessa. You chose to stay at home instead of meeting with me, correct?"

"I was just taking a break from work. That's all."

"Sure you were, with a yard of dick down your throat!" His statement terrified her more than the gun he was aiming at her from inside his car.

Did he spy on me in my home? What type of lunatic have I gotten involved with?

"But enough about that. Can you join me right now for a day out, or what?" he said, tapping the gun on the steering wheel with a crooked smile.

"W-why can't...Why can't we talk right here?" she stammered, never taking her eyes off him and the gun.

"I would rather take you for a drive somewhere in my car so we can talk."

"Where you tryna take me to?"

"It's a surprise. Now turn off your car, get out, and come to me...NOW! I'm afraid it's a little too late for begging, don't you think?"

Vanessa didn't say a word, so Kenny pressed on. "C'mon, Vanessa, you know you want to make it back home to your precious lil daughter. Now all I want to do is talk. It's really quite simple." He smirked and cocked the gun for her to see.

"You just want to talk?"

"That's it. I don't know what it is exactly, but you're not like any other woman I have ever slept with," he said, beckoning her to his car with several waves of the gun. "I feel like I'll do anything to have you...and I do mean anything," he added in uptight tone.

169

An uncomfortable silence invaded the line. It was painful and terrifying to hear his words, but she felt like she had no other choice but to listen. Vanessa sighed and then turned off the engine. Seconds later, she got out of the car. She held up a finger, telling him to hold on. She clicked over and called Casey. After a few moments of talking, she ended the call. Then she clicked back over to Kenny's line.

"You just want to talk right? Nothing more, right?" she asked in a nervous tone.

Kenney nodded positively as Vanessa walked towards his car, trying to look brave, but deep inside she was terrified and she didn't know what to expect.

Drunk In Love

Briana

An hour before the party started, Vanessa called Briana and told her that she would be running a little late.

"I thought you was with Casey and Anitra at the spa?"

"Ah, something c-came up," Vanessa stammered, looking over at Kenny who was staring down her throat. "Just tell the gang I'll be there before it ends, okay?"

"Why, Vanessa? Is there something wrong?"

"No. I'll be there, okay?" she said and hung up.

Briana hung up and poured herself a glass of wine. She moved to stand over by the window, thinking about Terrence. She spotted various red and yellow taillights moving on the highway from the skyline view.

Vanessa just don't know. I'll be glad when this party is over too so I can get back to my boo. But I'll never stand my girlfriends up for nobody, she thought, and then she walked into the bathroom. She plugged in her mother's expensive curling iron and looked in the mirror.

Without giving it a second thought, Briana found herself styling up her hair in crinkles of joy. After styling her hair, Briana walked into her mother's master bedroom and sat on the huge bed. She looked around the spacious master suite and got up to take another look around the spacious condominium. She didn't know how her mother could stay in such a huge place all by herself.

At least she does have something to show for her success in the fashion industry, but she stays on the go so much that she doesn't ever get to enjoy any of this, she thought, feeling the effect of mother's distance from her - which was definitely real and getting worse every year. Briana wished she could find a way to close the emotional gap between them, but she didn't have a clue on where to start. They both were stubborn women who wanted things their way and they gave you a choice to either take the highway or do things their way.

Briana returned to the bedroom to get dressed. She sat back on the bed. As she pulled on her panty hose, her mother's telephone began ringing. After several rings, the answering machine automatically clicked on.

"Yo, Evelyn, this is Terrence. Look, I'm sorry that you found out about us the way that you did, but you can never let Briana find out about us, our past, or what we did. You need to call me back soon as you get this message so we can talk things out."

After hearing Terrence's message, Briana became very nervous and her heart began racing. She stopped dressing at once and moved over to the answering machine. She replayed the message over and over until she memorized and verified that it was Terrence's voice. Her eyes started watering and her cheeks felt like they were being pulled away from her face. Her lipstick felt like Chapstick. Their good relationship was too good to be true, and now Terrence's skeletons had bolted from the closet, slapping her with a crushing blow that knocked the wind from her. She hadn't expected that kind of betrayal, that kind of insult, from Terrence.

I knew I should have taken things slow, but noooo, I just had to fall for the dick. Every time I fall, some bastard lets me crash land. Of all the women in Dayton, he had to go fuck my mother? My mother? Oh, it's really on now, she thought and rewound the message again; trying to will the tears rolling down her face to evaporate.

Listening to Terrence's smooth graveyard baritone, Briana fell into profound reflection. She weighed the two angers in her brain - that of the betrayal and that of her mother and Terrence's deception. The deception predominated enormously.

When Briana's anger subsided, she realized that she'd gone too far and she felt stupid at letting her heart open up so

Drunk In Love

much to a total stranger. For a moment, Briana contemplated the fright of losing that handsome stranger. She felt sickened with the realization that she was a fool overcome and blinded by love, knowing she'd just been inducted into that unkindly hall of shame class.

Vanessa

Right after Vanessa hung up; Kenny took her cell phone and turned it off.

"I'm sorry," Kenny mumbled and stepped on the gas.

Everything became a blur. Kenny turned the streets of Dayton into his own personal Autobahn and Vanessa tried to look directly into Kenny's eyes, trying to figure out if this was some sort of sick joke. But some reason, her vision became blurred. Kenny looked out of focus and Vanessa couldn't tell if the expression on his face was anger or relief.

Vanessa sat quietly, looking back and forth at Kenny's gun and out the window. She looked at people going about their ordinary lives. She started wondering if any of them had ever experienced the ordeal she was going through right then.

As Kenny sped through the back streets of Dayton, Vanessa had rows of perspiration trickling down the nape of her neck into her hair and soaking through the top of her Christian Dior blouse. A long stream made its way down her spine. But Vanessa didn't care. All she cared about was one thing: getting away from Kenny.

Yet there he was, sitting right next to her, more frightening, more horrid, and more dangerous than ever.

Is this one last hurrah? Or is it denial on his part? Or temporary insanity? she thought, hoping for the latter. She turned toward him. "Excuse me. W-What did you say?"

Kenny started droning on about something, but Vanessa couldn't hear him over the roaring engine of the Cadillac and the even louder noise inside her head.

"I said, aren't you happy that you joined me?"

"I don't know yet!" she replied in a near holler. *Hell no, I'm not happy to be with you! You just kidnapped me. I just want to get away from your crazy ass,* she thought and then

Drunk In Love

said, "You still haven't mentioned where we're going? I don't like serious, Kenny."

"Oh yeah." He smirked. "You just don't like it when you're not in control and I love it."

Before Vanessa could counter-speak, Kenny barreled into a sharp turn, his foot nowhere near the brake pedal.

"AAAAAAHHHHH! Stop this car! Kenny, stoooooop!" she shrieked along with screeching tires as the Cadillac lurched and seemed to have thoughts of flipping over.

Kenny tilted his head back and laughed maniacally into the translucent sunroof. "Stop for what? We're just getting started!" He giggled, ignoring all of the pain, desperation, and fear that danced across Vanessa's twisted face.

Briana

Briana didn't remember a thing after hearing the message that Terrence left on the answering machine. She didn't remembered letting her girlfriends and the male strippers into the condo, nor Vanessa's telephone call alerting her to the fact that she'd be late for the party. All Briana remembered was that Terrence had deceived her and laughed in her face while doing it.

Breathing hurt. Her heart felt so full of pain. Caught up in her thoughts, Briana had no idea that at that very moment, Casey was just two steps away inside the walk-in closet receiving oral sex from one of the male strippers, nor did Briana realize that several women along with a few strippers had come and left the bachelorette party while she sulked.

When Briana stopped crying and got her thoughts together, she heard some music blaring from the stereo in the empty condo.

"Anitra! Casey!" she called out after turning off the stereo. *Damn, where the hell did everybody go?* she wondered while walking into her mother's master bedroom. When she opened the door and looked inside, everything she saw was shocking.

Drunk In Love

Anitra

Hours passed at the party and Anitra was still partying like the party had just started. She felt so good to be wanted and chased by all the strippers that she decided to take a trip on the wild side with one of them.

Anitra looked at the party as a bachelorette's final wish to get whatever she wanted before jumping the broom. She figured that one of the strippers was really attracted to her. Caveman was his name and he wanted her badly. Anitra had been picking up on his vibe the whole night. The 6'3" dark chocolate-skinned bald Mandingo stripper danced in front of her face until she begged him to stop.

"I'll stop on one condition." He winked and continued humping her face, making the tent in his zebra-striped thong jab her chin.

"And what condition would that be?" she shouted over the loud music while her girlfriends and other women giggled, flirted with a few strippers, talked, and went on about the party like they were on another planet: Planet Hedonism.

Caveman leaned in her face until he could smell her breath. "Pull my thong off and walk me around this party like I'm your dog."

"What?" She gasped, placing a hand over her breast.

"Grrr... Woof, woof!" he barked, making her laugh.

"Boy, noooo! Uh uh! I am not doing nothing like that."

"Okay then, suit yourself. Two can play it like that!" he bellowed over the music as he backed up. "Have it your way!" He tore off his thong and began slowly stroking his rigidness in her face.

When Anitra saw the thick loving he had to offer, she got weak and said, "Where the leash, big man?"

"It's hanging up in the bedroom right over the bed." He licked his lips; winking at her while he jerked himself off. "Why don't you go get it and I'll be right behind you."

With her eyes never leaving the butt-naked stripper, Anitra walked briskly towards Briana's mother's bedroom. When she got inside the room and turned around, Anitra saw Caveman standing behind her, still playing with his hulking boner.

"You're very sneaky. I didn't even hear -"

He silenced her with a passionate kiss. Before she knew it, he had shoved his awfully long tongue down her throat. She felt her breath shortening and decided to pull away.

"You're kind of rushing things, aren't you?" she asked, and then she walked away from him. She moved over by the vanity mirror resting on top of the bureau. She looked in the mirror for a long moment, trying to get herself together. She couldn't remember the last time a kiss from a stranger evoked such hungry lust within her. Her skin still tingled with excitement. "I don't even get down like that," she added, trying to control herself.

"Well, you should. This is your last night to be single before you walk down that aisle," he pointed out while easing behind her, planting soft kisses on her neck and squeezing her behind lightly. She moaned from his touch, swaying her hips. "Why not make it memorable for yourself, for me, and allow yourself to have a dirty little secret? I'll never tell," he said, pushing her further over towards the mirror, hiking his hands up her flower print dress. "Mmm... I see you don't have on any panties." He smiled while his hands explored her body.

"I don't like them...never did," she panted, looking at him through the mirror and smiled at him as if she were seeing him for the first time.

"Come here," he growled, turning her around and kissing her again. This time he was greedy and aggressive.

Drunk In Love

"Mmm… H-hurry up before I change my mind," she moaned while he seriously stroked her ass. She turned on him while he massaged her behind. She smiled and began stroking his hulking manhood.

Although Anitra had every intention of getting married to Nathan, she figured there was nothing wrong with enjoying a little meaningless sex with one of her bachelorette toys. It wasn't the stripper's attraction or his aggressive nature that alerted Anitra that he wanted her. It was his rock-hard dick poking her in the navel. She had always been a sucker for a huge love muscles.

"You got it, baby," he huffed, picking her up. She wrapped her legs securely around his body as he carried her over to the bed.

He slowly worked his fingers inside her wetness, making her moan with each stroke. While their lips and tongues wrestled in a heated kiss, Caveman held her soft ass with his left hand, took his right hand, and guided his throbbing sausage inside her wet love canal.

"Sssssss… It's sooo big…so, so big!" she squealed, winding her hips very slowly like the second hand on a grandfather clock, but she grounded him very hard to make sure his impaling tool hit every inch of her pulsating honey pot. She started swaying her pelvis in slow, sensuous circles and ran her fingers down the muscles of his back.

He gripped her butt cheeks, holding her in the air, and fucked her hard with rapid thrusts until she gasped, begging for more. She pulled herself up on his neck, allowing his throbbing pipe to stand at full attention inside her pussy. The air between them was filled with moaning and grunting with each stroke.

"Aaaah!" She breathed in deeply as he ran his tongue over her dress, biting on her nipple. She licked the light sheen of sweat on his neck, savoring the taste of his chocolate skin. His forceful strokes caused her to inhale deeply and exhale moan after moan, begging for more.

"Grrr!" he growled, pumping faster and faster until her hips bucked and she shivered, moaning like she was having the best orgasm ever.

"Oh Lord, give it to me! Ah, yesss...I'm th-there... I'm so theeeerrreeee!" she howled, creaming all over his stabbing pole. She continued moving her hips as if she needed and wanted him to stay inside her.

Her arousing sounds of ecstasy made his dick swell more, urging him on to pump harder and harder until he began shaking. He couldn't resist the good feeling surging through his body any longer. He embraced her hard around the waist and slammed her down on his impaling love sword a few more times to a rhythm that sent him over the edge.

"Damn, your husband-to-be has got some good-ass pussy in his future, girl!" Whoooo... Got-dayyum!" He whistled and released a gush of hot semen spewing inside her sloshy cunt.

"Tell me about it." She giggled as he lowered her on the bed, wiped sweat from his head, and licked his lips.

"Thanks for a wonderful send-off, Caveman." She smiled and kissed him on the lips.

"Anytime, baby...anytime." He grinned and jerked his man meat until the last of his semen dripped onto the bed.

"You know I'm in the Yellow Pages. I'm just a phone call away if you ever need me, so if ole boy ain't hitting it right, you better call Tyrone!" he joked.

Anitra grinned, smiling down at his swinging dick, and then suddenly stopped when she noticed the expression on Caveman's face had changed after he turned to the right. Anitra also looked in the direction of the doorway and saw Briana standing there with a wide-eyed, shocked expression.

Drunk In Love

Vanessa

This is the end. Simple as that. Please God, don't let him kill me, she thought, knowing she was in deep trouble, but there was nothing much she could do about it. He had a gun on her.

"Get your ass out here!" he demanded with the gun up near her temple. "And try to remember, you have to get back home to your lovely daughter." He yanked her from the car fast before she could move and obey his commands.

Kenny saw the panic and fear in her pretty brown eyes. He wanted her to see the monster she had created so she'd always think about him -even when he wasn't around. He rushed her down a half block and then slowed down in front of his apartment. Kenny pulled a set of keys from his pocket before they reached the front door and Vanessa started crying during their approach.

"Bitch, open the door!" He shoved the keys in her hand and poked the gun in her ribs. "And shut the fuck up with all that damn crying."

After she put the key in the lock and turned it, Kenny pushed her through the door. "Thanks for coming over so we could finally have this chit-chat," he said in a friendly tone, which unnerved her.

Briana

"GET THE HELL OUTTA HERE!" Briana screamed at Caveman while he scampered around her and bolted from the bedroom. "What the fuck is wrong with you?" Briana directed all her anger at Anitra after the stripper left them alone.

"Girl, I can explain," Anitra mumbled, easing from the bed as she headed to the bathroom.

"Explain? Explain what!" Briana continued shouting, all the while following Anitra inside the bathroom. "You just cheated on your man - the same man that you're supposed to get married to in a few days. God, you're so trifling," Briana said, shaking her head in disgust.

"No, I'm not," Anitra said as she sat down on the toilet, releasing a stream of urine. "I just don't think I'm ready to get married right now. I'm scared to give up all the fun I be having while I was single." She stared at Briana's reflection in the mirror, wondering why Briana was crying. *Damn, you acting like I just cheated on you or something?* "I mean…I don't know what I mean." Anitra sighed while wiping herself several times. "Now don't get me wrong, Nathan is a wonderful man, but I don't think I am the one for him, Bri. I love dick too much, and honestly, I don't think I can get used to just one flavor."

Briana glared at Anitra, really getting pissed off about what she said. She looked from her and stared at her reflection in the mirror. Briana's face was distorted in tears and a mask of pain - nothing like her. Something inside her exploded. Everything she felt about Terrence's betrayal came out and she went off on Anitra.

"Bitch, you better learn to get used to one flavor!" Briana scolded her, scaring the mess out of Anitra. Anitra had never seen Briana that mad before. "Nathan is a damn good man. If you fuck this up, then our friendship is over. You need to grow the fuck up and do the right thing by him." She glared at Anitra until tears welled up in her eyes.

Before Anitra could utter a response, Briana stormed out of the bathroom and slammed the door so hard that the mirrors rattled a little. Anitra got up and moved over to the sink to wash away the leftover sins and juices marinating in her love oven.

When she finished, Anitra slid down to the bathroom floor, shaking all over. The flow of tears flooded her face. She felt guilty about what she done, even more so for enjoying the sex as much as she did. Briana reminded her that she did make a commitment to Nathan, but how long could she go on without having sex with other men?

Vanessa

An uncomfortable silence passed between them, and then Kenny ordered Vanessa into the kitchen at gunpoint. She backed up, holding her hands high in the air until she backed up against a counter top island.

"Kenny, what's wrong with you? Please let me go," she begged.

"Sorry, I can't do it. And FYI, nothing is wrong with me. Something is wrong with you for the way you tried to diss me."

"Kenny, I cou-"

"Shut up! Just shut the fuck up!" he snapped, moving closer to her. "Don't say one fucking word!"

Vanessa's body stiffened like wood when he opened a drawer and retrieved a butcher knife. "You just need some reassurance that you belong to me," he hissed and began cutting the buttons off her pricy silk blouse. Next, he cut off her bra, her skirt, and her thong. Vanessa came undone right along with her clothes. She went from paralyzed to limp. When she tried to squeeze her eyes shut, Kenny slapped her hard enough to get her full attention.

"Look at me, Nessa! Remember me for me." He feathered her body with the butcher knife.

Vanessa kept her eyes glued to him, doing as she was told. She knew her life depended on it. He just picked her up, prying her legs apart after sitting her on the countertop. After lowering his pants, Kenny pulled out his rigid manhood. Stroking his love muscle in one hand, Kenny picked up the gun and put it on her right nipple with his free hand - a memory she'd never forget, ever. It was exactly what he wanted.

"Nessa, if I can't have you," he snarled, forcing himself deep inside her, "when I want and where I want...then nobody,

Drunk In Love

and I mean nobody, ever will, including your husband, your precious little daughter, and your three fake-ass girlfriends. Now fuck me back like you did the first time I waxed dat ass." Vanessa did her best, arching her pelvis, humping back several times to meet his demands and violent thrust, but she avoided eye contact.

He slapped her again. "Bitch, don't you ever look away from me!" he growled, drilling her somewhat sopping tunnel. "Look at me now!" he demanded, sawing in and out, in and out of her pussy as hard as he could until he released a gush of warm semen deep inside her.

It was over for him - for both of them.

"Here's just a reminder before you go," he said, pulling up his pants. "If you ever tell a soul about what happened here today…" He trailed off, producing a photograph of her home from his pocket. The picture showed Vanessa's daughter playing with her father on the front lawn. Kenny held the picture up close to her eyes. Vanessa reverted back to being frozen again.

"I think the rest needs no explanation. Well, you get the picture, right?" He grinned while she processed his indirect threats. "Don't you?" he asked again, squeezing her face between his thumb and index finger.

"No, I won't say a word," she whispered, fighting back tears. "I promise… I won't tell a soul."

"That's a good girl," he said, releasing his grip. He tapped her lightly on the butt. "But just in case though, I'm going to be watching you." He produced another photograph and gave it to her.

Vanessa looked at the photo, her eyes widening in shock and fear, looking at her daughter sleeping peacefully in her bed. Vanessa knew there was only one way for the picture to be taken that close. *He had to be inside my home and standing over my baby's bed,* she thought and then looked at him, terrified.

"You know, she's a slight snorer. She never even heard a peep." He smiled.

"NOOOOOOOO!" she screamed. She ran at him, trying to rake his eyes out with her nails.

Kenny sidestepped her attack and slipped behind her. He put her in a full nelson wrestling hold and shook her until she calmed down.

"No, Kenny, no! God, please, no, Kenny..." she begged through uncontrollable tears.

"God can't help you now, Nessa," he whispered in her ear. "You belong to me now. Until death do us part."

After his declaration, Kenny escorted her from his house, still keeping her in a wrestling hold, and threw her out of his house. She tried to run back in the house, but he slammed the door in her faced, leaving her butt naked. Microseconds later, Kenny opened the door, threw her clothes out at her, and slammed the door closed, leaving Vanessa alone with her memories and him and all the evil things he was capable of doing to her family.

Drunk In Love

Girlfriends

DAYS LATER, the women's normal lives started spinning around and around, heading for the worst. After the rape, Vanessa kept her promise and didn't tell a soul. This affected her life at home and at work.

Coping with the physical experience of the rape, Vanessa spiraled down on to a terrible emotional path. Rather than clinging to her husband for support and strength, she withdrew from him. She avoided her husband whenever he tried to make love to her and show her some affection: no sex, no communication, just open bitterness. She knew Russell longed for the raw and passionate energy of their lovemaking. The rape's aftermath ruined everything. She needed time to heal.

Russell left her alone, figuring that she was on her period. Deep inside, her bitterness preyed on Russell, making him tense, magnifying everything that he felt. They'd just grown closer a few days ago—now this? It worried him.

Vanessa stopped going to work and handed all the responsibilities over to her assistant, who eagerly jumped on the task of running the show during her boss's absence. Vanessa knew that, and it worried her, because somewhere deep down, she believed that her assistant would want to be her own boss, competing against her in the catering business, and then where would she be?

Kenny continued calling her until she got fed up and threw away her cell phone. Vanessa bought a new one and only gave out the number to her girlfriends.

Casey had to bail her mother out of jail for assault on her little sister. It didn't help matters either when her mom called one night while she was in the middle of some mind-blowing sex with Ronzell. He claimed he understood her plight, but his actions told a different story. After that night, Ronzell started avoiding her, and ignoring her calls. Sensing his ducking stemmed from the incident at the mall, Casey felt hurt, cheated, and tricked. She was supposed to be the one doing all of that to him, not vice versa. But Casey kept calling him in the hopes of him answering because she was determined to get the last laugh. In the meantime, Casey buried herself in several upcoming cases she had to defend and the new arrival of her baby sister into her home.

Casey got temporary custody of her sister until the outcome of her mother's assault charge. Casey had assured the court and prosecutor's office that her sister didn't want to press charges, but Child Protective Services got involved, urging the state to press charges. Casey knew it was the law, but she felt that shouldn't apply to a mother disciplining her child.

Briana found herself back in therapy, crying over Terrence's and her mother's betrayal.

"Why don't you confront them both about the pain they're causing you?" the shrink suggested, hitting a nerve.

"Motherfucker, that's what I pay your dumb ass for, not to ask me stupid questions!" Briana rose quickly from her favorite futon. "If your stupid ass was listening to me in the first place, your stupid ass would've figured out that I'm not ready to talk, nor am I ready to confront anybody but you about this shit. But I forgot, you don't know shit!"

After the verbal assault, Briana stormed out of the office.

"I'll bill ya!" he called with a slight giggle as the door slammed.

During the drive home, Briana had received several calls from Terrence. She ignored them all. She wasn't ready to see, talk, or confront him yet. The pain of being betrayed and treated like a fool was still stinging her heart. But she intended to confront Terrence and her mother when she felt the time was right. For now, she couldn't go back to him.

As the wedding date grew closer, Anitra continued struggling with herself about getting married to Nathan. She

Drunk In Love

didn't really feel she could promise Nathan fidelity forever. How could she when all she knew was right now, the present! *How can I tell someone what my state of mind will be two years from now? It's impossible,* she thought, feeling pressured into marrying Nathan.

Anitra felt it was the right thing to do to avoid living a life like Casey - lonely and constantly hurting for sexual gratification. She wanted a love that always trusted, kept no records of wrongs, wasn't self-seeking, and was always exciting.

I have all the above in Nathan. So why am I running from it? Caveman, the big dick stripper, that's why. I need a variety of meat in my life. Since the night of passion at the bachelorette party with Caveman, I can't get him off my mind. Am I living a lie?

Anitra accepted her grim reality of living a lie, and that's what she decided to tell Nathan – as soon as she got up the nerve.

Casey

Before getting ready for work, Casey went into her sister's room, only to find her long gone. She called her sister's cell phone repeatedly and got the voicemail on every call. Casey went back into her room and called her mother.

"Mama, Justine is missing," she blurted frantically. "I checked on her before going to work and she's gone."

"Where did she go, Casey? It's eight in the morning."

"Mama, I don't know. This is really crazy, and it's scaring me."

"Calm down, Casey. She'll turn up around nightfall when she gets tired of ripping and running the streets."

"Mama, how do you put up with her shit?" She sighed.

"It's a motherly secret. Now it's your turn to deal with her fast ass. You wanted it so badly. Well, good luck. Buh-bye." She hung up without another word.

"I can't take this shit," Casey muttered while dressing for work. Casey found a pencil-colored D&G business suit with white pinstripes and a pair of five-inch peep-toe sandals. While slipping on her heels, her phone rang. She answered on the second ring.

"Hello?"

"Casey, are you awake?"

"Justine, where the hell are you?"

"Promise   that   you   won't   get   mad?"

"It's too late for all that. Now where the hell are you?" Casey pressed.

"I'm in jail."

"For what?" she gasped.

"Joyriding with my friend. Honestly, I didn't know that the car was stolen. We jus-"

"I'm on my way. Just sit tight."

Drunk In Love

The phone rang again, and Casey snatched it up, thinking it was Justine calling again. "I said I'm coming."

"Now how did you pull that off without me?"

"Oh, hey, Ronzell. I thought you were my sister." A smile quickly creased her face. She was pleasantly surprised to hear from him after the long absence. Even though she acted the playa, Casey was really feeling Ronzell like she'd never felt any other man. When he up and disappeared, Casey's feelings for him went down the drain. He had a good sex game and knew how to keep her wanting more, which she loved. After he stopped paying attention to her, she forced herself to move on and get back into her player lifestyle, treating every man she met like a piece of meat.

"So to what do I owe the pleasure of your call?"

"I've been thinking about you, that's all."

"In what ways?"

"You know, something simple like dinner, a movie, and whatever else comes to mind."

"I have some important errands to run today. I'll be done hopefully by eight tonight."

"Fine by me. I'll pick you up by nine then?"

"See you then." She smiled and hung up; knowing her time to get the last laugh on Ronzell had finally arrived: just hours away.

Casey quickly put that in the back of her mind. Grabbing her purse and keys, Casey bolted out of the house in a hurry to see about her sister.

After bailing her sister out of jail, Casey held open her arms as Justine ran up to give her a hug. Casey shivered at the thought of what might have happened to Justine if she hadn't called for help. Casey and Justine were very close. Casey was the only one who understood Justine. Their mother was old fashioned, too stubborn, and only saw things one way: her way or the highway.

"You okay, Sis?"

"Yeah, I'm fine. Does Mama know about this?"

"Not yet, but she will after I kill your fast ass," She threatened, pushing Justine towards the car.

Justine looked at her sister and then lowered her head briefly before resuming eye contact. "Casey, I'm sorry," she said, feeling horrible, knowing that she had just lost all the respect, love, and trust Casey had for her.

"Sorry my ass! You're kidding me, right?"

"No, Casey. Please believe me; I didn't know the car was stolen."

"And that's supposed to make everything cool? Justine, you betrayed my trust by sneaking off like that. I was worried sick about you. How do you expect me to get Mama to lighten up and bend some rules for you when you don't even do right while staying with me? I'm the last person in the world you're supposed to cross. You need to get something on your mind other than some dick," Casey scolded, and then told Justine that she was grounded for a month.

Justine looked at Casey, tears welling in her eyes. She got in the car and tried to explain. Casey ignored her and pulled off. When Casey returned home, she ordered Justine to go to her room.

"So now you treating me like Mama does, right?"

"No, you're treating yourself like that. I tried the other way, but you don't care. You don't give a damn. I gave you enough rope to hang yourself. You've taken my kindness for weakness for the last time. Now I'm putting my foot down."

"Casey, I'm sorry!" she shrieked, letting her tears tell how sincere and apologetic she was.

Casey raised her hand, silencing Justine. "Tell that shit to your pillow. Now go to your room, and don't come out for nothing, except to use the bathroom and get something to eat.

Drunk In Love

And if you sneak out again, don't worry about coming back to this house."

Casey followed Justine to her room and took her money, cell phone, computer, and TV set before leaving and slamming the door. Casey walked in her room and had to fight back tears. After the episode, Casey discovered that disciplining her sister hurt more than she thought it would. Casey dug into her feelings, finding the strength to stay firm in her decision.

She took a deep breath and called Ronzell. He'd been on her mind ever since his out of the blue telephone call.

He answered on the third ring. "What's good?"

"I'm just calling to see if we're still on for tonight?"

He took a deep breath. "I wouldn't want it no other way."

"Okay. Let's meet at the Dave & Busters near Dayton Mall."

"I'll be there. What time?"

"Around eight-thirty. Is that cool?"

"Yeah, I'ma see you then."

"Okay, bye."

After hanging up, Casey headed for the shower to freshen up. Now that the date was confirmed, she began thinking of ways to pay Ronzell back for neglecting her. Casey promised herself to pay Ronzell back, even if it took one more night of being around him to show him what he was missing out on. She would get the last laugh.

With that in mind, Casey stood under the hot water and lathered up her body with body wash, intent on doing the one thing she thought would give her some peace of mind.

Briana & Anitra

Briana and Anitra were just exiting Foot Fetish shoe store inside the mall when Terrence called for the umpteenth time. Briana allowed Anitra to persuade her to answer the call. Briana had been constantly crying to Anitra over the past several days about what happened, and Anitra was tired of hearing the same old sad love song. Anitra wanted to enjoy that peculiarly warm day in the dead of winter, not be sad and stressing over a man like Briana was.

"Bitch, you better talk to him or I will leave your ass right here!" Anitra threatened.

Under any other circumstances, Briana would've behaved stubbornly and told Anitra, "Go to hell!", but she had caught a ride with Anitra to the mall, which forced her to comply with Anitra's demands. Briana rolled her eyes at Anitra and reluctantly answered the incoming call. Listening to Terrence's voice, Briana could hear the worry in his tone.

Should serve his ass right for betraying me, Briana thought before speaking. "What do you want, Terrence?"

"I want you, baby! What have I done for you to just up and disappear on me? No calls or nothing letting me know if you're alive or what, and you have been ignoring my calls, for what? What's really good?"

Briana began wondering if Terrence truly had love for her. She hadn't spoken to him ever since she'd learned about his affair with her mother. "I've been going through some things, Terrence."

"Like what? Is it more important than us? It's that important that you have to face it alone? I thought we were doing good together. I thought we were better than that?"

Drunk In Love

WRONG! We were, until you fucked my mother before you met me and tried to hide the shit! "Look, T, I really don't have the time for this right now."

Anitra elbowed her in the side, and whispered, "You better talk to him, girl, or so help me God..." She held up a fist.

"Why don't you come over to my house later on tonight so we can talk about it?" she suggested, glaring evilly at Anitra, who smiled.

"Sure, what time?"

"Around nine. That'll give me enough time to get ready for your arrival." *And prepare some hot grits I'd like to throw on your no-good lying ass!*

"I'll be there. I love you."

"I know you do, T. Bye." She hung up and looked at Anitra.

"Now see, that wasn't so bad."

Briana burst into tears. "I don't think I'm ready to face him yet, Nitra. Gurl, I hate him so much for hurting me."

Anitra leaned in and hugged her. "You're ready and you'll get through this. I know you will." *I hope you will,* Anitra thought while hugging Briana in the center of the mall. During the supportive hug she gave Briana, Anitra started thinking about her fiancé Nathan and Caveman, the big dick stripper.

Decisions, decisions, decisions, she told herself, knowing she had to make some very important life-altering ones very soon before her scheduled wedding day.

Vanessa

Vanessa was having one of those days. No big surprise. Her computer system was down, plus on top of that, she continued to avoid her husband's love and affection and was working from home, which was killing her. Dejah was out of school for two days and giving her a splitting headache. Plus the fact that someone on her catering crew had mixed up the food orders. Re-routing a marriage reception's bucket of pork chitterlings and pork chops to an Islamic gathering for newly inducted Muslims only intensified the headache to a full blown migraine.

And it wasn't even noon yet.

Plus, for what seemed like the thousandth time - and it probably was - Kenny continued calling her house, stalking her. This type of stalking was a little scary for her.

But what can I do? He'll kill me if I go to the police, Vanessa thought while sitting at her desk in the far corner of the bedroom.

When her door opened, Vanessa looked up from her blinking computer and smiled, seeing Dejah skipping inside the room holding a piece of yellow notebook paper.

"Hey Mommy, what'cha doing?"

"Trying to get this dumb computer to work so I can do some work."

Dejah blinked a few times. "Uh, Mommy, this…um…some very nice man just gave me this note to give to you."

"What note, baby? C'mere," she said, growing instantly concerned and losing her smile. She thought for a second, *No, it can't be?*

Dejah ran over to the desk and passed her the note. "Mommy, I was on the front porch playing with my Barbie

Drunk In Love

dolls when this nice man walked up and gave it to me," she explained as Vanessa became frightened by the second while reading the note.

> *The longer you stay away from me, the angrier I get, Vanessa. Haven't you learned anything from our last date together? Vanessa, you are MINES!!! Now start playing the part. There's nowhere you can go, run, or hide. I will find you...just like now. Come to work tomorrow - or else. No more hiding, no more excuses. By the way, your daughter is looking lovelier with each passing day. Don't be the reason she ends up being an ORPHAN.*
>
> *See You Tomorrow.*
> *Love You,*
> *K*

In a split second, the color drained from Vanessa's face and her head began spinning. The note slipped from her hand and fell onto her desk with a silent thud.

"Mommy, what's wrong? Are you mad at me for talking to the nice man?"

"Dejah, baby..." Vanessa could barely talk. "Don't you ever talk to strangers. Ever. You understand me? It's dangerous, Baby, very dangerous," she said, her voice straining. "Now c'mon, we have to leave. We have to get to your Daddy."

"Yay!" Dejah cheered. She ran from the bedroom to get her shoes without a clue as to the fear her mother was experiencing.

Scared to death, Vanessa immediately grabbed the telephone and began looking out her bedroom window for any signs of Kenny. Tears streamed down her face as she dialed 911. She struggled to remain calm, her legs feeling like jelly.

"Nine-One-One. What's your emergency?"

"Oh, thank God! I'm…I'm…being stalked by someone who raped me several days ago," she muttered between gasps of air. Hyperventilating, she stared at the note on her desk and then back out the window.

"I'll connect you to the Victim's Crime Unit. Hold on, Ma'am," the emergency operator said and clicked over, leaving Vanessa feeling abandoned.

Ripe with panic, Vanessa slammed down the telephone and ran to the front door. She locked it quickly before glancing out the living room windows, searching for any signs of Kenny.

Why is he doing this to me? she wondered as her body was engulfed by an inferno of fear, sweat gushing from every pore. Vanessa ran into the kitchen and found a butcher knife. Her hands trembled holding it. She clamped her eyes shut, wishing the evil would just disappear and never return.

"HEEELLLP MEEE!" she cried out. "Russell, where are you? Baby, I need you!"

Seconds later, it was if her prayers had been answered.

"Mommy, Daddy's on the phone!" Dejah came running into the kitchen, holding out the cell phone to her.

Vanessa's breathing returned to normal. Some of the color had returned. She opened her eyes, slowly at first, then wide. She breathed out a long sigh of relief and then took the phone from her daughter. "Hey, baby, what's up?"

"I'm just calling to check up on you. You seemed very distant this morning. You okay?"

NO! I've been raped for cheating on you with a stalking maniac! she wanted to confess, but simply stated, "Now I am after hearing your voice. I love you."

"Do you really?"

"Now where did that come from?" she gasped, looking at the phone.

Drunk In Love

"It came from you, and the way you've been acting lately. You don't treat the people you love that way. I can't even touch you anymore without you jumping out of your skin. I don't feel any love coming from you, and it scares me. It's like I don't even know you anymore."

"Baby, baby," she sighed. "I'm trying to get past something. Believe me, it has nothing to do with you, I swear, baby. Please, just bear with me on this."

"For how long?"

Until I get Kenny out of my life! "I don't know. Please, just be there for me."

"Yeah, okay," he said and hung up abruptly.

That's when it got ten times worse for her. The trembling became a series of brutal spasms that hooked her body, causing her to drop the butcher knife and cell phone, forcing Dejah to take several steps backward.

"Mommy, what's wrong!" Dejah asked, beginning to get scared.

I did something very bad. Now it's disrupting my life, my marriage, and all of our safety.

"Nothing, baby. Mommy's just a little sick," she lied, and Dejah took a step closer.

"Are we still going to see Daddy?"

"No, he's very busy today."

"Mm-kay." Dejah sounded a little disappointed. She took off a second later, running out of the kitchen to finish playing with her Barbie dolls.

Vanessa didn't want to go to work and face Kenny, yet she knew she had to if she wanted the nightmare to end. All she could do now was wait for his sick infatuation with her to dissipate so she could move on with her life - the only best choice that she saw fit.

Or she could follow through with her call to the police and have Kenny arrested for rape and stalking, which was a choice that would ultimately destroy her marriage once Russell found out.

Vanessa laid on the kitchen floor in her lovely home crying alligator tears, trying to figure out what she could possibly do to find peace in an ever-growing crisis that was threatening to ruin life, as she knew it.

Drunk In Love

Anitra

Her body shuddered when she walked in her house after dropping Briana off. Caught completely off guard, she walked slowly on wobbly legs, feeling her body temperature rise, hearing her favorite Jodeci CD playing softly.

She couldn't believe what lay before her. Lining the floor in the hallway were rose petals. Her heart started beating heavily as she followed the trail leading to the kitchen. Nathan appeared seconds later naked, holding a long-stemmed white rose.

Staring at him and his dick swinging with bewildered eyes, Anitra noticed his slight grin. He walked up to her, gave her the rose, and then kissed her.

"I just wanted you to know how much I've missed you today. And I'm happy you're going to be my wife." He pulled her to him and helped her strip out of her clothes. She went with the flow, caught up in the moment and his attempt to show her love.

After getting her naked, he led her to the dining table and pulled back a chair, allowing her to sit. The table was covered in a white cloth with fine china place settings and cinnamon-scented candles burning in the candleholders in the middle. A bottle of Dom P. Rose chilled in a bucket of ice resting to the side. As he gathered the plates to fill them with food, Anitra felt a tumble of excitement in her stomach, leaking down to her slit. She took a deep breath of the rose as he returned with a plate full of greens and macaroni and cheese with fried fish and cornbread on the side.

"I hope you like it. I got skills, you know." He smiled, grabbing the champagne bottle and popping the cork. After pouring some bubbly into the glasses, he gave her one, and then raised his in a toast.

"Baby, this is a toast to you, for being my life and everything I've ever dreamed of in a woman. I just wanted to let you know I'm honored and grateful that you decided to spend the rest of your life with me." He clinked her glass with his, and then gulped down his drink. "Now if you'll excuse me, I'ma go get my dessert while you eat."

Anitra started eating, and then paused after seeing him crawl up under the table. "Nate, what are you doing?"

He didn't say a word until he reached the meaty fold of her pussy lips and slipped his tongue inside her saturated slit.

"Sssssss... Mmmmmm! Nate, boy!" She gasped in a mouth full of air, spreading her legs wider, allowing his face to get all the way up in her twat. The heat of his wet tongue felt wonderful on her clitoris.

Anitra moaned, closing her eyes and enjoying the last of the food she was chewing. He ran his big hands along her thighs, massaging her feet while he chowed down on her wetness. Anitra's guilt was getting the best of her. Here she was, one of the luckiest women in Dayton - in the world for that matter, to have a man who truly loved her - and she had cheated on him.

Her mind was consumed with uncertainty, doubts, and thoughts of Caveman and thoughts of marrying Nathan. The bomb tongue loving he was dishing out did nothing but seriously complicate the entire situation. Climaxing in record-breaking time, Anitra pulled lightly on his head. He forcefully spread her legs wider apart and explored the nether-regions of her love oven.

"Ahhhh, Nate, baby...ohhhhhh!" she moaned continually, biting her bottom lip in pleasure as he licked the inside and outside of her pussy, slurping every drop of her orgasm until she sprayed his tongue with more oozing pussy juices.

Sensing she was primed and ready for penetration, he pushed her chair away from the table, all the while fingering

Drunk In Love

her tight canal. Rising up, he wiped her juices from his mouth and kissed her softly on the lips. She kissed him back strongly, forcing her tongue into his mouth, getting turned on by the taste of her own sweet nectar on her snaking tongue.

While they kissed passionately, she found his hardness and started stroking it back and forth... back and forth...up and down. Instinctively he picked her up from the chair and started licking her hard nipples.

"Ssssss... C'mon, Nate... Mmmm... Fuck me, baby," she moaned, squeezing his erection as he laid her on the floor.

He ran his tongue over both her dark nipples as she guided his shaft with her hand between her thighs directly on to the warmth of her tight, hot, wet hole. He lightly touched the inside of her sweet walls, urging her to open her legs wider, allowing him to go deeper and deeper inside. Her wetness made him pound her sweet pussy with greedy urge. Long-dicking her aggressively, he palmed her soft ass, enjoying the feel of his dark bone thrusting in and out of her creamy slit.

"Yessssss, daddy! Oooooh...mmm! Fuck, yesss," Anitra moaned, swaying her pelvis upward rhythmically to the music that their slapping sex organs made. The sounds of Jodeci's "Forever My Lady" sounded so good to both of them that they began humping each other with powerful force.

"Aaaaah...NAAATTTTEEE! I love you! Ooooooh, shit!" she squealed with joy, releasing another orgasm all over his stabbing pole.

"I L-l-l-love you t-t-tooooooo!" he gasped, exploding his warm load deep inside her contracting love ocean.

As they lay on the floor, basking in the aftermath of the leg-shaking union they'd just shared, Nathan feathered her body with his fingertips, causing her body to spasm and jerk uncontrollably.

"You're so amazing, you know that?" he told her, planting soft kisses on her shoulder blades and neck.

"You bring it out of me. I love you." She kissed him on the lips, then got up and walked off to the bathroom. Before she had made it to the bathroom and closed the door. Nate went out like a light.

She sat on the toilet, not believing what had just happened. She dragged her hands all over her face, fighting back the tears. She just had the best sex of her life with a man that loved her - but all she could think about was Caveman, the stripper, which she'd tried to bury away during sex with Nathan.

Hanging her head down, Anitra let the guilt wash over her until she eventually let the tears fall freely. She hadn't yet figured out what she wanted to do. And even more importantly, she didn't know what her life would be like if she made the right or wrong decision, which she knew, she had to do sooner or later.

Decisions, decisions, decisions...

Drunk In Love

Casey

Dave & Busters was semi-packed, as usual. Adults were enjoying the chance to act like kids, playing video games, having fun without the risk of being scrutinized. Casey arrived at ten minutes after nine and ran into an angry Ronzell at the bar. His facial expression told her that he was upset behind waiting on her, but he didn't actually tell her how he felt.

Casey immediately ordered a drink, ignoring him. She got a kick out of that. Just as her drink arrived, she heard his sexy baritone.

"Thanks for finally showing up."

"You're welcome." She smiled and went back to sipping her drink.

Ronzell started laughing. "Okay, I see what's happening."

"And that would be?" Casey turned on her barstool to face him. She cleared her throat, looking at him dressed in a form-fitting turtleneck and a pair of dark grey corduroys. She wanted to eat him alive, but kept her hormones in check. She was determined to keep the promise to herself.

"It's that time of the month for you, huh?"

"Not hardly, boo. I wouldn't have come out tonight to see you if it were. I'm not the dick-teasing type."

"Then why the cold shoulder?"

"Don't take it personal. I have a big case that's heavy on my mind," she lied. "But you're just what I need to get my mind off of things."

"Thanks for the compliment." He chuckled, nearly making her cream in her panties.

"Anytime, boo. Now let's have some fun."

"What do you have in mind?"

"Um… how about some virtual tennis."

"Let's do it."

Casey wanted to do it, all right, but not the way he had in mind. She beat him badly in virtual tennis. He was highly disappointed, being a man and all. His ego got the best of him. After virtual tennis, they moved into Virtual Daytona 500 Racing. He kicked her ass in speed racing, getting a sweet taste of revenge. That's when Casey started getting frustrated. She hated to lose at anything; that's why she had out that night, to win. She beat him at three-point shooting. She knocked down four more baskets than he did that sailed through the bottom of the nets one after another.

"I'm badder than the baddest bitch that you seen thus far...I'm the baddest bitch!   Ah haaa! I beat dat ass!" she teased, blowing imaginary smoke off of the fingertips of her shooting hand.

"You got off a few lucky shots." He chuckled, trying to contain his anger at losing to a female. "I'll bet you if we play again, I'll win hands down."

"You get no second chances here, mister," she playfully said, but she meant every word. They stayed at Dave & Busters for another hour or so, allowing the sexual chemistry between them to build up to an all-time high.

Casey felt so good being around Ronzell again - playful and lighthearted, just like old times. They discussed what they'd been doing in their lives during their ninety-day intermission from dating. Casey learned that Ronzell had been in jail for not showing up for jury duty. *At least, that's what his excuse is for avoiding me,* she thought as she started reminiscing about all the fun they once shared.

Be strong, bitch! Don't fall weak again! she told herself as they headed for their prospective cars.

Ronzell walked over to her car and nervousness hung in the air for Casey. She wanted to kiss him. However, Casey began debating with herself about whether he'd think she was still an easy booty call if she allowed the kiss to happen.

Drunk In Love

"Well, Casey," he said, gazing deeply into her eyes after she unlocked her door and stood in the doorway of the driver's side.

"Well, Ronzell," she mimicked after he hesitated.

"We shouldn't end such a wonderful date on this note."

"Why not?" she queried, playing hard to get.

"You have no idea how long I've yearned to be near you again. Every single day I spent in jail away from you just killed me inside. I wanted to call you and spill the beans, but I never had the nerve. Sounds dumb, I know, but I didn't want to lose you, Casey."

She battled with her thoughts as Ronzell took her hand and kissed her palm.

"Have I lost you, Casey?"

She shook her head. "Not at all. In fact, I'm glad you had the nerve to open up to me now. Otherwise, I don't know what would've become of us after tonight."

"Shut up!" she blurted before she quickly realized that she was talking out loud.

"Excuse me? I didn't say anything."

She giggled. "I know, I was just talking to my girl intuition."

"And what did it say?"

"It's a girl thing. You wouldn't understand," she said, unable to hold in the way she was blushing.

He glanced at his watch. "You wanna take in a late movie at my crib?"

"Is that a hint?"

"Pretty much. I'm the type of man who knows what I want, and basically I want you - the only woman who can complete me."

"Smooooooth operator." She giggled nervously.

"No, I'm not," he replied seriously. "It's my heart speaking to a woman I truly adore and want to spend more quality time with.

"I think I want to do the same."

"Then let's go to my place, catch a movie, and fall asleep together," he suggested, licking his lips.

"That's all we're going to do?" she asked, taking a deep breath before exhaling.

"If you want." He smirked, and she felt that he looked enticing enough to eat and make love to all night long, or until his engine broke down.

"That sounds good to me."

"Lead the way, Mr. Ronzell."

He kissed her again and made sure that she got to her car okay before racing back to his car with pussy on his mind. He pulled up beside her and told her to follow him. Casey smiled, and then pulled out behind him as he drove off into the night...

In his car, Ronzell also smiled like a Cheshire cat, watching his booty call for the night follow him. Even he had to admit that his game flowed smoothly. *The jail sob story works every time,* he thought while speeding to his house.

Ronzell thought about Casey for a second longer. The carnal cover slid out of place, and then Ronzell grew hard. While speeding home, Ronzell drove towards something that he'd never forget for as long as he lived.

Drunk In Love

Briana

Briana had her Usher CD *"Confessions"* **streaming** through the Sony sound system in the walls, trying to give Terrence a hint to confess about his sins. She spent the night sitting across from him, staring at him eat, and listening to the reality of their relationship, mainly sexual. She heard it in the sounds of his chewing and smacking that filtered through her ears and throughout her body. The noises reminded her of his annoying ways - the man himself was slamming, but tonight it was all about the pain that he'd caused her, and she intended to let him have an ear full.

There had to be at least fifty scented candles burning in her place, which was exactly how she envisioned it: a candlelit dinner, some wine, and a full-blown argument - the perfect closure. Briana even shocked herself by sitting quietly through the steak, lobster, and fettuccini dinner she'd prepared for Terrence. It was definitely a first for her - being nice before the break-up.

Over dinner, she glared at him. As she did so, her feelings for Terrence started transforming into hate. The hope for finding love had finally disappeared in her heart, and it had taken Terrence's betrayal to make it happen, to make her heart turn cold.

Terrence pushed his empty plate away and stared at Briana lovingly. "Mmm, mmm, mmmph! Baby, that was so delicious. Thank you."

"Yeah, whatever!" she said in a nasty tone before grabbing his plate and moving away from the table.

Terrence eased behind her as she reached the sink. He hugged her from behind and kissed her on the neck. "You just don't know how much I've missed you," he whispered in her ear.

"Wow, lucky me!" she snarled, moving away from him. She was sick to her stomach. She regretted following Anitra's dumb advice. She just wanted to confront him and throw him out of her house, not play any mind games, which she hated. Briana turned on Terrence with an open hand and swung hard, slapping him ferociously, unleashing her wrath.

"BIT- WHAT WAS THAT FOR!" he bellowed, rubbing his stinging cheek, looking surprised.

Briana stepped back away from him, giving him a disgusted look. "For lying and hurting me." She actually felt good, getting it off her chest. She knew now that his betrayal was true after noticing the shocked expression on his face. He looked like the cat that got caught swallowing the canary.

He swallowed hard, recovering well. "Bri, what the hell are you talking about?"

"Don't 'Bri' me, motherfucker!" she hissed, storming into the living room. "I'm talking about this!" Briana pressed a remote control button and folded her arms across her breasts, glaring evilly at him. Within seconds, Terrence's taped answering machine message replaced her Usher CD streaming through the sound system on repeat.

"Bri, baby, I can explain!"

"I wanna see you try, you low-down piece of shit!" she raged.

"See, it's like this..." he started, moving closer to her grabbing her arms.

"Get the fuck offa me!" she yelled, pulling her arms free of his grasp. "Don't touch me! Don't you ever fucking touch me!"

"Terrence, how could you do this to me? And of all people, with my MOTHER?"

"Bri, I want -"

"Save the shit! I gave you a chance to confess your sins, to cleanse yourself, to be honest with me before this day, but you still held back, which is bad." Her words stung him.

Drunk In Love

He almost wanted to lash out angrily at her, but he felt that two wrongs didn't make a right. He noticed her look of unyielding heartbreak, a look that surpassed all the tears, because tears could never capture the depths of the pain he'd caused. "Bri, don't..." He paused, staring at her. She stood before him as a stranger now. He saw a woman torn between anger and heartbreak because of his actions. He saw a woman who was unable to trust and love, all because he had failed her.

"Terrence, it's already written in stone. You did this to us, not me."

"C'mon Bri, let me make it up to you. Just tell me what I have to do to prove my love to you?" he said, giving her a puppy-dog look, expressing his remorse and everything else with his sad eyes that his mouth left out.

"Stay the hell away from me, Terrence," she said with fire in her eyes while backpedaling to her bedroom door.

"It's over. Please get out." She went into her room, slammed the door, and locked it.

"Briana! Briana, open the door! Let me explain! Briana!" he demanded, banging on the door.

She dove on the bed, burying her face in a pillow, her hands raking the sheets with her nails.

"Terrence, get the hell out of my house before I call the police on you!" she screamed out.

"Bri, you can't end things like this!" he called.

"I just did, you no-good bastard! It's over!" she yelled back.

Terrence stood on the other side of the door for a moment, hoping that Briana would change her mind. An uncomfortable silence lingered for several moments as the naked truth filled the space between the door and their relationship. When it became clear that she wasn't budging, Terrence turned and left with a defeated finality that he'd never known before.

Briana heard his footsteps shuffling away from her bedroom door. She sat up on the bed. Her hands still trembled in anger and sorrow. She listened over the next few minutes until the noise of her stereo shut off and the sound of a slamming door caused her to investigate. Briana stuck her head out the bedroom door and didn't see him.

Thank goodness, Terrence has left, she thought while walking through the apartment to make sure that Terrence had really left. She locked the front door and then cut on her stereo system, searching the CD changer until she found her *"Waiting to Exhale"* CD. She remained on the couch for the rest of the night, listening to Mary J. Blige's song "I'm Not Gon' Cry No More" memorizing every word. She accepted it as her new theme song.

"N-n-n-not gon' cry-eye… Not this time, 'cause you're not worth my tears," she sang along, allowing the tears to flow while she stared up at the ceiling. She was pissed at Terrence and her mother, no doubt about it!

They hurt me. What the fuck did I do to deserve this shit? she thought as her mind drifted back to Terrence. She thought he was the one - Mr. Right!

No, forget him! He intentionally hurt you. Yes, he had to go. There'll be others. It's his loss, not yours!

But what about my mother? I can't just shut her out of my life?

Why not?

She's my mother. She gave me life.

She also ruined it for you!

Point taken. Briana didn't know what to do. She'd seen and experienced a lot of things in her life up until this point. That was it. She was done with all the foolishness of trying to find love. Now she felt like love was just a myth, sometimes seen in the movies and written about in novels for entertainment. She wondered what lucky sister would snag up Terrence after tonight.

Drunk In Love

He was definitely a prize catch, some woman's Mr. Right - just not hers. And her mother was the blame of it all. She was the next person on her shit list to confront.

Casey

As soon as they entered Ronzell's house, they started making out. Gripping Casey's ass, Ronzell could feel her excitement in every kiss. Pulling off his shirt, Casey kissed every part of his muscular chest.

'C'mon, baby. Let's take this upstairs," he huffed while she snaked her tongue along his torso. Lust geysers shot through his loins. His throbbing man meat demanded freedom from his chinos.

"Why wait?" she moaned, going for his belt buckle.

Once Casey had his pants around his ankles, she smiled and massaged his engorged love stick. She stared at it briefly until she came to her senses. "Ronzell, how would you like to fuck me?"

"Doggy-style of course. You know how we do it." He winked. He wanted her; at least for tonight. After that, she could go to hell for all he cared. He'd seen many men, along with his friends, die and go to jail behind chasing women like Casey, and he didn't want to follow suit.

Without responding, Casey pushed him roughly on his back and stood up.

"Wh-what's up, baby?" he asked, looking confused.

He opened his mouth slightly, watching her back away.

"Your weak-ass game, Ronzell, that's what!" she snarled, reaching the door. "You think I'm one of them naïve freak bitches you're used to dealing with? Not hardly! I'm glad this is the last time I will ever see you. I'll never forget this memory, and the look on your dumb-ass face." She chuckled and walked out the door.

Standing in the doorway, she turned and laughed again. "Ronzell, you almost had me for a minute. Well, at least you

Drunk In Love

thought you did. Peep game, Ronzell. I don't ever get played; I always play niggas. Have a nice life, dummy."

With that said, Casey slammed the door with a triumphant feeling. Now she could move on with her life after closing this chapter.

Thinking quickly, Ronzell vaulted towards the door to stop her. He didn't want Casey to leave. Well, at least not until he got some pussy.

"C'mon, Casey, what am I supposed to do?" He stood in the doorway, giving her a sad puppy dog look.

Casey walked back over to him, grabbed his dick, kissed him, and then she shoved him back in the house and left. "Use your hand and your imagination, you silicone fake-ass nigga!" She burst out laughing while walking off to her car.

"Fake-ass bitch! Fuck you!" he bellowed, then slammed the door. Ronzell walked over to the TV where he kept his porn collection. He stared at the various DVD titles for a brief moment, and then grabbed one he wanted to watch. *I knew I shouldn't have called that hoe. Damn, she got me! She got me good as a motherfucker. Fuck it, I got to get off some type of way,* he thought as he put the DVD in the machine then pressed play.

Sitting on the sofa, he started stroking himself. When he saw the porno stars enjoying a steamy anal scene, he moaned and licked his lips, wishing he could bang Casey like that.

Fake-ass bitch, you got me good!

He continued jacking off long and fast, unable to reach a climax. Casey was on his mind.

You won't stop this nut tonight, bitch! Matter of fact...

He started imagining himself and Casey replacing the porno actors who fucked away on the scene. He picked up the pace and started stroking faster and faster while watching himself long-dick Casey's tight bunghole. Seventy-two seconds later, he exploded all over his hand happily. In his mind, he just had sex with Casey.

Yeah, bitch, I still got mines off, he thought as he hopped off the sofa, cut the TV off, and headed for the shower.

Lathering up his body with liquid soap, Ronzell tried, but he couldn't get Casey off of his mind. As the hot water relaxed him, Ronzell began wondering if he made a mistake by playing with her.

Drunk In Love

Briana

Briana took several deep breaths before knocking on her mother's door. She'd been fighting with herself about confronting her mother over the last seventy-two hours. Once her shrink suggested that she should confront every problem that was affecting her life and causing her stress, Briana took his advice.

"I'm coming!" Briana heard her mother from the other side, and she trembled with rage.

How could she be my mother and be so insensitive? She's a real bitch! There's no way I could ever let my child run around town with somebody that I ever dealt with. She's sick, or she just hates me, she thought as the door opened.

"Hey, baby, what a surprise." Her mother smiled as Briana entered the condo. "I thought you were Wayne. We're going out tonight. I think he's going to propose."

All you ever think about is you! You selfish bitch! What about me and what I'm going through? What about my love life that you destroyed? I hate you! Briana wanted to yell, but she kept her cool. "Ma, can I ask you a serious question?"

"Sure, baby, come in here and sit on down with your mama." She patted the sofa, beckoning Briana to take a seat.

She remained standing, tapping her left high heel rapidly. Evelyn caught the action and suspected that something was wrong with her daughter. Immediately she felt bad for not being there for her daughter when she should have been. "What's wrong, Briana?" she asked with genuine concern, looking at her.

No matter how bad the circumstances will be, the price of telling her off will be worth it, Briana thought, allowing the tears to flood her eyes. "You ain't shit!" she raged. "You just can't see me happy, huh?"

Evelyn searched Briana's face. "What are you talking about, Briana?"

"You and Terrence fucking, that's what!" she yelled, and her tears stopped abruptly.

Ouch! Even though she's wrong, her accusations sting a little. Is this her way of disrespecting me for not being a part of her life? No, she knows better than that. She must really be in pain, Evelyn thought while staring at Briana.

Immediately, Briana turned cold despite her love for her mother. "Your no-good snake ass can't talk now, can you?"

"Just shut your mouth, Briana!" Evelyn's anger made her get hot. "Don't you ever talk to me like that! I am still your mother!"

"Unfortunately by birth only!" Briana spat saucily with venomous precision.

Just like that, their relationship was over. All the good times and bad times were all official memories to Briana. No tears would come now. In time, they would, but Briana felt strong-willed and independent, and she figured she could move on with her life without her mother.

Being strong willed herself, Evelyn refused to give Briana the satisfaction of knowing her words just hurt her - damn near crushed her heart. Searching Briana's eyes for any signs of emotional forgiveness yet receiving none, Evelyn mumbled, "I never meant to hurt you. Briana, I love you more than anything in this world, baby, but if you want to be stubborn and pout about things that you have no knowledge about, then I guess you should leave."

Briana backed away from her mother, never breaking eye contact, but she felt the shock and delayed reaction in her muscles.

I guess you should leave... The words kept echoing in her mind. No apologies, nothing. At that moment, Briana wanted to vomit, but she wouldn't give her mother the satisfaction. "I

Drunk In Love

don't have time for this shit! Just know that you destroyed my life, and I'll never forgive you for that! Ever!"

"I done told you about your damn mouth!" Evelyn warned, and quickly told her that she never had sex with Terrence. She went on to explain that Terrence came into her life during a vulnerable time after the divorce with her father.

"I mean, we cuddled a little and kissed a few times, but that's as far as things went, Briana, I swear. Terrence wanted more but I couldn't give it. I was an emotional wreck over your daddy. Briana, listen to me, baby. I really think that man loves you, and the only way you'll know is if you give him the test."

"I don't have time for any damn tests!" she hissed. "He failed the test when he didn't tell me about you two cuddling and shit!"

"Chile, I done told your ass about your nasty mouth! Now shut up and just listen. If you get him to offer you his last piece of food, then you can get his heart, and everything that comes with it."

"You're a very sick woman, you know that?" The rage seeped from Briana's tone.

"No, I'm not." Evelyn remained calm. "Just think about it. That one little action shows sacrifice, unselfishness, and a commitment to please you in an unconscious way. Just give it some thought and try it."

"You try it!" she snapped. "You can have him now! I'm through with his ass and you for good, bitch!"

With that, Briana turned away to allow the tears to flow freely as she stormed out of the condo.

"I will, the next time a good man like Terrence comes into my life," Evelyn said shakily after the doors slammed on her and her daughter's relationship forever.

Casey

After dumping Ronzell and getting the last laugh, Casey's demeanor changed and she had a whole new outlook on life. She wasn't going to take shit from anyone anymore - especially not a man. She went into a zone after that night with Ronzell, leaving her sister Justine to find her own way through her growing pains and promiscuity. She was still very caring, but she felt like she had to deal with herself first before she could interfere in Justine's life. That made it impossible for Justine to ask her sister's opinion about boys that she wanted to date and other mixed emotions she had been going through.

Casey looked at her watch, setting the timer for her two-mile run. She stretched, and she couldn't wait to hit the path and enjoy the fresh air. Everyone was late, as usual.

These hoes always late. I'ma start working out alone, she thought. Looking up, Casey noticed a high-yellow brother sporting sweats and a tank top, hustling to get near the bench Casey occupied.

"Excuse me; I was wondering if I could get a moment of your time."

"What for?" Casey snapped playing the mean role, even though she liked everything she saw in the husky built 5'8" man with huge biceps and cat-grey eyes.

"For real, lil mama, I'm lame as hell when it comes to this, but you fine as hell, and I just had to let you know it. Can I take you out sometime?"

Casey laughed inside. She saw his apparent nervousness to get her to go out on a date with him. She sensed his discomfort. "Well, what are your intentions? I know you just don't want to take me out. There's always a hidden agenda?" she asked, knowing he wanted to screw her.

Drunk In Love

"Lil mama, you ain't never lied." He smiled, revealing even white teeth with a chipped tooth up front, which gave him character. "You so fine, got-dayyum!" He sighed. "Need I say more?" he asked while extending his hand.

"No, I catch your drift." She shook his hand. "You shouldn't treat every woman you meet like a piece of ass," she told him, taking all the wind out of his sail.

Casey sensed the lust in his eyes, knowing her body was the culprit that attracted this monster to her. Casey had been a male magnet since the day she reached puberty. The men in the world did nothing but make her ego worse, giving her all the power her heart desired.

"So what you saying, lil mama, you ain't feeling my Mack-Daddy vibes?" he asked, drawing a slight grin from her.

"No," she said flatly. "You'll have to come better than that, hon."

"How am I supposed to do that?"

"For starters, you try to catch me, if you really want me!" Casey told him, and she took off running.

The guy had a problem with keeping up, but he didn't stop chasing her. Casey admired his determination. She saw that he was out of shape and she didn't want to torture him anymore. She stopped after a mile and let him catch up.

Casey walked over to him and patted him on the back. He was bent over, panting and breathing hard, trying to catch his breath.

"You know what you want, I see?" Casey giggled.

"Lil mama… I would…have run… Hold up." He coughed, trying to get himself together. After a few minutes of wheezing, he turned his attention back to her. "I'm Adrian, and in regard to your comment, yeah, I definitely know what I want, which is you."

"You don't even know me. I could be a crazy stalker or something."

"Well, you just gone have to make me know it then."

"Boy, you silly."

"What's your name?"

"Casey," she said, wanting to stop him from going in the dismal direction she foresaw. "Adrian, you seem to be an okay guy. Don't get yourself caught up in something you can't handle."

"I can handle anything you can throw my way, Casey."

"Oh yeah? What if I wanted you to eat my sweaty pussy right here, right now? Could you handle that?" she said, trying to keep a straight face.

"Just because we outside don't mean shit, lil mama!"

"And if that's what I wanted from you right now, you could handle that?"

"Hell naw, you got me on that one."

"Your words are overrated, in my opinion."

"And you scared to take a chance on me, in mines," he countered.

For a moment, they remained silent while studying each others body language. Casey wanted to save him because she figured he deserved more than what she was willing to give.

But he keeps asking for it, she thought. "So you think I'm scared of you?"

"I say what I mean, and I mean what I say."

"Wow, you actually put that together rather well. I'm proud of you." Casey was intentionally being a smart ass, trying to turn him off, but he wasn't budging.

"Look, Casey. I know damn well, you ain't make me chase you for a whole mile and a half just to play games? Either you gon' fuck wit' a nigga or let me move on, dayyum."

"Every time I turn around, it's guys like you sniffing up my ass, trying to hit and quit it."

"Who ever said anything about quitting it? I don't do that. I only been with four women my entire life, and that's 'cause they cheated on me and hurt me, even though that ain't

Drunk In Love

your business. What I'm saying, Casey, is I'll be the one to be there for you - until you get tired of me."

Casey studied Adrian. She could see his needs to express his feelings for someone. Maybe in a few years she would understand, but for now, a dick was a dick to her. *You had one, you had them all,* she thought. "Adrian, hon, I'm sorry. I'm definitely not the woman for you. I like to have sex with different partners when I want, and where I want." The tone of her voice had an arrogant edge that stung him.

He was pissed, but didn't let it show. "You're just going to do me like that, huh? Okay, fuck it then, let's just have sex and get it over with then."

"Boy, you're determined, aren't you?"

"We met today for some reason, and I don't think it would be fair to either of us if we didn't find out what that reason is." He gave it one last try.

"Why did you have to say that?" Casey asked, pouting like a little girl who had been told to do something against her will.

"Because I'd really like to see more of you."

Adrian Phillips had always treated women with the utmost respect—just like the Queens he felt they were. He always managed to pick the wrong women to fall for. At 27, he had been through more heartache and pain over love than a leading start in a daytime soap opera. One day, he got himself together, forgetting about his last girlfriend. He had been dating women and searching for love ever since.

"I told you what I'm about, Adrian, so don't go getting any ideas about falling in love."

"I'll only take what you give me, how about that?"

"You know what? I can live with that." She smiled and they exchanged phone numbers.

They walked back to the bench where they first met, and he kissed her on the cheek. "Thanks for the work out. I'll call you!" He walked away, leaving Casey to blush and her friends

Briana and Anitra staring on in disbelief with their mouths hanging wide open.

"What?" Casey laughed at her friends after he left. "You acting like you ain't never seen no dick before." She took off running, causing her friends to chase her, throwing question after question about the fine brother she just had in their presence.

A dick is a dick, Casey thought as she avoided all the questions, replaying hers and Adrian's meeting over and over in her head while they jogged.

Drunk In Love

Vanessa

Vanessa stared blankly at the dimly lit computer screen on her desk inside of her office at work. Her thoughts traveled everywhere at once, but they always came back to one thing: Kenny! She looked at her watch, hoping that the minutes would speed by, ending her day before Kenny got a chance to confront her. She made sure that he had plenty of work to keep him busy for eight hours and as far away from her as possible.

Vanessa feared that Kenny's temperament would push things to spin out of control. Her fears weren't about the things Kenny had threatened to do to her. It wasn't even about her anymore. The thing that scared Vanessa most was the possibility of losing everything that meant something to her, Russell and Dejah and her family. It was a possibility that seemed more real with every threat that Kenny threw her way. Vanessa knew that if she didn't get rid of Kenny very soon, her life would never return to normal and she'd never enjoy loving her family again.

Vanessa sensed this because she loved Russell and Dejah in a way that allowed her to crawl into their skin and become what they were: love and happiness. She had breathed in their essence when they awakened in the morning and greeted her with loving hugs and kisses over breakfast. She tasted it when Russell laid down and made love to her all night. She always sensed their moods and experienced their pains. Her own mood rose happily with Dejah's beautiful smile and skin and fell gloomily with Russell's anger.

The thoughts reverberated in her mind as Kenny suddenly entered her office, startling her.

"You can never give me enough work to keep me away from you," he said, and then he banged his fist on her desk as she looked away.

"Kenny, you really need to stop all this," she said shakily. "We need to be adults about this and end things off on a good note, not a violent one. Kenny, I'm married. Please let me live my life."

Kenny looked her up and down, his brown eyes lingering on her perky breasts and wide hips insistently pressing against her tight-fitting wool dress. He felt like she wore the dress especially for him.

Vanessa lowered her head, feeling ashamed and disgusted that he was literally raping her again with his eyes. She sighed and eased her chair under the desk, trying to hide her body away from him.

"Don't gimme that married shit!" He exploded with rage, staring at her through a haze of lust and anger. "You was married when I fucked you the first time. Ain't a damn thing changed!"

It has, Kenny. You're acting like a fucking maniac - no, you are a maniac, she thought before answering him. "You're right Kenny, but I was vulnerable at the time. I mean...we both shared something special. But all good things come to an end. Why can't you move on and let things be?"

"Because I don't want this to end." He walked around her desk and pulled her chair out. "Not yet, anyway. It's just beginning to get good."

She smelled his cologne as he leaned over her and she got scared with each passing second. "Please, Kenny," she begged, standing to face him. "You already raped me. I didn't turn you in. That should be enough. I mean, damn, you act like I owe -"

Kenny rushed her, pushing her on her back over the desk. "AHHH!" Her screams were covered by his hand.

Pulling up her dress, he grabbed her thighs and his hand moved upward hurriedly to the soft flesh above them, ripping

Drunk In Love

off her panties. For as long as she could, Vanessa fought and struggled, knocking the computer and other knick-knacks off the desk and onto the floor until he backhand slapped her and roughly entered her warm center with two fingers. His other hand gripped her hair roughly, holding her in place. Forcing her legs apart, he ripped her dress and bit down on one of her nipples through her bra.

"Kenny, puhleeeeeaaassee stooooppp!" she cried softly. "You don't have to take it again. Please."

Relenting in his aggression, Kenny smirked triumphantly while Vanessa leaned up, reached down, touched and caressed him, then squeezed his throbbing love stick through his jeans. "Kenny, this has got to stop before you destroy us," she said softly while loosening his pants.

He looked in her eyes. Even with the increasing infatuation he had suffered behind her good pussy, Kenny knew she was right, but he'd gone too far and didn't know how to act if he couldn't have her when and where he wanted.

Sliding down on her knees, Vanessa freed his hardening phallus and jerked him until the helmet-shaped head brushed her pouty lips. It sickened her to do the act of fellatio on him, but that's all she could think about to avoid being raped again. Kissing the head of his dick and the sides of it with every part of her mouth, Vanessa looked up at him, took a deep breath, and swallowed his thick meat deep inside her torrid mouth.

"Ah, yeah, Nessa... That's it, baby... Yessss, right there, baby... Suck this dick... You love my dick in there, I know you do... Ah, yessss," he moaned, looking down at her bobbing head. He threw his head back with pleasure, clenching his ass cheeks tightly together, giving into the moment. He felt like he had her under his spell again. He didn't know for how long, but the pleasure he was feeling right then was all that mattered to him.

Glancing up at him, Vanessa sucked and licked him slowly as if he was the last lollipop on Earth. Then without the slightest hesitation, she bit down on his hulking boner as hard as she could and growled until she tasted blood. She pushed him away from her and got to her feet quickly, swinging wild punches at his face until she staggered backwards several steps and fell on his back.

"AAAHHHH!   AAH-AAAHHHHH-AHHHHH!" he screamed in pain, curling into a fetal position after crashing to the floor. Blood oozed from the sides of his rapidly deflating dick while he rolled around on the floor, not believing what she had just done to him.

"AAAAHHHH, I'm a kill you, bitch! I'ma kill you! AHHHHHH! Oh my God! Bitch, you are sooooo dead!"

"Fuck you, you sick bastard!" she screamed. She began kicking him as hard as she could. Her pointy-toe heels hit the side of his ribs and face with dull thuds. Pain shot up her ankle, forcing her to stop. She bolted from her office screaming rape and looking for help.

Now she'd be rid of Kenny for good.

Moments later, Vanessa told her assistant that Kenny just tried to rape her inside her office. Vanessa's assistant saw her boss's partially torn dress and bruised cheek, which corroborated her teary eyes accusations.

"C'mon, girl. I got your back."

They rushed to a phone and reported the incident to the police. After the call, Vanessa's assistant rushed to Vanessa's office in hopes of restraining Kenny until the authorities arrived.

Opening the door, the brunette cautiously looked around the office to see where Kenny was before entering. Once she saw that the blue drapes covering the open office window had been ripped down and several broken figurines laid on the floor, she knew Kenny had fled the office in a hurry, making himself look more guilty of Vanessa's criminal accusations.

The brunette turned quickly and rushed back to Vanessa's side. "I'm so sorry, Vanessa, but Kenny's gone," she said sadly. "He's nowhere in there. He must've left through your office window."

Taking in the terrifying revelation, Vanessa collapsed to the ground in a shivering mess. While cowering in the corner, Vanessa began wondering when and where Kenny would turn up next.

And what will he do once he finds me?

Anitra

The following afternoon, Anitra was leaving her job, heading for her car when someone called her name. Turning to see who had called her, Anitra recognized Caveman, the hung stripper. Immediately she got moist after seeing him, remembering the night of lustful passion they shared.

Caveman smiled and extended his hand.

Anitra took a step back, still watching his hand as if it were some form of deadly toxin. Nathan immediately popped in her head, and she thought about how sincere and genuine his love was for her.

Caveman's smile faded quickly and he lowered his head. "I thought that was you. How have you been?"

"Just fine." She nodded, flashing her engagement ring. "And about to get married."

"Oh, I see. You sure it's what you really wanna do?"

Not really, but I can't hurt Nathan like that. He's too good to me to get that type of treatment. "You know you're way out of line for asking me that," she snapped. "What damn right do you have?" She got louder, drawing stares in their direction.

Caveman threw up his hands in mock surrender, taking several steps back, regretting his decision of stopping her. "Hey, it must be that time of the month for you, huh? I'm totally sorry. I just thought I'd speak, since I haven't heard from you since the party."

Anitra searched his eyes, finding genuine honesty in them. But she knew she had to stop this now before she went too far again. A sudden hardness appeared on Anitra's face. "Listen up, Caveman; you got what you wanted from me that night, okay - a good fuck. That's it, that's all it was. There ain't shit to talk about and there never will be. I'm getting married."

Drunk In Love

Caveman chuckled. "You hoes kill me! And you wonder why we call y'all bitches, skeezers, sluts, and freaks. Hoes like you ain't shit! You probably got a good nigga pussy-whipped, and you out on the town 'round here fucking off on him."

Anitra grew so hot with anger that she couldn't concentrate for a moment. "Motherfucker, where do you -"

"See ya' round, HOE!" Caveman laughed before turning and walking away.

"Punk ass! You better run!" she yelled before answering her phone on the third ring. "Hello."

"Hey, gurl, it's me, Briana. What'cha doing?"

"About to blow a fuse. I just ran into someone today from my past."

"Oh yeah, what's up?"

"He just made me realize that marriage is not the thing for me."

"Hold up, hold up... Come again?"

"I can't go through with it, Briana. I can't marry Nathan."

"Oh, hell no! Where are you, gurl?"

"Outside my office."

"Don't you move. I'll be there in ten minutes."

As soon as she ended the call, Anitra called Nathan and got his voicemail, which was a relief. She didn't have the guts to tell him that she didn't want to get married, so she left the bad news on his voicemail.

Anitra felt that there was simply too much dick walking around in Dayton to be somewhere tied down to one. After ending the call, Anitra started to feel nauseous over hurting Nathan. She climbed in her car, hating the fact that Caveman, a mere stripper, had been right about her. She was just a freak who loved dick more than being in love.

Briana

It took less than eight minutes for her to reach Anitra's job. As soon as she confronted Anitra, she pushed her hard and got up in her face.

"You wanted to act like a child, then c'mon, let's do it!" Briana shoved her harder. "I told you it would be over for us if you didn't do the right thing. Now we 'bout to fight about it right here and damn now!"

Anitra looked at Briana, biting her quivering bottom lip. "I'm not going to fight you. If you want to throw all we have away over a man, then fine!" she screamed as she walked away from her.

Briana knew Anitra was mad; she could see her fists balling at her sides. She went after her. She didn't know what to say or do to get her to stay with Nathan. Briana didn't want her to give Nathan the pain that Terrence gave her. She didn't know if it would be the same, but she couldn't imagine it being that much different.

She stopped her and said, "You wouldn't want no man to do that to you. How did you come to this decision anyway?"

"I saw Caveman today."

"Caveman? Who the hell is that?"

"Caveman, the stripper from the party you caught me having sex with."

"And what happened?"

"Nothing. He just made me realize I can't get married right now. It'll be like I'm living a lie, Briana."

Briana gave Anitra a hug and led her back to her car. "I'm sorry for blowing up on you. This shit with Terrence is really fucking with me. The last thing I want for you is to feel this pain and let you make Nathan feel that pain. Gurl, it really hurts. Please reconsider."

Drunk In Love

Standing by her car in silence, Anitra broke down crying, and Briana was glad to be getting through to her.

Twenty minutes later, they sat in Anitra's office in silence. Anitra cried, and then cursed Briana for being right and grew silent. She cried some more, cursed Briana some more. Briana let her vent until she felt Anitra was finished and ready to talk.

"Okay, now that that's out of your system, what's your next step?"

"Next?"

"Yeah, don't act like you don't have a wedding day coming up!"

"Briana, this shit is too much, for real!"

"Yeah, well you better get a grip, because you have a man who really loves you and you have to make a choice about him. Now what are you going to do?"

"I don't know. I feel like I'ma lose you if I don't get married. I mean, how can you take his side over mines?"

"I'm not taking his side. I was just upset over the whole situation. We're family, girl. We're more than cousins; we're sisters. I'm not going anywhere. But I think that you should at least give that man a chance to love you."

"I don't know, Briana," she cried. "I just don't know if I can do it."

"Just make sure you give me my money back for the bridesmaid dress I paid for if you don't go through with the wedding." Briana smiled, then stood and walked over to Anitra.

They hugged, and Anitra cried harder than she ever had in her life, remembering the message she left on Nathan's voicemail.

Casey

The crowded courtroom erupted with obscenities and loud booing after the jury passed down a not-guilty verdict for Casey's latest client, who'd been charged with six counts of capital murder. People were nearly standing on top of each other trying to get at the man accused of murdering their kinfolks.

"Order in the court! I say, order in the court!" the Judge demanded, banging his gavel.

The courtroom grew silent. "Mr. Millhouse, you need to thank your lucky stars and kiss the ground that your attorney walks on. I still cannot believe how the jury negated all the incriminating evidence against you. But -"

"Objection, your Honor. This case is over," Casey reasoned.

"You're right, Counselor," he said tightly. He turned back to the defendant. "You're free to go, young man, but here's a warning to you: don't ever let me see your face in my courtroom again."

"Oh, you won't," Mr. Millhouse grinned and started getting acquainted with Casey. "So where do you wanna go out to celebrate?"

"I'm happy for you, Mr. Millhouse." She smiled, closing her briefcase. "But I don't think it would be such a good idea."

"Why not? 'Cause I gang bang? You know, I'm really feeling you, especially after you got me outta the frying pan."

She giggled a little. "I never knew that."

He took her hands into his. "Damn, you're soft. Will you marry me right now?" he said, getting down on one knee.

"You're silly." She smiled, pulling away, noticing him for the first time: his butterscotch skin, shoulder-length dreadlocks with red-dyed tips, and sparking bourbon eyes. A worthy catch, indeed.

"Only about you. So am I gonna get to see you ever again, after today?'

Gurl, what the hell, you only live once, she told herself as she wrote down her number for him. "That's up to you," she said, handing him her business card.

"What chu' mean?"

"If you can stay out of trouble long enough and clean up your thuggish ways, I may be able to fit you somewhere in my busy schedule."

"Bet that up, shawty." He smiled while sliding her card inside his blazer pocket.

Casey watched as Jonet Millhouse, aka J-Man, a known Piru Blood gangbanger left the courtroom smiling back at her, all the while avoiding the angry and cursing mob.

Later that night, Casey went over to Olive Garden to meet with Adrian. It was the first time she'd seen him since the day in the park and he looked even better, wearing an orange sweater vest, pinstripe button-down shirt, multicolored tie, and dark jeans with some lace-up leather oxfords.

Adrian got up and pulled out Casey's chair so she could sit down. He pushed her chair in and took a seat. The mood in the restaurant was okay between them.

"I'm glad you came out tonight, Casey. Thanks."

Adrian would be getting in between her legs in no time at the rate he was moving. He was so adorable to her. Casey liked him very much. She noticed how much he went out of his way to cater to her. She looked into his handsome, innocent baby face, studying him closely. For the most part, Casey saw him being her boy toy for more than the average month she allowed men to have. She felt he did deserve that much.

"No need for that. I just want to see what the reason is behind us meeting?" she reminded him.

"Only time will tell as the date progresses," he said without blinking.

Casey looked at him in disbelief. She couldn't believe how much arrogance he was showing all of a sudden. Casey had a feeling he was playing a role he wasn't used to - a role that would get him burned in the long run.

Adrian was glad that Casey agreed to go out with him. He knew that she didn't have respect for good guys like him, but he wanted the chance to show her that he could be taken seriously. He stayed the same just as the day he first met her, making her laugh in spots. He figured he must have been doing something right, because they were two hours into the date and she didn't show any signs of wanting to end things.

He took her bowling, planting some memories of his own by beating her the first two games. Adrian must have done something, because Casey refused to leave until she won a game.

"This my racetrack here, Casey. You thought I forgot about how you kicked my ass in jogging the other day." He talked trash, bowling another strike.

"You missed that, huh?" Casey countered, throwing a strike as well.

She couldn't believe how quickly she got used to the game and throwing strikes. Her reason to keep playing wasn't just to learn the game; she wanted to win. That's why she was so willing to accept his trash talking.

"Hell naw!" He threw a strike and winked at her.

"Well, I'm going to show you that I can kick your ass in anything." She made her feelings known, throwing a quick strike.

"I hear you, lil mama…I hear you. You wanna make a bet?"

"What's good?"

Drunk In Love

"If I win the next three games, you'll hang out with me for the next three months."

"And if you lose one game?" Casey challenged, raising an eyebrow.

"That ain't gon' happen, but let's just say if I lose to you... you move on with your life, and just leave me with a good night kiss."

"You got a bet, Mister!" she said, hoping that he wasn't better than what he appeared to be.

After losing the first two games by a large margin, Casey was sure that Adrian would be in her life for the next ninety days. Pouting and rolling the ball, Casey cursed when she didn't roll a strike.

Adrian laughed and decided to throw the final game. He didn't want her to feel obligated to hang out and date him. He wanted everything to take its natural course. After seeing the triumphant look on her pretty face, Adrian felt that look was rewarding enough for the time that they spent together that night.

"Well, it looks like you lose!" Casey teased playfully.

"Yeah, I guess my lucky horseshoe ran out."

"Aww... You poor baby, give Mama some sugar!" Casey laughed as they embraced and shared a sensual, long tongue kiss that gassed her head up and made her weak in the knees as they capped off their date. There was no doubt in her mind that she'd be seeing him again.

Vanessa

At 2:55 p.m., Vanessa arrived at Dejah's school and scanned the area. Even though she didn't see anything strange or any signs of Kenny, she still felt scared.

The police told Vanessa that they'd call her as soon as Kenny was apprehended. That was four days ago, and her nerves were on edge ever since waiting for that call. She also didn't want to give Kenny the satisfaction of instilling fear in her and disrupting her life, so she continued on with life as if things were normal.

She recognized one of Dejah's teachers immediately after getting out of the car. The portly white woman waved at her but remained silent. She then ushered Dejah through the front door.

"Hey, Mommy!" Dejah beamed, running into Vanessa's arms and hugging her lovingly.

"Hey, baby," she cooed. "How was school today?"

"Okay, I guess. That is, until that ugly boy Ronald Bledsoe started messing with me."

"What did he do?"

"Things."

"What things?" she asked while they walked towards her car. Looking at her daughter and then looking around, Vanessa didn't see nothing out of the ordinary. She put Dejah inside the passenger seat and kissed her.

"Mommy, stop it! People are watching," Dejah whined.

Vanessa followed Dejah's gaze across the parking lot and fear paralyzed her. Kenny's car sat across the parking lot.

Kenny got out of the car, and then looked around the parking lot and across the street before making eye contact with Vanessa. He smiled before making the gun signal and

Drunk In Love

pointing at her. She stood there terrified and watching him, oblivious to the activity going on around her.

Kenny looked at her with serious eyes and mouthed, "Bang! Your husband is dead!"

Vanessa held up her shaking hands over her mouth.

Kenny jumped back in his car and pulled off like a NASCAR racer coming out of a pit stop. Vanessa slammed the passenger door and ran to the other side of the car in hopes of getting to her husband before Kenny. Vanessa sped out of the parking lot, and called Briana. She got no answer. She tried again, praying for her answer. When she didn't answer, Vanessa dropped her phone in her lap.

"Shit!" she fumed while weaving through traffic.

"Mommy, slow down! You're scaring me!" Dejah said and began crying.

"It's okay, baby, don't cry," she muttered, patting Dejah's thigh. "We just have to get to Daddy." *Before the monster does,* she told herself. She picked the phone back up to dial Casey's number.

Casey answered on the third ring.

"Casey, oh thank God! It's me, Nessa. This is an emergency. I need you to call the police and send them to my house right now. I really think that my husband is in danger."

Before Casey could respond, Vanessa hung up and applied pressure to the accelerator, speeding home to save her husband from a lunatic that would stop at nothing and was willing to do anything to control her life and possess her body.

Vanessa

When Vanessa made it home, she jumped out of the car, looking worried. She ran straight past Casey, Briana, and Anitra, anxious to see if her husband was okay.

A huge cop with a red beard stopped Vanessa as soon as she reached the front door. The cop got angry when Vanessa yanked away from him.

"Ma'am, stop!" the cop ordered, and then he asked if she was the one responsible for calling the police.

Vanessa looked back, nodded, and then opened the front door. "Russell!" she shrieked. "Russell, baby, you home?"

The huge cop followed her inside the house, making eye contact briefly with a male figure walking down the stairs.

Vanessa ran up to Russell and hugged him tightly as she could. "Baby, I'm so glad that you're not hurt. Oh my God, I was so scared for you!"

"Why, what's going on?" Russell tried not to show the concern he was feeling. The alarms immediately began ringing loudly in his head.

Vanessa didn't say anything.

"Ma'am, we have better things to do with our time, like really serve and protect the citizens of Dayton," the cop admonished, giving Vanessa an evil look.

Casey, Briana, Anitra, and Dejah entered the house on the end of Russell's question, throwing worried looks at Vanessa. The huge cop looked at Russell for a second, and then nodded, holding his hat. He didn't feel the need to hang around.

"Thanks, officer. I got it from here." Russell smiled nervously and the cop nodded again and left the premises.

Drunk In Love

Once the cop left, Casey closed the door. Russell looked at his wife with serious eyes. "Baby, what the hell is going on? Talk to me."

Vanessa glanced around and noticed everyone staring at her like she had gone insane. She took a deep breath.

"Russell, baby, I've done something very terrible. Now it's threatening our safety and our future together." She began crying, feeling horrible as if she already knew the end results behind her infidelities.

With wide eyes and agape mouths, Casey's, Briana's, and Anitra's stomachs dropped like a runaway elevator in a skyscraper, listening to Vanessa confess to Russell about how she'd cheated on him with a man who turned out to be a psycho-stalker that raped her once and tried to rape her again just four days ago in her office.

Russell looked at his wife, but remained silent.

"Baby, I am so sorry. I don't know what I was thinking. Baby, I don't want to lose you over this."

"Don't worry, baby, everything's going to be all right." He mumbled words of comfort and hugged his wife, but the pained expression written all over Russell's face said the total opposite.

Casey

To get away from all the drama going on in Vanessa's, Briana's, and Anitra's lives, Casey decided to hang out with Jonte Millhouse at Diamond's, an expensive restaurant in downtown Dayton.

Apparently, he's trying to impress me. She blushed at the thought.

When she exited his fire engine red Dodge Magnum, Casey drew stares in her blue form-fitting Roberto Cavalli Cocktail Dress.

Jonte Millhouse's eyes were immediately drawn to her thighs. Even though he hated the blue color she chose, he couldn't deny the fact that she was wearing the hell out of the skimpy garment. She blushed a little after noticing his mouth-open gaze.

"Your keys, sir?" the valet requested with a cordial smile.

"Yo, don't crash my baby, Mane." He handed over the keys, then took Casey's arm into the crook of his and headed for the restaurant.

Once inside, they were shown to a table and seated. Casey felt like a piece of meat, noticing his eyes fucking her.

Who the hell does he think he is? she thought, her eyes stretching wide. "Mr. Milhouse -"

"Please, call me Tay, baby." He winked, his eyes moving back to her breasts.

"Yeah, you're looking at me like I'm some fried chicken or something."

"Is that a bad thing? Do you have something against fried chicken? I mean, damn, you're gorgeous. I didn't expect you to look more beautiful than you did in court, that's all."

"Thanks, I guess." She grinned, blushing a little.

Drunk In Love

A waitress approached and asked if they were ready to order.

"For starters, gimme a straight up Hennessey." He smirked, glancing at Casey. "Whatever you want is on me." He winked, making her tingle a little inside. "Just knock yourself out."

"I'll have a glass of Moet Rose, please."

"Coming right up," the waitress said, giving them a Hollywood smile, and then she disappeared to the back of the restaurant. Five minutes later, she returned with the drinks and took their food orders.

Jonte ordered a shrimp and lobster platter. Casey ordered a shredded jack cheese Texas broiled steak dinner.

Casey glanced at Jonte. She felt that he had potential to be her toy for the week. For starters, she could get wet and excited from looking at him. Also, he was a bad boy, a thug, and she longed to have a bad boy at her disposal to play with. *He's totally opposite from Adrian,* she told herself.

She began thinking about what came along with his bad boy persona - the street life and his promiscuity. Casey thought about what their next date would be like and where he would take her. She thought about the adrenaline rush of sexing someone from the wrong side of the tracks and being his down-ass chick. It made her smile inside.

"Damn, Earth to Casey. What you're thinking about, lil mama?"

She cut up her steak in small portions, thinking about how she should answer him. She didn't want him to know that she was thinking about him. She didn't want him to know he had some type of emotional effect on her. She finally looked up at him and smiled.

"First of all, I am not your lil mama, and secondly, I was thinking about how long it's going to take for you to leave the street life alone?"

"Damn, lil-" he caught himself. "I mean, why you so caught up on that? I dig you for you, so why can't you dig me for me?"

"Because that will never give me any guarantees that you'll be around long enough for me to dig you, or whenever I need you. Tay, you're an endangered species. All of your kind are either locked up or dead. Honestly, I can't see us being more than friends unless you change your lifestyle." She surprised herself with that statement.

He sipped his Hennessey and stared at her.

Casey's eyebrow's raised. "What, did I say something wrong? Or you just don't like the truth?"

Jonte scanned the restaurant. He shrugged. "I just want to experience the good life, but I always got a problem when I'm in the hood. Niggas always tryna get a rep off me."

Casey sipped her champagne. "Listen to me, Tay. You can live that other side of life. All you have to do is put your pride to the side and just walk away from the hood and everything else that's preventing you from reaching your goals."

"So tell me this…" He leaned in closer, placing his tattooed-covered forearms on the table. "If I do this as you suggest, and end up fucked up and dirt broke, will you still be down for me?"

"Yes," she said quickly, surprising herself. Taking in his innocent smile, Casey looked into his eyes, which seemed to be saying, *I can believe you're realer than most women, and I like that.*

Jonte remained silent for a moment, absorbing all the positive vibes he was getting from her. He knew she was very capable of being wifey, but was pursuing her really worth giving up his street fame, rep, and fortune?

"Now what are you thinking about, Tay?" she asked while taking a sip of her drink.

"About you and me being together for the long haul."

Drunk In Love

Casey smile at the thought, then caught herself. "Whoa, homeboy, we still have to make it past the first date."

Jonte relaxed and laughed. At that moment, he began to imagine sharing a future with her, thinking about how he'd look coming home to her and their kids, which was a good place to look forward to. He looked at her again, gaining a new found respect for her. At first, he just wanted to fuck her brains out and keep it moving. Now, after chilling and getting to know her and learning that she cared about his well-being, Jonte really warmed up to her, feeling genuine love from her.

"I already flew past the first date. I'm already tuxedoed out and playing Jagged Edge, hoping that you meet me at the altar in your white dress," he crooned with a light chuckle.

Casey giggled with him, now knowing that she wanted Jonte to become more than a weekly play toy. She'd never met anyone who was so into her, which scared and intrigued her. She felt that Adrian was okay, but he didn't excite her like Jonte. She felt the sparks instantly with him. With Adrian it took a while, which she didn't like.

Hours later, after enjoying a Kat Williams comedy show and several drinks at an after-hours pool hall, Jonte dropped Casey off at home. While walking her to her front door, they held hands like high school kids in love.

"I hope you had fun tonight?"

"I truly did. You're fun to be with, Tay." She smiled.

He turned and faced her. "Casey, this is no bullshit, I really like you."

She smiled but didn't respond.

"Did you hear me?"

"Yeah. So I take it you enjoyed yourself tonight?"

"Put it like this…" He leaned towards her and kissed her gently on the lips. "Does that answer your question?"

"Mmm." She licked her lips. "Yeah, it did."

Their eyes met, and Casey was expecting him to kiss her again, this time long and passionately. He just smiled, revealing his deep dimples as he backed away.

"So when can I see you again?"

"I have to think it over first. I'll call you, okay?"

"Yeah, you do that, so we can star -"

Casey pulled him towards her and gave him a very passionate kiss. Her pussy pulsated as she creamed in her panties. She didn't know what he was going to do to her, but whatever it was sure felt good and she didn't want it to end.

Drunk In Love

Casey

Casey opened her door, pulling Jonte inside with her. She gave him a long, sensual kiss, expertly unbuttoning his shirt. He licked and kissed the sides of her neck, running his hands all over her body. She was so soft to touch. He couldn't believe he was inside her house about to tap that ass on the first date.

They slid out of their clothes like they were on fire. She couldn't keep her hands off of him. Reaching for his manhood, she held it in her hands, stroking it, radiating the warmth of his smooth, stiffening rod he had to offer.

"Right here...right now," she whispered, squeezing his shaft. "Fuck me, Tay. Fuck me."

She led him down to the floor on his back and slipped her tongue into his mouth. He sucked her tongue hungrily. Working him on his side, Casey gripped his boner lightly with her small hand and guided him inside her naturally-lubricated treasure hole.

"You don't need no streets. I can give you the world and more. All you have to do is fuck me real good," she told him, as she grinded back and forth, sucking his dick with her warm tight pussy.

They were on their sides, facing each other in a nice sensual rhythm, when he looked up and spotted a younger version of Casey standing on the stairs watching him. He tried to pull out and alert Casey, but she pulled him closer to her and fucked him even faster.

"Goddamn, Casey!" he whispered, squeezing her naked ass and watching Justine stare at them with her mouth open.

He started getting off on being watched by her as he slid his fat man meat in and out of Casey's tight wet tunnel of love. He waved at the girl on the steps beckoning her to come down to him, and smiled while slowly guiding his stiffness in deeper and deeper and deeper into her sister's clenching hole.

Justine stood still for a minute, and then tiptoed back upstairs to let her sister do her. She was horny, so she reached for her young pussy and began slowly fingering herself to an explosive orgasm.

Back downstairs, Tay had Casey shuddering while holding her right leg up in the air, grinding his stiff pole deeper and harder into her filled-up pussy. The deep fucking felt too good to her. Casey tried to push his hairy balls up inside her.

"Mmmm...boy... Mmmm, shit!" She moaned as he eased his dick out until just the head was rubbing against her outer pussy lips.

He began rubbing it against her clitoris until she roughly squeezed his dick and rammed it back inside her well-oiled depths, trying to keep the heavenly feeling going.

They switched positions and he penetrated her from behind, squeezing her ass with every thrust. After going hard in that position for a few minutes, he extracted his boner and went downtown. She sucked his dick while he ate her pussy in the 69 position. They then moved upstairs, where he titty-fucked her and she licked the head of his dick every time it came near her mouth through the warm flesh of her cleavage. By the time she reached her sixth orgasm, he was just building up to his first, giving her the dick and no other feeling like it in the world. She no longer thought a dick was just a dick.

"Awww, fuck! Fuck me, daddy... fuck meeee!" she urged, loving it, watching his huge sausage slam inside her pink ocean.

He tickled her clitoris with every thrust of his dick to add to her pleasure. She was in heaven and climaxing again all over his pounding muscle, making both their thighs wet from her pussy juices and sweat. Long stroking her wetness drove him crazy.

"Whose pussy is this?"

Drunk In Love

"It's yours, daddy, it's all yours, Tay."

He slammed his dick in her harder and harder and harder, loving the cries of her passion. "I said, whose pussy is this?"

"It's yours....Jonte Milhouse... Oh my Gawd, I'm cuuummmmiiiiinnngggg!" she exclaimed, releasing a liquid lake of cum over his expanding muscle.

"That's what I th-tha...ohhh, shit! Aaaah...oh my ugggghhhhh..." he stammered, sounding retarded as his spewing warm load shot deep inside Casey, causing them both to shake, rattle, and roll.

Casey didn't know when exactly it happened, but it did. All of a sudden, he was the center of her world, and she was completely drunk and high on his loving. She held on tight to him as if he was a dream come true.

"What the Hell? Oh my God, boy, oh my God!" She kissed him passionately, pressing her body against his. They felt so right together. Even after the thug loving he just put on her, Casey wanted him more than ever before. The Love Bug had just bitten her and she never even saw it coming. "You know what time it is, right?"

He looked at her, puzzled. "What's cracking, lil mama?"

"You mines now. You belong to me, so all the other little bitches you got on the side, you can just tell them the dick is off limits from now on. Do you think you can do that for me, daddy?"

"I'll see what I can do."

"What!" she snapped. "Tay, don't make me hurt something over you, boy! Oh my God...mmm... mmm...mmph...oh my God," she moaned. She grinded against him until she closed her eyes, exhausted and dazed. She dreamed of Jonte, of the perfect union of their bodies - explosive, leg-shaking, and very mind-blowing and memorable. She twitched in her sleep, having her first wet dream in years.

Casey

At 10 a.m. the following morning, Casey's telephone rang, waking her from a fantastic dream. Jonte kissed every spot on her body as if he'd never see her again, and they made love all night long, until the sun came up.

Looking over to an empty bed, she saw the note and knew it wasn't a dream - it really happened. Grabbing the phone, Casey read Jonte's scribbled note:

> *Casey, you truly rocked my world, and changed my life. I can longer go back in life after meeting you and experiencing that bomb-ass pussy. My blessing from above has arrived in the form of you. As much as I didn't want to leave you, I realized that we might have rushed into things. There are a lot of things I want to tell you and share with you. I know it's quick but you need to know that I LOVE YOU, for real.!!! Hope to hear from you soon...*
>
>

I Love You,
Jonte

"Aw, he so sweet." Casey smiled before answering the phone. She knew without a shadow of a doubt that she had to see him again.

"Hello?"

"Hey gurl, what'cha doing?" Briana's voice sounded cheerful on the other end.

Casey's voice was a little groggy as she answered. "Well, it's kinda early, and I'm still tryna get over this dick hangover."

"Damn! It was that good? Who is he? What's his number?"

"None of your beeswax." She giggled.

Drunk In Love

"Anyway, I was just talking to Anitra again and trying to convince her to at least talk to Nathan. The man has been ringing my phone off the hook looking for her ass. Oh, she's getting married, whether she likes it or not. I spent too much damn money on this shit."

Hearing the anger in Briana's voice, Casey sighed with a deep breath. "Why don't y'all come on over? Maybe we'll come up with something to make everybody happy."

Briana jumped on the opportunity. "I have to trick her ass into coming over. So we'll probably hook up with you in a few days. Love you, bye-bye."

Hearing Briana hang up, Casey hung up and sniffed her sheets. Smelling Jonte's lingering Issey Miyake scent mixed with the leftover odor of their sex sent her hormones ringing. They were getting more out of control every time she thought about how he hit her G-Spot and sent her into climatic oblivion.

They had been great together sexually. She felt as if she were giving a part of herself when she took him inside her instead of simply taking. She had not felt that way in a long time. She felt like a high school girl a day after making love for the first time with her crush. Casey jumped out of bed and headed for the shower to get fresh and clean for what she wanted to do today.

Casey started wondering what it would be like to actually love someone. What they shared was banging sex, nothing more, but she had never felt as strongly about any other man in her life.

She thought about Anitra and her upcoming wedding, which made her turn over a new leaf and stop freaking. She thought about Vanessa and her marriage, which had lasted for so long before Vanessa decided to cheat.

What is the secret about love and relationships? Is it all chemical? Am I missing something that other women have? she thought. She instantly got the urge to see Jonte again. There was something about him that fascinated her and she just couldn't put her finger on it at the moment. She wanted to know if what she felt for him was a product of the sex they shared or something more. Would she want him because of the bomb sex?

Yes, of course. What more was there to it? A man I slept with one time. Why should he matter, when none of the others I screwed in the past mattered? Casey thought, and then she figured that she'd never find the answer by using logic, the lawyer's tool.

What to do? What to do? she wondered, having trouble keeping thoughts of Jonte off her mind, which was a first. Usually after she sexed a man, they became a distant memory, but not Jonte. He'd remained heavy in her thoughts, which scared her.

Jonte had a strange effect on her. Perhaps the mysterious way he'd entered her life was the cause for her desire. Perhaps it was the passion of their lovemaking. When they were in bed, she held him so tightly, then when she thought he was giving himself to her completely, she suddenly felt him stop, which implied a disinterest during the act. It confused, yet entranced her to the point where she wanted to solve the mystery beneath the surface of the muscular body that held her last night.

Yes, I definitely need to see you again, Jonte, she told herself while showering. The more she thought about the previous night, the greater she desired him. She lathered herself up, daydreaming about what her next encounter with him would be like, and how he would react to her after getting between her legs on the first night.

Forget him, gurl, there's no future for y'all, she told herself, but her heart said differently. Another decision was being made due to one question: what if Jonte Milhouse was her soul mate?

She slid her hand between her slit and discovered wetness. She wanted to hold Jonte; she wanted to ride him and

Drunk In Love

make him commit himself to her. But she knew that would be a mistake. She figured that he was the type that had to want her before he committed himself.

But he's done that in his letter, right?

Yep, she thought, letting her mind race to the memories of Jonte's face buried deep in her sopping pussy, sucking her dry. She thought of the way they touched and how she melted into him. They stroked each other hungrily, and she forgot where she was and who she was during the desperate lovemaking. He sawed inside of her with violence and passion until her body arched and her eyes closed tightly, releasing tears of euphoria, all the while digging her nails into his back. Then came the gasp, the moan, and shaking legs of the ninth mind-blowing climax.

The next thing Casey knew, she was playing with herself and fingering her fiery love tunnel, urging herself onto a gushing climax, all the while thinking about Jonte, who couldn't have been a more perfect way to start the day.

Anitra

Anitra arrived at her place of business and went straight to her office. Her assistant John entered the office moments later with a cup of steaming walnut-flavored coffee brewed just like she liked it.

"Thanks, John." She smiled at him, taking a seat behind her desk.

"Anytime you need me, just call on me, Ms. Stamos."

"How long have you been working here, John?"

"Ever since I got out of the joint... Going on about ten months now, why?"

"No reason." She took a sip of coffee and looked at him. "Actually, there is a reason. I'd like to know why you're so infatuated with me?" she asked, catching him off guard.

"Huh, say what?"

"You heard me. I mean, just a few weeks ago, you kissed me, risking your job and everything, and I'd like to know what have I ever done to make you so infatuated with me?"

"I guess it was all those times of seeing you on TV while I was locked up. You know jail fucks up the mental and makes you want to make love to every woman you see on TV. You were just one of my favorites and I told myself if I ever got the chance to do it, I'd eat out your pussy and ass as soon as you left the track all sweaty and wet," he said, licking his lips, which made her coochie twitch in anticipation.

"You just talking, boy. You -"

"I can show you better than I can tell you," he cut her off. "All you have to do is go run around the block and get sweaty as you can and come back in here. I bet you I drop to my knees and lick that sweaty kitty-cat," he said, making her smile.

"John, you don't make no sense." She shook her head. "That'll be all."

Drunk In Love

"You sure? 'Cause I can hit you off right now and give you a good day to remember right here at work while you browse the web," he offered.

"You know what? I think you full of shit. Lock that door and come put your mouth where you want to right now," she said, hiking her pencil skirt up around her waist.

"Shiid, you ain't got to tell me twice!" John bolted over to the door, locked it, and rushed back to her desk.

"On your knees, soldier," she commanded and he obeyed. "Now crawl over here and get some."

By the time he crawled over to her desk, she had her skirt raised and her thong slid to the side so he could see the meaty folds of her pussy lips. He licked his lips and inched forward. He couldn't believe what was happening to him. It was like a dream come true.

"You sure you don't want to run around the block first and get that thang all sweaty and wet for me?" he asked, causing her to close her legs.

"I knew you was full of shit! Just -"

"Open your legs back up and I'm a show you I ain't never bullshittin'."

Anita slid her legs open a little wider as he moved in closer and began sniffing at her exposed sex like a dog. Anitra palmed the back of his head, urging him on, feeling the electricity between them. John eased his hands in the strap of her thong and helped her remove them, all the while rubbing up and down her long, toned legs.

"Damn, you're so soft," he said huskily. "I could tell you was from watching you jiggle all those years."

He kissed the inside of her thighs and hot shivers ran up and down Anitra's back. He lifted her legs up and placed them over his shoulders. He began kissing her butt cheeks, not once but several times. His nibbling lips moved to her clitoris. Then his lips covered the folds of her pussy lips with sweet passion. As soon as he made contact with her love tunnel, her pussy flamed. Her whole body tingled with thrills from his oral pleasure. Her pelvis moved to the gentle licking of his probing tongue and she was his for the taking.

Her hard nipple burned and she felt herself getting wet. She moved her hands up and down his head, her fingers digging into his scalp. Stroking her swollen lips, he used the heel of his hand to massage the top of her coochie. He rubbed up and down and around and around, causing her to lift her groin against his strokes. She rocked her pelvis up and down, up and down while he jacked off her clitoris. He teased her moist pussy lips with his longest finger. Gradually he worked his probing tongue and finger inside her, using his finger to tease the entrance of her vagina for a long minute while his tongue worked up into her slick channel. The way he worked her pussy over sent her reeling.

"Ooooh shit! Sssss…boy, what are you doing to me?" she cried, humping onto his stabbing tongue.

"Nothing…absolutely nothing…" he said after stopping suddenly. He got to his feet quickly and rushed to the office door.

She looked at him as if he lost his ever-loving mind. When he started to open the door, she emptied her lungs in a long stressful sigh. "You can't leave me like this, John, please."

"There's a time and place for shit like that. If you want some more, you set up the place and time and I'll be there," he said as he left her office and closed the door.

Sitting behind her desk with heart and pussy thumping wildly, Anitra smoothed down her skirt. She grabbed the telephone and called up Caveman. He answered on the third ring.

"What it do?"

"I have an emergency that I need for you to handle."

"Who this?"

Drunk In Love

"Bachelorette party, leash, fucking?" she gasped, feeling the flames in her coochie that she needed extinguished.

"Oh, 'sup wit' ya, lil mama?"

"No talking, need dick like now." She sounded retarded while trying to catch her breath.

"Sorry, I can't help you. I don't hit the same pussy twice. Hoes like you ain't worth my time." He laughed and hung up on her, leaving her with a fucked up look on her face.

Anitra slammed down the phone and got up quickly. She left her office to go find John so she could make him finish what he started.

'Cause if he don't, I'm going to fire his ass so quick, she thought. She couldn't believe how she let John get out on her like that. As she walked around her office, thoughts of Nathan popped in her head. She didn't know what was happening to her. One minute she wanted to get married and then the next, she was back to her old ways, being a slut.

Something has got to give, she told herself as she stopped in her tracks. At that moment, she realized that leading the life of a slut wasn't worth all the hassles. She turned on her heels and returned to her office to retrieve her battery-operated dildo, which should hold her over until she got the real thing in her life again.

Casey

After getting dressed, Casey walked into her sister's bedroom to talk to her. She opened the door and got an eye full. Casey saw Justine riding some boy in the reverse cowgirl position. Casey damn near lost her mind.

"Justine!" she yelled, and to her surprise, Justine didn't stop riding the dick.

"Get out, Casey, and respect my privacy!" Justine yelled, looking at her and continuing to ride the dick faster and faster.

"Oh, I'ma respect my foot up in your ass!" Casey rushed over to the bed and began beating the brakes off of her little sister. After slamming Justine's naked behind to the floor, Casey looked over at the naked man with fire in her eyes.

"And you, get the hell outta my house before I call the cops on you!" she yelled at the stockily built young man who sat on the bed just watching her beat up on her little sister.

"Psst," he sighed in frustration. "Ay, Justine, you can come with me so you ain't got to deal with this bullshit up in here," he said, getting up slowly, going for his clothes.

"What!" Casey snapped and looked at him, sneaking in a look at his hanging boner. *Damn, he's big! How the hell Justine fit all of that inside her,* she thought and then went with the flow. "Yeah, Justine, just get the hell on outta here and go with your little boyfriend. Just see how long that lasts before another piece of ass comes along and he leaves you out in the cold."

"I hate you, Casey!" Justine raged, shoving her back roughly. "You such a hypocrite. You can have all the sex you want around here, but I can't have any. You think I ain't see you fucking that man on the living room floor last night? Yeah, and you ain't respect me enough to take it up to your bedroom, so why the fuck shouldn't I be allowed to get some dick?"

Drunk In Love

"Bitch, do you pay any bills around here?" Casey raged while the guy got dressed.

"No, but you was having sex like nothing was wrong with it, so I felt I could do the same. You ain't have no problem before when I told you I was doing it."

"Yeah, there's a difference in hearing and actually seeing it. Listen to me, when you get your own place and support yourself, then you can do what the fuck you want, or better yet, just go ahead and leave with this loser. I bet you he don't have a pot to piss in or a window to throw it out of."

"FYI, old lady, I have my own apartment and make good money," he bragged, throwing on his windbreaker. While they were arguing, he eased his pistol inside his waistband, making sure to keep it out of sight from Justine's crazy sister.

"Doing what?" Casey asked in a nasty tone.

"None of your business, but I can take care of lil mama right here if she wants to ride out wit' a nigga. You ain't said shit."

"You need to watch your tone with me, young man," Casey checked him.

"I'm through up in here," he said. "Yo, Justine, you coming or what?"

Justine looked at Casey, who crossed her arms over her breasts waiting for her to answer the life-altering question. Justine then looked at her male friend, who waited at her bedroom door for an answer.

"Weezy, just give me a second to talk to my sister and I'll be out to talk to you before you leave."

"Yeah, whatever, but if you ain't out there in five minutes, I'm out, and you're ejected from Weezy's world for life," he said before walking out and slamming the door.

As soon as the door slammed, Justine flopped on the bed, still naked as the day she was born. She looked up at Casey with sad puppy dog eyes, making Casey melt.

"Casey, I'm sorry if you think I was being disrespectful, but I just thought it was cool since you were doing it."

Casey sat down on the bed beside her. "Justine, I love you," she sighed. "I just don't want to see you get hurt or become something that you're not really ready to live up to. Now Mama told me about your episode with having sex with those two boys at one time. That's just straight up nasty, I ain't even gon' front, and now I catch you in here with another boy putting a foot-long dick in you, what? You don't expect me to go off on your ass? All you're doing now is making yourself a freak. If you're going to do that, then you need to get something out of the deal instead of some dick. Those niggas can pay for all the shit you be asking me to buy your fast ass."

"Casey, I'm not no freak. Those boys I had in Mama's house paid me $600 dollars to do that. They both were virgins and I was just helping them out, I swear. Now Weezy's a totally different story. I have been seeing him for close to a year now and he knows nothing about the episode at Mama's. I really like him Casey, don't ruin this for me."

"You really like him?" Casey grilled.

"Yes, I do. He's my boo for real."

"Then why did you cheat on him?"

"I don't know. I mean $600 is a lot of money and I couldn't just pass that up. Plus I knew those boys ever since we were little, so I didn't look at it like that. I just looked at it like they was paying me to help them out."

"You think you got all the sense, huh?"

"No, I just got a little bit of sense." She grinned, making Casey laugh. "So you not mad at me no more?" Justine asked, batting her eyelashes at Casey.

"Of course I am, but you're getting older and I can't stop you from taking the dick if that's what you really love doing."

"No, I just love him, Casey. Weezy's my everything," she answered quickly.

Drunk In Love

"Well, get dressed and go out there and tell him then." Casey smiled and gave her sister a comforting hug.

Casey left Justine's bedroom and went outside to confront Justine's little boyfriend to see what he really did for a living to earn money. She also wanted to lay the law down about being respectful to her at all times. *If he's going to be in my sister's life, then he's going to have to learn how to respect his elders and he can't be no thug or none of that shit,* Casey thought as she left out the front door.

Nathan Welch

Kenny

It took a while for Kenny to get a sense of Vanessa's regular routine and mandatory appointments. There hadn't been much leaving the house or reporting to work, since their last rocky encounter at the office - a very painful encounter that cost him several stitches in his love muscle. But he had seen enough of her out and about activity to know that she was trying to live a normal life again without living in fear of him. Maybe it was even a taunt directed at him - at least that's what he gathered from it.

So it was revenge and revenge only that brought him to her home and out of hiding from the Ohio police's APB out on him. He hated Vanessa for having him strung out on her pussy. He'd been in love with her since the first time he ever laid eyes on her at a job seminar. Then she had eagerly slept with him, urging him to make love to her with animalistic enthusiasm. He'd poured his heart and soul into it, and she just wanted to end it all - like it was just that simple!

He remembered the assault in her office, what had happened, the disfigurement she'd caused, and because of it, how he was a wanted man on the lam. Dayton's finest would be looking all over for him now, and one day they'd find him. He just didn't think that they would find him right here.

Not today.

From where he was watching with the high-powered AR-70 Assault Rifle resting in his lap, Kenny couldn't see too much movement in Vanessa's house. He figured the house was holding his sleeping beauty Vanessa.

She's probably out like a light; don't have a care in the world. Wrong, bitch! he thought, knowing they had to get up and leave the house sometime.

Drunk In Love

And he'd be right there waiting to mow them down like irritable weeds with his deadly rifle. For now, he was settled in where he was, waiting patiently to get his revenge.

A bleep of a soap opera skit ran through his head, something Erica Kane always said when he used to watch *All My Children* during his prison bid.

"Beware: the anger of a rejected heart is deadly…"

I AM THEE, Kenny thought while watching and waiting, perfectly still in the ever-lightening dawn.

I AM THEE…

Casey

Several hours later, Casey sat in a restaurant with Adrian for lunch. He was surprised at the sudden invite and rushed over to the place to meet her. He brought her a dozen long-stemmed roses, which made her smile and feel bad inside.

"So Adrian, the reason I invited you out to lunch is because I have been thinking about us."

"Us?"

"Yes, and I don't think it's going to work. Don't get me wrong, you're a very handsome guy and we click and all that, but I have somebody in my life now."

No you don't, stupid bitch! All you had was a one-night stand with a big dick gangbanger. You're not sure he's going to be with you again!

Well, that's a chance I'm willing to take.

This guy is safe for you, Casey. He's smart and works for a living.

Fuck playing it safe. I need a thug in my life. Them other niggas ain't loving me right!

You such a fucking hypocrite. You want a thug, but your sister can't have one in her life? Bitch, please!

Shut the hell up already, she told herself off while looking at Adrian's expression change from happiness to sadness. Even though he tried to hide his disappointment of being kicked to the curb so soon, he failed miserably.

"You had somebody in your life when I met you, so why you telling me this now? Why you ain't tell me that before I chased you around that damn park?"

"Adrian, boo, I'm sorry if I led you on, but honestly, you deserve a woman way better than me. I'm so fucked up in the relationship department that it don't make no sense and I'd rather let you fly instead of being tied down with my baggage."

Drunk In Love

"I like being tied down," he said, making it hard for her to just up and leave him.

"Adrian, there's other women out there in the sea for you. I'm just not the right one, dear." She leaned over the table, kissed him gently on the cheek, and tried to leave.

He stopped her by pulling on her arm. "Nope, you can't leave until you finish your food. I don't care about you dumping me, but you gonna give me all this time right here before you walk out of my life for good. I just want to remember you the way you are."

"Aw, you really make a girl feel special and guilty at the same time."

"You know what they say, nice guys always finish last." He smiled and dug into his food.

"That's not true, Adrian, and don't ever let anybody tell you different."

"The proof is in the pudding. I came in last trying to make you my woman, so I can't do nothing but believe it, but it's cool. All things happen for a reason, right?"

"Exactly." Casey smiled and took a sip of wine.

They held a stimulating conversation over lunch, sharing their views on love, relationships, and other facts of life. Casey felt bad cutting all ties off with Adrian, but she felt it was necessary in order to focus on the object of her desire: Jonte, who had her stuck on stupid after giving her that thug passion.

Briana

The following morning, Briana persuaded Anitra to take a ride with her. By the time Anitra realized where Briana was going, they were parking in front of Casey's house. After they entered Casey's house, Briana and Casey came up with a plan to go at Anitra with everything but the kitchen sink to persuade her to marry Nathan.

Briana wasn't sure why she felt the need to tell Casey and Anitra about the argument with her mother now, but she wanted Anitra to have some sort of grief about the hurt she was causing Nathan. Maybe she wanted Anitra to have the love that she couldn't obtain herself. More than a month later, Briana still remembered Terrence's silky voice blaring on her mother's answering machine with nightmare clarity.

"Anitra, I've been thinking about your situation lately," Briana began taking a seat on Casey's sofa. "It's been on my brain a lot and I'm telling you now, girl, you need to marry that man."

"Aw shit, here we go again," Anitra sighed while sipping her coffee.

Casey and Anitra gathered around close, sipping coffee, acting like this was one of their usual *Waiting to Exhale* talks - minus Vanessa.

"That's right, here we go again, 'cause you blowing a good man, and I'm not about to let you do it on my watch. I mean, for him to put up with your ass and call around town looking for you even after you dissed him, he has to be a special man in so many ways...so many."

"Shut up, Bri, you don't know shit!" Anitra protested. "You supposed to have my back, not take his side on nothing!"

Casey smiled, and then said, "Chill, gurl, she just wants to see you happy. You can't fault her for that."

Drunk In Love

"Why we're talking about my life all of a sudden?" Anitra complained.

"Because lately I realized that time is our enemy, and we're supposed to be happy with what little time we do have left. That's why we're talking, okay?" Briana said.

Casey and Anitra listened in silence, and Briana talked for a long while about missing Terrence, hating herself for kicking him to the curb without investigating the matter further. Eventually, Briana choked up, letting them see her cry about Terrence and cry about her life.

"I loved him so much, like he was a physical part of me. I still do love him, I guess. I just don't want you to fuck up your life like I did."

"Over potential love," Casey added. "I mean, it's partly my fault for living the life we've led for so long, isn't it?"

"What do you mean, Case? It's not that at all," Anitra responded with an apologetic tone.

"Yes it is," Casey blurted. "I remind you of the freedom of choice, right? I remind you of not being tied down by one dick every day. Every time you see me, you remember that's the life you'll be leaving behind. Ain't that right?"

Anitra gave her an affirmative nod. "Maybe there's some bit of truth in that. But you remind me in a good way, the best way. It's all about good, Case."

"No, it's not," Casey said, not taking her eyes off of Anitra. "I didn't know it until the other night, but I want that tied-down dick. I want to wake up to a man I love every morning until I die. And the playa lifestyle is over for me. Trust me on that."

Briana looked at Casey and then around the room as if a camera crew might suddenly burst into the room screaming, "You've been Punk'd!" Briana knew Casey was going to put her two cents into the matter, but she had no idea that she was going to come this strong.

Casey continued telling them what happened in court and how she might have met her soul mate. She told her girlfriends the truth about falling in love as she knew it. She shared most of the details of Jonte's lovemaking, where his empathy and compassion came from, and she revealed that she never saw it coming.

When Casey finished and couldn't talk anymore, Briana had tears of joy streaming down her face. Anitra had to wipe away a few tears of guilt herself and then she heard firecrackers capping off Casey's beautiful testimony of finding love. Then they all heard it, louder!

Brraaap!

Pap!

PAP!

The sounds went off again like cannons going off on the 4th of July, and they all jumped and dove under the coffee table.

Pting!

Pting!

Pting!

Briana crawled over to the window and to take a peek and see what was going on.

Suddenly the rapid gunshots exploded again, and Briana's stomach dropped in shock and horror as she made eye contact with the shooter.

Drunk In Love

Girlfriends

Briana's eyes opened wide in horror while peering in the direction of the street. She saw Anitra's fiancé, Nathan, standing on the sidewalk holding a big handgun and dressed in his white wedding tuxedo.

"Anitra!" he bellowed. "I know your ass in there! Get yo' ass out here and face me like a man! Get out here now!" he raged and then more gunshots followed, this time shattering windows, and hitting furniture.

"Anitra, it's you know who," Briana said. "Listen, y'all stay put while I go out there and try to talk some sense into him."

"You better hurry up before he shoots up my damn house! Crazy motherfucker!" Casey scoffed as Briana rushed out of the house, holding her hands up in the air like she was surrendering.

Casey and Anitra eased towards the windows to be nosy while Briana began screaming bloody murder at Nathan for coming through the neighborhood like a madman and shooting up Casey's house.

Meanwhile, Anitra's tears were flowing everywhere. She really felt bad for hurting Nathan, and more importantly, hurting her chances at happiness.

Nathan kept yelling, "Anitra, why? Why you doing this to us? I love you, dammit!"

Briana didn't listen as she continued moving across the lawn towards Nathan. Nathan turned the gun on himself and placed it against his right temple.

"If this is how you want it to end, then so be it!" he yelled. "It's fine with me! I don't care anymore! Your love is all that matters to me. You hear me? Anitra!"

Yes, I hear you baby, Anitra answered inwardly while looking out the window. *I hear you loud and clear, baby!*

So now what? Am I supposed to jump and take you back because you're threatening to kill yourself? Is this payback for hurting you?

Even though she loved him with every fiber in her being, she felt like he was trying to run game on her by performing like that. Nothing made much sense anymore to Anitra after seeing his actions.

Anitra stared on as Briana and her man faced off on the front lawn. Justine was upstairs, looking out her bedroom window, not missing a thing. She couldn't wait to tell her girlfriends at school about all the crazy drama that was happening around her sister's house.

Outside, Briana moved in and hugged him. "I know how you feeling, Nate. Just calm down and let me talk to you."

"Why, Briana? I didn't cheat on her or none of that shit, and she just up and leaves me. I went to jail over her ass and this is how she gonna do me?" He cried as Briana pulled him into her arms and began rubbing his back in a comforting manner.

"Let it out, Nate. It's okay to cry about it, baby, I'm here for you…I'm here," she said soothingly while hugging him. Somehow, during the embrace Briana managed to get the gun out of his hand.

After seeing that, Anitra bolted outside.

"It's going to be all right, Nate." Briana patted his back soothingly while he cried on her shoulder.

"I don't think so, Briana," he sniffled. "She just up and left me for no reason. I've done nothing but be good to her, and she kicked me to the curb like trash… Why, Briana? Why!" he cried louder, startling her.

"Because I was scared!" Anitra said.

Drunk In Love

Briana turned and moved away from Nathan as Anitra's words invaded her ears. Briana began giving Anitra an evil look as Anitra walked up to him. Briana stood beside Nathan, looking over-protective like his mother. Briana silently prayed that the two would make up and get married.

"I was scared of not being able to love you like you need to be loved," she told Nathan. "I mean, you came into my life unexpectedly. Then you changed it forever by loving me the way you did. I guess I didn't know how to accept it."

"I guess you didn't." His voice trembled as he moved closer to her. "I didn't know how to accept your rejection. It nearly ate me alive over the last week. Baby, I can't breathe, let alone live, without you."

Anitra felt crazy inside, pulled in so many directions. She thought she would come apart not having Nathan in her life.

What the hell was I thinking? she thought as Nathan embraced her and gave her a kiss, all the while touching her cheek.

"Baby, I love you and always will," he said and then kissed her softly.

While they held each other tightly, Briana looked up at the heavens and mouthed, "Thank you, Lord." She felt like her prayers had been answered.

At least one!

"Hey!" Casey screamed out the window and everyone looked at her.

"Sorry to ruin the happy reunion, but we have to get over to Vanessa's now! It's another pussy-whipped man shooting up her house!"

271

Vanessa

The memories of her infidelity always haunted Vanessa whenever she sat down to eat breakfast or any other meal with her family, the one-night stand she had with the madman from her job and the horrific rape, which led to the in-house separation from her faithful husband.

Russell decided to work things out with Vanessa solely on the strength of Dejah's welfare. He didn't want to explain to his daughter why he left her mother and her and only came to visit them on the weekends. That's the road he wanted to take, but the love Russell had for his daughter and Vanessa made him stick around for now. By staying, Russell chose to sleep in a different bedroom and not talk to his wife. He only talked to Vanessa during the family meals; that was it!

"Hey Daddy!" Russell heard Dejah calling him, which brought him hurtling away from his thoughts - back to the kitchen table in the house where he lived with his beautiful daughter and the Betrayer!

Then he heard Dejah asking, "Daddy, can we go to the park today? Just me, you, and Mommy, you know, like old times?"

Dejah was quite the slickster and more focused than ever. Vanessa saw the crazed and angry look in her husband's chinky brown eyes - a look that screamed that he wanted to tell Dejah the truth once and for all.

"Dejah, baby, why don't you and Daddy just go to the park? Mommy has a lot of work to do. Maybe I'll go with you guys some other time."

Russell grunted in disgust as she finished talking. He glared at her evilly.

This cheating-ass bitch has some nerve! Now she's lying to our daughter! What's next?

Drunk In Love

"Okay Mommy," Dejah said joyously before turning to her father. "Daddy, you can take me -" she suddenly stopped in mid-sentence and just bad-eyed her father. "Daddy, what's that?" Dejah asked, pointing at the red pinpoint of the laser on his chest.

Russell looked down and saw the red dot moving slowly up onto the Polo horse emblem near his heart. It didn't take a rocket scientist to figure out what the red dot was.

What the fuck! he thought before going after his daughter. Fear consumed Russell as he instinctively grabbed hold of his daughter and dove quickly to the kitchen floor. Microseconds later, rapid gunfire penetrated his sham of a Happy Home.

Vanessa

The wooden wingback chair still rocking splintered apart as Russell and Dejah hit the ground. Loud metal pings sounded as stray bullets raced through the air in their kitchen, ricocheting off the cabinets and refrigerator.

"Nessa! Call the police now! Go! Go! Go!" he yelled, shielding Dejah with his body.

Vanessa didn't have to be told twice. She dropped into a crouch and sprinted for cover and her cell phone.

Russell lifted Dejah and crawled for all he was worth to protect his seed at all costs. He also wanted the gun upstairs in the closet, which was like two football fields away from the action.

More shots followed, penetrating his house, stifling his thoughts of going for the gun upstairs. One shot came so close that he heard it whizzing by his head.

Vanessa suspected the gunshots were coming from the woods directly in front of her house. *It's Kenny!* That much she did know. She didn't bother to look, not yet. Reaching her purse, Vanessa dumped out the contents and grabbed her cell phone. An explosion of glass followed.

Vanessa stayed low, terrified, face pressed against the shiny hardwood covered floors in the foyer, and pressed Number 2 on her cellphone: the speed dial service to Casey's house.

Another shot came. More explosions of glass followed.

"Hello?" Casey spoke.

"Casey! Oh my God! Call the police! This maniac is shooting up my house!"

"Go figure! We just had that problem. Stay behind something. I'm on it, gurl. You just stay outta the line of fire. We on our way."

Drunk In Love

After Casey hung up, Vanessa chanced taking a look out the window and spotted Kenny in plain view spraying the front porch. She ducked just in time to feel shards of glass raining on her. *This sick bastard won't stop shooting,* she thought. But that was the least of her worries.

"Mommy! Mommy! Mommy! Help me! Daddy is bleeding! Mommy, I'm scared!"

Vanessa heard her daughter's voice coming from the living room - all the way across the house - and her baby's voice was hoarse with panic.

"I'm coming, Dejah! Don't you move! Just lay still and don't move!" she yelled as she jumped up, seeing Kenny heading closer to the house, maybe forty yards away.

Kenny raised the gun just as their eyes met.

The moment of truth.

Revenge, a dish best served piping hot!

I AM THEE, Kenny thought, and roared as he pulled the trigger, sending a half a dozen shots racing into the house, delivering death wherever they impacted.

Girlfriends

When Nathan pulled up in his Blue Chrysler 300-C, he along with Briana, Casey, and Anitra spotted Kenny sweeping the house with automatic gunfire.

Who would be sick and crazy enough in the head to go after a woman at her house? With her kids? Briana thought as Nathan told her to give him the gun.

"Yeah, bitch! You thought it was over? Huh!" Kenny roared as several slugs struck Vanessa in the stomach and back.

Neat lines of crimson holes opened up along Vanessa's shapely body.

Inside the house, Vanessa dropped quickly like she'd run into a wall. She just laid there quivering pathetically, trying to breathe, but it hurt too much.

"Mommy! Mommy, help me!"

Once Vanessa heard Dejah's crying, she pulled herself together, ignoring the pain. She even welcomed the pain as she crawled towards her daughter.

Back outside, Kenny kept his finger on the trigger and sprayed Vanessa's car in the driveway with heavy gunfire. More glass shattered. Then his gun emptied. Looking wild-eyed as he went to reload, Kenny could hear police sirens screaming in the distance and screaming voices coming from inside the bitch's house.

Children. Then he heard a voice coming from behind him. A male!

"Yo, back up and drop that gun, you sick motherfucker!"

Drunk In Love

Kenny turned around slowly and saw a man standing there with a gun in his hand. Three women stood behind a car, staring at him.

The bitch's friends, Kenny thought. He ignored Nathan's demands, reloading the rifle like he wasn't even there aiming a gun at him.

"This has nothing to do with you! You need to get the fuck back in the car and leave!" Kenny snapped. "Before I kill your superhero ass!"

"You sick motherfucker!" Nathan shouted, taking aim. "You're stalking a married woman! Outta all the women in Dayton, you chose to stalk a married woman!"

Slamming the fresh magazine home, Kenny fired aimlessly at Nathan, striking the car. Then something inside told him to run. Listening to his inner voice, Kenny took off, charging out of the driveway. While running to his car, Kenny continued shooting at Nathan's car, forcing him and the women to take cover.

Once Kenny got in his car, he sped away, feeling safer, better, and satisfied with making the bitch's life a living hell.

Girlfriends

Suddenly Vanessa's husband bolted from the house carrying his gun. He looked around wildly until Nathan called him over to the car.

"I saw him leave. C'mon!" Nathan yelled.

"Baby, be careful!" Anitra cried as Russell bolted past her, running up to Nathan's car with blood smeared on the side of his face.

All the women along with Nathan could tell he got shot, maybe grazed by one of Kenny's shots.

"I will, baby! Y'all go inside the house and check on Vanessa and the baby!" Nathan ordered in a serious tone. "Go now!"

Then they sped off in hot pursuit of Kenny's car, going to God knows where.

As the women ran inside the house, several police cars were speeding into the cul-de-sac.

"Nooooo! Nooooo! Help us, God!" came Casey's horrific screams as the cops climbed from their cars with guns drawn.

Inside the house, Briana frantically went to work, trying to revive Vanessa's unconscious and bloody frame. Blood seeped through Vanessa's shirt, forming a small puddle under her.

Briana plopped down on the floor over Vanessa and began performing C.P.R. Dejah appeared at a slow run, puzzled by what was happening, unsure of what to do next. Anitra could see streaks of blood on Dejah as she picked her up and decided to leave the house.

Once Anitra got her to the front door, Dejah began screaming for her mother, and the sounds were heart wrenching for Anitra.

Drunk In Love

"Nooo! Put me down nooo! I want my mommy! Mommy! Mommy!

"Get her outta here!" Briana yelled, and then went back to doing all she could to save her friend from dying.

"Fight, Nessa. Don't you leave us like this. C'mon, gurl, fight, damn you!" Briana cried, doing everything in her power to revive Vanessa, her best friend.

But Briana's efforts just weren't good enough.

Nathan Welch

Kenny

After getting his revenge against the bitch who ruined his life, Kenny sped down I-75, attempting to leave Dayton for good and escape the clutches of the law before it was too late. Seeing the blinking red gas light on the dashboard, Kenny couldn't believe his luck.

Why the hell is this happening to me right now? he wondered. He suddenly made several dangerous swerves through Interstate traffic until he made it to the next exit and got off the highway. Speeding around the curvy exit ramp, Kenny glanced in his rearview mirrors and could've sworn he saw the same blue Chrysler 300-C following him that he had just left behind at the bitch's house.

Spotting the Exxon gas station on his right, Kenny pulled into it and stopped at a pump. He wanted to see if the blue car would do the same.

It did!

Figuring it was the same guy he'd already taken shots at back at Vanessa's, Kenny made sure to slam another fresh magazine home in the AR-70 before cocking it and getting out of the car.

You wanna play Good Samaritan? Then take these hot missiles for your troubles, Kenny thought while nervously eyeing the blue car as he ran up to the gas station attendant's window, yanked a woman by the neck, and quickly raised the rifle to her head.

"Cut the pump on now so I can fill it up or this bitch right here gets it!" Kenny yelled at the attendant.

A look of fear and shock stayed on the woman's face as she pleaded for the gas station attendant to do as ordered. People in the vicinity started screaming for help and scrambling for safety. The gas station attendant had no choice but to do as he was told. He cut on the gas pumps and triggered the silent alarm, alerting the police to a robbery in progress.

Seconds after the kidnapping, Kenny made the woman pump the gas into his car at gunpoint.

Nathan and Russell moved forward with their guns drawn, shocked by what was happening, somewhat unsure of what to do next.

"Hurry up, bitch!" Kenny demanded, keeping his eyes on the two armed men standing in front of him. Kenny recognized the bitch's husband and flipped out. "Stay back, or this bitch's death will be on your hands! You think I'm frontin'? Try me!" he yelled at Russell and Nathan.

While the standoff continued, Nathan backed off as several state trooper and local police cruisers made their way into the gas station with blaring sirens, blocking any hopes of escape that Kenny had.

With adrenaline surging and sweat forming on his brow, Kenny looked around wildly, noticing that the cops were surrounding him and blocking off all exits. Kenny felt that he had a very slim chance of making it out of the gas station alive. *Going back to jail is not in the equation,* he told himself.

"Freeze! Drop your weapon and step away from the woman, now!" a voice blared from a police bullhorn as Kenny held the crying woman in a chokehold.

"Please! Don't let him kill me!" the woman cried hysterically for help.

Several cops closed in on Kenny, causing him to flinch.

"Back up! I'm telling y'all! Back the fuck up!" Kenny demanded.

"Stand down! Stand down!" the voice ordered the approaching cops over the bullhorn. Seeing the suspect was about to pull the trigger, the cop holding the bullhorn decided to try a more peaceful approach to the deadly situation.

"Please, Sir, this doesn't have to end this way! I'm sure we can -"

Suddenly a shot exploded from a gun.

"AAAAHHHH! Oh my God" the hostage screamed and ran for cover.

Kenny felt a crushing blow in the center of his forehead that sent him crashing hard into the steel gas pumps. For a second maybe, Kenny stood on his tiptoes, looking surprised and in shock - dead on his feet. He glared out at the bitch's husband, and then fell over face first.

Russell dropped the gun and raised his hands high in the air in surrender as several cops rushed him, pointing guns at his head, yelling demands for him to lie down.

When the cops finally got everything under control, Russell sat handcuffed in a police car, looking at Kenny's corpse lying sprawled next to the gas pumps. A little distance away from the scene, Nathan stammered over his cellphone, filling Anitra in on everything that just happened.

Drunk In Love

Girlfriends

One week later, as Vanessa's mahogany and titanium casket was being lowered into the earth, two armed police escorts stood beside a handcuffed and shocked Russell. Crying hysterically, Russell's pain and hurt could be seen and felt by everyone in attendance. Casey, Anitra, and Briana cried more than all the mourners at Vanessa's funeral. They had lost more than a friend; they had lost their sister, and it felt like a part of them had died with Vanessa.

A few people that knew Vanessa were shocked to see her daughter, Dejah, sitting quietly without a single tear. While the service went on, Dejah watched her father, who kept looking up at the sky like he was trying to find some answers from God as to why his life has turned out this way? His wife was dead, and now he was fighting a capital murder charge for killing the sick lunatic who took Vanessa away from him and their daughter - the same lunatic who destroyed three lives with his violent actions. Now the future of his daughter's welfare weighed heavily on the outcome of his murder trial. Russell couldn't shake the scary thoughts of living life and raising Dejah without Vanessa being around, but coming to grips with the possibility that he might have to do it from behind prison walls terrified him.

Vanessa was his everything and he never got the chance to reconcile their problems. He was just angry and beefing with her for a moment, but he was going to forgive, forget, and take her back. Kenny took all that away from him.

Vanessa was gone forever and the only trace of her presence left was Dejah. Listening to the choir sing their version of "It's So Hard to Say Goodbye to Yesterday," Russell lowered his head, closed his eyes, and reluctantly said goodbye to Vanessa - the love of his life.

Not knowing if he'd ever be the same again, Russell waved at his daughter during his walk back to the awaiting prison van with the two things in mind: beating the murder charges and getting back home to his daughter, because he truly felt in his heart that Dejah needed him.

Drunk In Love

Casey

"I got some good news," Casey said after walking up to her client.

Russell smiled for the first time in months since losing Vanessa. "What's up, Casey?"

"Well, it's been six days, and they still have not reached a verdict, which is very favorable for us." During the forty-five day trial, Casey had presented a temporary insanity defense to the jury of mostly women whom she'd selected, knowing they were wives and mothers - the perfect jury panel. Casey painted Russell as a loving father and husband who lost his mind and did the only thing he knew of to protect his family from a monster who continuously threatened their lives. Casey also presented evidence of Kenny's psychopathic behavior and rape attacks on Vanessa, which ultimately forced Russell into temporary psychosis.

Through a painful heart and teary-eyed defense, Casey was able to present several trained psychiatrist's testimonies over the objections of the prosecution. They all testified in Russell's defense, claiming that such traumatizing actions threatening the livelihood of a man and the lives of his wife and kids could send any sane person into a psychotic state, a serious mental illness marked by loss of or greatly lessened ability to test whether what one is thinking and feeling about the real world is really true.

Russell played his part by testifying that he didn't remember seeing anything after witnessing his bleeding wife lying unconscious on the floor. Through a teary-eyed testimony, Russell told the prosecutors, "The last thing I remembered was the police arresting me."

When the prosecutor's psychotherapist testified that Russell could have blacked out and returned to reality after committing the murder, Casey knew the trial was won. She was just waiting for the not guilty verdict or guilty by reason of insanity. Either verdict was a win.

Russell gripped the cell bars in the holding area, hoping the twelve people holding his future in their hands ruled in his favor. He had a little girl in society who needed him.

"So keep praying for the best," Casey said, touching his hand, and invading his thoughts.

"Maybe you'll be home in the next couple of days."

"Man, I sure hope so. I miss my baby girl, Dejah." He sighed, extending his hand to Casey.

"She misses you too." Casey smiled warmly.

"Thanks,   Casey.   You're   the   best."

"Don't mention it. I'll be waiting in the courtroom if you need me for anything, Okay?"

"Okay," Russell said. He sat down on the iron bench, watching as Casey left the bullpen area. As soon as she left, Russell got down on his knees and began praying to the Creator to lift him out of the storm he was currently trapped in.

Drunk In Love

Girlfriends

The following day at 2:45 p.m., the Honorable Judge Clifford Hamilton looked over his horn-rimmed glasses at Russell while he sat at the defense table holding Casey's hand. The jury had reached a verdict.

The Judge read the verdict and looked at the foreman of the jury. "Jury, in the capital murder charge of Ohio versus Russell Jergens, Docket Number OH-187-09314, have you reached a unanimous verdict?"

"Yes, we have, your Honor," the portly and balding white man stated, causing Russell's whole body to shake. He could feel the butterflies having a race in his stomach as fear and nervousness consumed him.

"Will the defendant please rise."

Russell and Casey stood together still holding hands.

Briana, Anitra, and Nathan, along with various news reporters, all stood up in the rear of the courtroom.

"Mr. Foreperson, what is your verdict on the charge of pre-meditated capital murder?" asked the Judge with a stern face.

"We, the Jury, find the defendant..." The portly man looked over at Russell, pausing for dramatic effect.

For Russell, Casey and the rest of the courtroom, it became suspense city!

"Not Guilty."

Russell released a sigh as Casey's face was etched into a goofy smile, and the courtroom erupted with cheering and clapping.

"Order! Order!" the judge shouted, banging his gavel. "Thank you, Jurors. You're dismissed."

As the jury and several news reporters filed out of the courtroom, the Judge began going through several papers.

Once he finished, the Judge told Russell that he was going to have to do some jail time for the unlicensed firearm he possessed during his arrest.

Casey raised her hand. "Your Honor, if I may say something?"

"Make it quick!" Judge Hamilton snapped.

Judge Clifford Hamilton was the worst that they could have gotten for trial. Almost eighty years old, Hamilton was so erratic that many attorneys filed affidavits of prejudice against him rather than risk his unpredictable rulings at trial and subject themselves and their clients to his very strange mood swings and temper tantrums. Casey took on the challenge. She figured if she could win in his courtroom, it would solidify her career and certify her as a real defense attorney.

"Given the facts and circumstances around this case, and the loss my client has suffered with the passing of his wife, I'm asking the Court's mercy in granting my client time served with some type of extended probation. My client has a young daughter waiting on him in society. He's now the sole provider for the child."

"I see. But what does this have to do with having an unlicensed firearm, Counselor?"

"Your Honor," Casey gasped, not believing the Judge's inconsideration. "This man has just lost his wife. His *wife*. Never mind. Your Honor, people make mistakes. My client's made one, and regrets it fully. Do you think his daughter should have to lose her only parent because of a mistake? My client is truly sorry for his mistake." *Have a heart, you miserable old bastard,* Casey wanted to add, but she left well enough alone.

"Is that so, Mr. Jergens?"

"Yes Sir, Your Honor. I just want to raise my little girl and be a productive citizen and role model for her."

"Is there any objection from the prosecution?"

Drunk In Love

"Your Honor, with all due respect, murder is a serious crime…" The prosecution began the protest and made several requests for jail time.

"With all things considered, I hereby sentence you to serve six years."

Russell's knees buckled and his body began shaking uncontrollably.

"With all of it suspended but three years to be served on supervised probation." The judge looked at Russell again and gave him a weak smile. "Sir, I want you to know that I am truly sorry for your loss. You're free to go. This court is adjourned."

"Thank you, your Honor." Russell smiled as Hamilton banged his gavel on the bench.

"Thank you, Lord!" Casey exhaled as Briana, Anitra, and Nathan rushed over to the defense table and showered Russell and Casey with congratulatory hugs and kisses.

Epilogue
18 Months Later

Nathan and Anitra's wedding was held on the Bell of Louisville's huge riverboat. And the people in attendance occupied all four levels of the historic riverboat as it cruised along the Ohio River, holding the loving couple who came out to jump the broom.

Casey held her sleeping ten-month-old daughter in her arms, whom she named after Vanessa in memory of her slain friend. Casey's fiancé Jonte Milhouse got arrested and indicted on several murder and racketeering charges one month prior to Casey giving birth to their child. Casey was currently working along with Jonte's attorney to prepare a good enough defense to cause reasonable doubt at Jonte's upcoming trial.

A smiling Russell sat in the crowd with Dejah propped up on his lap, applauding the happy newlyweds. Russell's days now were filled with one purpose: providing for Dejah every chance he got, because he knew that tomorrow was not guaranteed.

The wedding lasted for an hour. Briana never noticed it with her head cast down to the floor the entire time, fiddling with a diamond-studded butterfly-shaped ring that Vanessa had given her over one year ago as a birthday gift. Several minutes later, Briana looked up directly into her father's smiling gaze.

"Hey, darling. I met an old friend, and I told him about you. Do you have a second? I want you to meet him. He's an okay guy."

"Sure, Daddy." Briana took his hand, allowing him to lead her over to the buffet table near a man who stood with his back to them.

"Hey there, old pal. Here's my lovely Briana!"

Drunk In Love

When Terrence turned on her and smiled, Briana's heart nearly stopped. With a shocked expression, Briana glanced at her smiling father with disappointed eyes for setting her up.

"Go ahead, baby." Briana's father winked. "Please give the man a chance before he worries me to death about you."

Angered about the sudden set-up, Briana backed away. "I'm sorry, Daddy. I c-c-can't do this," she stammered as she began walking away. Ever since learning of his affair with her mother, Briana had gone out of her way to avoid Terrence. But for some reason, Terrence didn't get the message and just wouldn't give up.

"Briana, please stop!" Terrence called, chasing behind her. "C'mon, gimme one second, please!"

Suddenly the music stopped and the crowd grew quiet. As all eyes focused on them, Terrence stopped Briana and pleaded for her to give him another chance.

"Why the hell should I? Huh?" All the hurt and the anger she felt seeped from her tone. Briana watched him intently, standing there quietly, thinking and hoping that he'd come up with a good reason for them to reconcile their differences.

"Because the third times always a charm," he joked nervously.

But he didn't come up with the right answer, and Briana returned to her seat, mentally moving on with life, more confused than ever about his intentions for stepping to her on a day like this.

Briana's evil look alerted Terrence that his answer wasn't the right one. Briana leaned back, breathed deeply, and composed herself. This wasn't good. There was too much adrenaline involved. She wasn't thinking straight, like some high school kid trying to get over a stupid crush. Just silly!

After gaining a little control, Briana felt she had herself in hand, and spoke quickly. "I mean, honestly, Terrence, my mother? How can we ever get past that, let alone start over after being apart for so long?" She stared at him intently, searching with her questions for far more than she had asked.

Terrence tried to read her eyes. He was afraid to express what he really felt in his heart. He was afraid of making a fool of himself. He'd already done that twice, and still gotten rejected. Terrence was really afraid he'd already lost her. But he knew that now was the moment to speak and lay his crying heart out in the hope she saved him from drowning without her love.

"Briana, baby, listen. I came after you for a third time because I still love you. I never stopped loving you, and I never will. I need you, Briana. Now can we discuss our future over some cake?" he asked with an innocent smile, holding up a plate with a slice of wedding cake. "C'mon, just a second is all I need," he begged, grabbing her hand and gathering his courage again to pursue the woman he loved and get her back in his life.

Following Terrence to a nearby table, Briana awkwardly stared around the ballroom and noticed that everyone was watching her and giving her "go ahead" nods. Briana felt like a dam had burst inside of her, setting free emotions she'd thought she would never feel again for him. Sitting down, she stared at Casey, Anitra, and her mother.

Doing a double take, Briana looked at her mother again. Quickly remembering the gem her mother gave her about the test, Briana decided to go for it all. This would make or break her future at any chance of finding love.

"It's only one slice left, Terrence," she said sheepishly, looking at him. Suddenly she got frightened, afraid of what he'd say next. Her whole world and happiness hung on his response.

"It doesn't even matter, Briana. You can have mines. Here… Here you go," he said and spoon-fed her. "How does that taste?" he asked over the loud applause of the cheering and whistling crowd.

Drunk In Love

"Mmm... it's wonderful." Briana smiled, closing her eyes, knowing that Terrence was really in love with her.

Now that she had him back in her life, she didn't ever want to let him go. Briana wanted to find out if anything more than what they had before was possible between them. She'd sensed that possibility when he fed her his last piece of cake - the ideal man for her, just like her mother predicted.

"Here, lemme get that for you." He leaned in and wiped the icing from her lips. "Briana, baby, I'll never love no other woman like I do you. You're all I need to get by." He mimicked Method Man's famous one-liner from the classic hip-hop duet with Mary J. Blige.

When their lips locked in a passionate kiss, Briana began feeling like there was still hope for her to get all the love she needed...

About The Author

Nathan was born in Washington, DC and was found guilty in 1996 and sentenced to a lengthy prison sentence. Over the past decade, Nathan has been entertaining various inmates with his page-turning Urban Tales. He is the author of A Killer'z Ambition 1 and 2, Convict's Clique and the ebook short story Wrong Move.

Nathan Welch – 09314-007
PO Box 2000
Bruceton Mills, WV 26525

In Stock Now!

 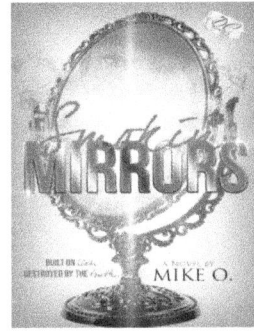 

Coming Soon

Order Form

DC Bookdiva Publications

#245 4401-A Connecticut Avenue, NW

Washington, DC 20008

dcbookdiva.com

Name: _____

Inmate ID _____

Address: _____

City/State: _____ **Zip:** _____

QUANTITY	TITLES	PRICE	TOTAL
	Que, Dutch	15.00	
	Smokin Mirrors, Mike O	15.00	
	Dynasty By Dutch	15.00	
	Dynasty 2 By Dutch	15.00	
	The Commission, Team DCB	15.00	
	Trina, Darrell Debrew	15.00	
	Secrets Never Die, Eyone Williams	15.00	
	Dynasty 3, Dutch	15.00	
	A Killer'z Ambition, Nathan Welch	15.00	
	A Killer'z Ambition 2, Nathan Welch	15.00	
	Lorton Legends, Eyone Williams	15.00	
	Convict's Clique, Nathan Welch	15.00	
	A Beautiful Satan, RJ Champ	15.00	
	Above the Law, Dutch	15.00	
	A Beautiful Satan 2, RJ Champ	15.00	

QUANTITY	TITLES	PRICE	TOTAL
	Tina, Darrell Debrew	15.00	
	A Hustler's Daughter, Pinky Dior	15.00	

Sub-Total $_____

Shipping/Handling (Via US Media Mail) $3.95 1-2 Books, $7.95 1-3 Books, 4 or more titles-Free Shipping

Shipping $ _____

Total Enclosed $ _____

Certified or government issued checks and money orders, all mail in orders take 5-7 Business days to be delivered. Books can also be purchased on our website at dcbookdiva.com. Incarcerated readers receive 25% discount. Please pay $11.25 per book and apply the same shipping terms as stated above.

www.ingramcontent.com/pod-product-compliance
Lightning Source LLC
Chambersburg PA
CBHW071111250626
47159CB00002B/695